PRAISE F

THE L

"The glamorous cast of characters in Anita Abriel's *The Life She Wanted* captivated me from the start, while the unforgettable setting had me dreaming about stepping inside every mansion in wealthy 1920s New York. But I adored Pandora most, the novel's plucky heroine whose single father works at one of the region's grand estates, giving Pandora entrée into a world of glittery formal balls and suitors with deep pockets. And while Pandora seems like she's on a path to good fortune, her story shows us it's rare that life turns out as planned—no matter how much money you have. For anyone who loves a sweeping rags-to-riches tale, Anita Abriel's novel delights!"

—Brooke Lea Foster, author of *On Gin Lane*

"A compulsively readable coming-of-age story set against a dazzling Roaring Twenties backdrop, *The Life She Wanted* had me flipping pages late into the night. Full of intricately researched history and characters you'll root for, Anita Abriel's latest proves it might be a long and winding road, but true love always finds a way. Fans of *The Gilded Age* will devour this treat of a novel!"

—Kristy Woodson Harvey, *New York Times* bestselling author of *The Wedding Veil*

"This is a fast-paced historical read that examines the roles of men and women in the 1920s, what was accepted and what was not, and the idea that sometimes what you are looking for is right in front of you."

—*Booklist*

AMERICAN HOUSEWIFE

ALSO BY ANITA ABRIEL

The Philadelphia Heiress
The Life She Wanted
A Girl During the War
Lana's War
The Light After the War

AMERICAN HOUSEWIFE

A NOVEL

ANITA ABRIEL

LAKE UNION
PUBLISHING

Published by Lake Union Publishing, Seattle

www.apub.com

Amazon, the Amazon logo, and Lake Union Publishing are trademarks of Amazon.com, Inc., or its affiliates.

ISBN-13: 9781662525537 (paperback)
ISBN-13: 9781662525520 (digital)

Cover design by Faceout Studio, Amanda Hudson
Cover image: © kolderal, © Gusztáv Galló / Getty; © Pushish Images, © Somyk Volodymyr, © Pixel-Shot / Shutterstock

Printed in the United States of America

To my mother

Chapter One

There was no point in trying to explain her feelings. Teddy wouldn't understand. How could he? He might be in love with her and want her to be happy, but he was a man.

Sometimes Maggie didn't know herself why she kept turning him down. She was a modern woman, who adored her independence and her career. But at the same time, she loved the idea of marriage, of having a husband, children, a family.

And she was quite sure that she was in love with him too. She had been ever since they'd met two years earlier, at a charity event sponsored by CBS Broadcasting for the New York Public Library. Teddy was speaking about being the "voice of Pathé News" reporting from England and France during World War II.

"I came to New York from a small radio station in Rochester," he said to the men and women who were assembled in the library's rotunda. "Radio was perfect for men like me—with a honeyed voice like Cary Grant but without his looks."

Teddy had been wrong on both counts. He sounded nothing like Cary Grant, who had a smooth British accent. Teddy talked more like the American movie star Gregory Peck—a confident tone with a slight lilt. He resembled Gregory Peck too. He was tall, with brown eyes and wonderfully thick brown hair that flopped over his forehead.

The women in the audience responded by clapping their gloved hands and smiling flirtatiously under their hats.

Teddy pretended not to notice them. He kept talking, giving the briefest description of being sent to northern France during the war, how difficult it was to get out the news when grenades were exploding around him on the front lines. How he had practically kissed the ground when he arrived back in the United States, and how New York was the greatest city in the world and he never wanted to leave again.

It was only at the reception that Maggie realized he had noticed her. He came over to her, carrying two glasses of champagne. He was even more handsome up close. His eyes were hazel, not brown, and there was a dimple on his cheek.

"It's only five p.m. How do you know I want a drink?" she asked. "And why do you think I prefer champagne?"

"I don't," he admitted, handing her a glass. "But if you're already holding a drink, no other man will offer you one. And champagne is the safest bet. I've been to these events before. The cocktails are watered down and taste terrible."

They talked for an hour—about how she grew up on a farm in Pennsylvania and, ever since she was a girl, dreamed of living in New York. There wasn't enough money to send her to university or secretarial school, so when she arrived, she didn't know what she'd do. But she was determined to stay. Living in New York was as certain as sitting down to listen to *The Adventures of Ozzie and Harriet* on the radio every evening or knowing that the following morning the cows would be up at 6:00 a.m. for their first feed.

She got a job through a temp agency delivering coffee at CBS. One day, the female voice in a radio commercial came down with laryngitis, and she was asked to fill in. That led to more radio commercials. She was the voice of the wife preparing a JELL-O salad during *The Frank Sinatra Show* and the voice of a coed brushing her teeth until they smelled minty fresh on *The Pepsodent Show*. She even did some television commercials. She stood on top of a Whirlpool washing machine and cracked eggs into a bowl of Deluxe cake mix. The previous year, Deluxe Baking Company gave her a radio program where she and a female guest sampled Deluxe desserts. At the end of each show, she read the recipe off the box, and the guest would croon that she had to get a box of Deluxe devil's food cake mix to keep in her own kitchen.

"I've never done anything brave like report from the front lines during a German ambush," Maggie said when she finished.

Teddy let out a little laugh. His eyes crinkled at the corners, and something warmed inside her.

"I'm the least brave person you'll meet. At the base, I kept a broom under the bunk because I was afraid of mice." He toyed with his drink. "That's the thing about war—you don't have to be brave. The draft board doesn't care what you're afraid of, they'll send you anyway. When you get there, you'll find things to really be scared of and wish you could spend every day sweeping the floor for mice."

Maggie felt a tug at her heart. He was so serious, she had to do something to lighten his mood.

"I'll let you in on a secret if you promise not to tell anyone." She leaned forward conspiratorially.

He crossed his hands over his chest. "You're talking to an Eagle Scout. Whatever it is, I won't tell a soul."

"Deluxe Baking Company is the sponsor of my radio show, and I don't know how to cook."

Teddy looked at her in astonishment.

"I thought all women knew how to cook," he said. "My sister is married, and she cooks roasts or meat loaf every night. I don't know how her husband, Andy, doesn't weigh two hundred pounds. And my mother has a maid, but she still loves to bake."

Maggie shrugged. "On the farm, I was outside doing chores. There was never time to learn. We didn't have much money, and I was an only child. As I got older my parents counted on me helping out in order for the farm to survive. Now my studio apartment only has a hot plate and a kettle. Besides, it seems silly to cook for one person."

"You can't eat out all the time on a radio salary," Teddy persisted. He glanced at her left hand. "Unless you have a wealthy boyfriend or fiancé."

Maggie blushed. "I don't have either. There's always coffee and pastries at the studio in the mornings, and I can usually find a salad nearby for lunch. Dinner can be tricky, but I've gotten good at ordering takeout. Wonton soup and egg rolls from a Chinese restaurant can last for days."

Teddy shook his head. "One thing I learned when I came home from the war was that good nutrition is more important than anything." He placed their glasses on a sideboard and took her arm.

"Where are we going?" she asked.

"To Delmonico's for their famous prime rib."

Maggie tried not to show her excitement. She wanted to go out with Teddy. He was good looking and fun to talk to. She loved the way his face crinkled into a smile when he described how much he loved New York. And unlike some of the men she met, he really listened to her when she talked. But her bank account was treacherously low.

"I never expect a man to pay on the first date, and I can't afford it right now."

"Then we won't call it a date. We'll say it's a public service." He led her to the exit. "The voice of Deluxe Baking Company can't faint on the air."

They took a taxi to Delmonico's on Beaver Street and ate prime rib followed by baked Alaska for dessert. Maggie learned that Teddy grew up in Westchester County. He enjoyed his childhood—there was plenty of room to bicycle and play baseball—and he loved his parents. His father sold insurance, and his mother was involved in charity. He went to university in Rochester but went to England to report for Pathé News and never graduated. When he returned from the war he didn't want to go back on the radio, but because so many servicemen came home at the same time, jobs were scarce and he couldn't think of anything else.

The dinner was followed by lunch hours spent feeding the ducks in Central Park, bowling on Friday nights, and catching the latest films at the New Amsterdam and Lyric theaters. Teddy was funny and romantic. He brought her flowers once a week, and he loved museums as much as she did. Nowhere was she happier than at the Met on a Saturday afternoon, marveling at how far she was from the farm and how much of New York was left to explore.

Now it was two years later, and Teddy asked her to marry him at least once a month. She always replied that she couldn't imagine marrying anyone else, yet she still felt guilty when he slipped his grandmother's sapphire-and-diamond ring back in the box. How could she say yes when there was a part of her past that she couldn't share? And marriage itself scared her. She had worked so hard not to rely on anyone else for her happiness and sense of security. What if something happened and she was alone again? She couldn't face it.

Teddy didn't seem to mind her refusals. He always shrugged them off, and they'd go to a favorite restaurant. He wouldn't mention marriage again for a few weeks, and they'd go back to being happy together.

Until lately. Lately, he had become more persistent, as if he needed her to say yes to lift him out of the despondency that enveloped him now and then, like a sudden rain shower on an otherwise sunny afternoon. The despondency that she guessed resulted from the war years he rarely talked about. When they started seeing each other seriously, she caught glimpses into his past. The sound of an airplane flying overhead could make him flinch. He rarely ate French food. And there were the constant night sweats, when he'd wake up and his side of the bed would be drenched with sweat. She had read about men who came back from the war changed forever. She couldn't help worrying that his despondency might grow worse. It wouldn't make her love Teddy less; love wasn't like that. But what if one day he woke up and didn't want to be with her anymore, or needed a new life altogether?

"A man wants to see you." Her assistant entered the broadcast booth where she was preparing her show notes. "He's waiting in the lobby."

Maggie set her papers on the desk. There was forty minutes until airtime. She had time to talk to someone.

A tall man wearing a dark suit and yellow tie sat on the sofa in the reception area. Maggie noticed the gold band on his ring finger and his lizard-skin watchband.

He jumped up and extended his hand. "Tommy Fischer from Deluxe Baking Company."

Maggie shook his hand and sat opposite him.

She wished she could offer him a cup of coffee to hide her nervousness, but a cup was already sitting in front of him. This could be about only one thing. She had read one of her lines wrong, on the last show. It was for lemon supreme pound cake, and she instructed listeners to use a quarter cup of cooking oil instead of a half cup. Someone must have written to the show and complained that their cake was too dry.

It was her own fault. The print on the recipe boxes was so small, and she should have worn her glasses. But even though she was on the radio, the people in the studio would have seen her, and attractive young women didn't wear glasses, even for reading. Teddy had encouraged her to get the new hard contact lenses that just became available. Maggie had tried, but they kept falling out.

"I see my assistant already brought you coffee," she began. "Can I get you anything else? A pastry or a muffin?"

"My wife has me on a strict grapefruit diet, since we're going to Florida on vacation." He patted his stomach. "Though don't tell my boss. Deluxe Baking Company is a bit like Lucky Strike cigarettes and smoking. Lucky Strike keeps telling their customers that cigarettes don't cause throat irritation, and they even use doctors in their commercials. Deluxe wants viewers to believe they can eat as much cake as they want without gaining any weight."

Maggie poured herself a cup of coffee. She had seen the commercials for Lucky Strike with doctors proclaiming that cigarettes actually made their throats feel better. But she had also heard Teddy's cough, after he'd finished his third pack of Camel cigarettes of the day. Still, cigarettes were different from desserts.

"Deluxe Baking Company products are only made with healthy ingredients. They're written on the side of the box," Maggie said.

Tommy smiled approvingly. "That's what Deluxe Baking Company would like consumers to think. You have such a winning, believable quality, even more so in person, than on the radio. We knew you'd be right for the position."

"I'm afraid I don't understand," Maggie said, puzzled.

"*The Maggie Lane Radio Show* has been such a success, we want to move it to television. Except we're going to rename it *The Maggie Lane Baking Show*. You're going to bake desserts on the air instead of just sample them."

Maggie almost spilled her coffee. If she tried to bake on television, it would become obvious that she didn't know how to cook. Even when she went to Teddy's apartment for breakfast, he whipped up pancakes or scrambled eggs while she read out loud to him from a newspaper or magazine.

"You want to give me my own television show?"

"That's an interesting way to put it." Tommy gave a little laugh. "I promise we won't take it back. That is unless the ratings fail." He handed her a piece of paper from the stack on the coffee table. "Given the research we've done on *The Maggie Lane Radio Show*, that's not going to happen."

Maggie glanced at the rows of numbers.

"You've researched my show?"

"We're the sponsor." His voice was patient. "Your demographics are just what we're looking for. Your main audience is twenty- to forty-year-old housewives, but you bring in teenage listeners as well. They see you as a fun older sister."

Maggie felt like she was standing naked in front of a complete stranger. Deluxe Baking Company had analyzed everything that made her radio show work. What if those things didn't translate to television?

She wasn't a trained actress. The same audience that loved listening to her on the radio might not like watching her on their television sets. She couldn't afford to fail. The radio program was the whole reason she was able to stay in New York.

"Well, I'm glad, but surely you want someone who is beautiful," she said. "That lovely young actress Angela Lansbury. Or Doris Day might like to do television."

Maggie was confident in her looks. Her light-brown hair fell in natural waves, and she had large green eyes. And she'd always been told she had good legs. That probably came from years of riding horses on the farm. But starring in her own television show was something else entirely.

"On the contrary, we want someone that viewers will trust. That 'girl next door' quality," Tommy said. "Viewers will write in with questions, and you'll give answers on the air. It won't all be related to cooking. You'll teach them how to iron a bedspread or read an encyclopedia."

Maggie opened her mouth and then closed it. She rarely ironed. When she got the radio show she splurged by taking her clothes to the laundry. And even though she loved to read, her bookshelves weren't big enough to hold a set of encyclopedias. But with the money she earned on television, she could afford everything New York had to offer. Visiting any museum, no matter what the entrance fee. Taking a taxi when she wanted to go somewhere instead of missing the sights by riding the subway. And if the show did really well, she could achieve her dream: an apartment in a doorman building on Park Avenue.

She patted her hair and took a breath. It wouldn't help to sound too eager. "It's a very interesting offer."

Tommy glanced at his watch and stood up.

"We hoped you'd think so. I have a meeting. Why don't you talk about it with your husband and we'll go to lunch tomorrow," he offered. "On second thought, bring him too. It's always nice to meet the star's spouse. The Waldorf at noon?"

Maggie was about to say that she wasn't married. But before she could get the words out, he was gone.

~

It was 6:00 p.m. Maggie had to go home and change. Teddy was picking her up, and they were going to Ruby Foo's Den for dinner.

May was one of her favorite months in New York. It was warm enough to wear a dress without a sweater, and there wasn't any of the summer humidity. May came with the floral decorations on Fifth Avenue, new exhibits at the Natural History Museum, and outdoor theater productions in Central Park.

She glanced at her reflection in a store window. She was wearing a blue pinpoint dress with a white cape collar and white sleeves. A pair of white gloves was folded over her purse, and she wore navy pumps. Her whole wardrobe was conservative. She couldn't afford the kind of clothes that were so dramatic you could wear them only once. Simple dresses, and blouses and skirts, complemented her prettiness. Could she really become an actress on television? When she thought of actresses, she imagined glamorous film stars like Lana Turner, who had sultry eyes and pouty lips. Or Veronica Lake, who had inspired every woman in America to color her hair with her snaky blond hairdo.

But she wasn't going to be in the movies. She was only going to host a baking show on television.

What would Teddy say? He'd be proud of her, of course. But he was less ambitious than she was. The GI Bill helped pay for his apartment. And his parents were well off. His mother was always offering to buy him furniture, but Teddy refused. He was twenty-nine years old. It didn't matter that he spent three years in England and France and had seen things that had somehow broken parts of him. Or that he lived in one of the hardest cities in the world to earn a living. He couldn't accept financial help from his parents.

It was one of the things about Teddy that puzzled Maggie and made her wish he let her in on his thoughts. Teddy was open about his happy childhood and being close to his family. Whenever they were all together, Maggie could see how much he and his parents loved each other. She had tried to discover the reason over the years, but whenever she broached the subject, Teddy closed up.

Maggie loved her own parents. When she moved to New York, she called them once a month and spent an hour on the phone telling them about the museums she had visited and her walks around Central Park. If they had been able to give her money to start her new life, they would have done so happily, and she would have accepted. One day when she was successful, Maggie hoped to start sending them money. That's what families did for each other. She couldn't understand why Teddy wouldn't accept help from his parents.

A man passed behind her. He had a dark crew cut and angular features. She turned abruptly, and her heart hammered the way it always did when she thought she saw Jake. But it wasn't Jake. It was one of the dozens of men in New York who resembled him.

She started walking, trying to calm down. She passed the Strand Bookstore and went inside. She told herself that she was going to see if they had the new Nancy Mitford novel, but that wasn't the reason. She had met Jake in the Strand six years ago. Whenever she stood there now, surrounded by shiny book jackets and inhaling the woodsy smell of the bookshelves, she felt like he was standing in front of her.

∼

It was February 1944, and Maggie had been in New York for two months. She had hoped the weather would be milder than winters on the farm. But it rained almost every day, and when it didn't, the skies were low and gray. She wished she could afford to see a Broadway musical or eat dinner in a nice restaurant. The only work she'd gotten was through a temp agency, and it barely covered the rent and her small food budget.

"You don't want to read that." A young man pointed to the book she was holding. "My mother read it and said it was quite disturbing."

Maggie had just picked up *Rebecca* by Daphne du Maurier. The cover illustration was of a young woman standing on a cliff in front of an old house.

She placed it back on the stack. "What should I read instead?"

The man walked around and selected books from different tables. He looked to be in his early twenties. He was in uniform, and he was very handsome—dark hair, blue eyes, and the kind of smile that you couldn't forget.

"I'm Jake Pullman," he introduced himself. He handed her a book by Agatha Christie. "It's a little scary too, but in a good way. She writes murder mysteries."

Maggie turned it over and read the back-cover copy.

"I'm Maggie Lane. To be honest, I don't really like murder mysteries. I prefer love stories."

Jake picked up *The Last Tycoon* by F. Scott Fitzgerald and a thick book by an author named Margaret Mitchell.

"I'll take this one." She read the title: *Gone with the Wind.* She had seen the film but never read the book. "It will last me for weeks, and I'll get my money's worth."

Maggie noticed that his shoulders were broad beneath his uniform. He had a sharp jaw and very white teeth.

She had been lonely since she arrived in New York. It was hard to make friends her own age. Jake was so attractive, and she wanted to be brave. She suddenly had an idea. She had never asked a man to lunch or dinner. But she was hungry, and she didn't want to eat alone.

"You saved me from buying a book that I'd hate," she said. "Why don't we go to the lunch counter at Woolworth's? I'll buy you half a turkey sandwich as a thank-you."

They sat on stools at the counter, and Jake told her about growing up in Ohio. His father owned a pharmacy, and his mother was the town librarian. He came to New York in 1941 to attend medical school. But after Pearl Harbor was attacked, he enlisted instead. He was on leave and was returning to the South Pacific in two days.

"Were you afraid?" Maggie asked, wiping a spot of mayonnaise from her mouth.

The turkey sandwich was quite tasty. Turkey and lettuce and tomato with mayonnaise and mustard on white bread.

"As frightened as I was reading Agatha Christie." Jake laughed. "I could have avoided the draft. I had three cavities, and the navy only allows two." He ate a bite of his sandwich. "But I lied on my papers, and they didn't check very thoroughly."

Maggie asked why he went to war if he didn't have to.

He shrugged and picked up a pickle. "What's the point of cutting up cadavers so I can help people later when I can make a difference now?"

They talked about Maggie's childhood on the farm and her dream of coming to New York.

"I joined a temp agency, but so far I haven't received much work," she admitted. "Sometimes I think I should go back to the farm. My parents are getting older, and at least I was useful. But then I get this choking feeling"—she pointed to her chest—"and I'd do anything to stay."

Jake poked at a piece of lettuce.

"I'm glad you came, and I don't think you should leave." He looked at her, and his eyes seemed even bluer. "When I'm in the South Pacific I want to imagine you sitting right here. The loveliest girl in New York eating a turkey sandwich at the lunch counter at Woolworth's."

They finished their sandwich and walked up and down the aisles until it stopped raining. Maggie insisted on buying Jake a small bottle of aftershave. She couldn't afford it, and she'd never bought a gift for a man before. But she imagined him sitting in a foxhole far from home, and her heart turned over.

She handed it to him. "That's so you'll smell good for the pretty nurses."

"I'll take it, but I won't use it until I see you again." He slipped the bottle in his pocket. "On the first day of my next leave. I'll write and tell you when it is."

Maggie could tell that Jake wanted to kiss her. She wanted to kiss him too. She'd never felt that way before. As if her body was lit by a small spark. She told herself a kiss wasn't possible. They were in a crowded aisle of Woolworth's, and they met only a few hours earlier.

She reached into her purse and scribbled on a piece of paper.

"It's a deal. Here's my address and phone number."

~

Maggie brought her mind back to the present. She and Jake happened so long ago. She had barely been eighteen when they met. She never would have started seeing Teddy if she hadn't been ready to fall in love again. And she did love him. A grown-up love that was so different from the starry-eyed first love she had felt for Jake.

So why hadn't she accepted Teddy's marriage proposal? Was it because she was afraid things might change and ruin what they had? Or was it something else, a stubborn desire to take care of herself? Whatever it was, perhaps it was time to rethink her refusals. True love was hard to find, and she didn't want to lose Teddy.

She took the Nancy Mitford novel to the cash register and gave the clerk a five-dollar bill.

Teddy was picking her up in an hour, and they were going to have cocktails and go out to dinner. Then she'd tell him about *The Maggie Lane Baking Show*.

Chapter Two

The Chinese restaurant was called Ruby Foo's Den, and it was on Fifty-Second Street. The dining room was on two levels, with red velvet booths separated by bamboo screens. The walls were painted green, and the ceiling was hung with glass chandeliers.

They sat at a table in the balcony. Teddy looked handsome in a navy sport coat and striped tie. A red handkerchief was folded in his breast pocket. Maggie ordered chop suey and chicken chow mein. Teddy asked for blond miso soup and pork chow mein and Ruby's Crisp Chicken. There was a platter of Ruby Rolls made with shrimp tempura and crab and avocado.

The evening had started with two highballs that Teddy fixed at Maggie's apartment. Neither of them were big drinkers. Teddy refused to give in to the "middle-aged" spread that was the result of a desk job and too many 6:00 p.m. cocktails. He jogged in Central Park after work and played squash three times a week.

Maggie planned on telling her news at the apartment, but something stopped her. He was in a particularly good mood, and she was afraid that saying she was going to have her own television show while he was a voice on the radio might ruin it. Even if Teddy wasn't ambitious, he could be proud, and she didn't know how he'd take it. It was better to wait until they were at the restaurant. Teddy loved Ruby Foo's Den. The owner knew him and usually added a plate of chow mein to his order at no charge.

"We can't eat all that food," Maggie said, eyeing the platter heaped with rolls and the side dishes of garlic noodles and spicy fried rice.

"It's not all for us. Mrs. Silverman in apartment B can't leave the building because her sciatica is acting up. Edna Miller on the third floor broke her wrist, and her husband doesn't cook. They've been living on her daughter's casseroles, and her daughter went out of town."

One of the things Maggie loved about Teddy was his generosity. Even if he lived paycheck to paycheck, he got his shoes shined weekly because he wanted to support the shoeshine stand, and he always gave delivery boys and waiters an extra tip.

"You can't feed all the old women in your building," Maggie protested.

"We all help each other. Mrs. Silverman brought aspirin when I had the flu, and Edna lent me a Band-Aid when I cut my finger." Teddy shrugged. "I don't want to talk about the women in the building; I have something exciting to tell you." He reached into his pocket and took out three packets of cigarettes.

"These are for you."

Maggie said she didn't understand. Teddy knew she didn't smoke. And Teddy loved his cigarettes. They were part of him, like the silver watch he wore that his parents gave him for his twenty-first birthday. He was more confident when he had a pack of Camels in his breast pocket, and Maggie tried not to question it.

"You can do whatever you like with them. Give them to the guy behind the counter at the newsagent or the women in the stenographer pool at CBS. They love to smoke. It's how they maintain their trim figures."

Teddy was right—almost every desk on the typist floor held a pack of cigarettes and an ashtray. The cigarettes suppressed the women's appetites, so they didn't have to worry about eating too many french fries on a date. Maggie had tried Teddy's Camels several times, but she didn't like the taste.

"I had a meeting with Roger Harmsworth this afternoon. I'm quitting smoking to celebrate," Teddy said.

Roger was Teddy's producer. Maggie had gently suggested that Teddy approach Roger about giving him a national radio program instead of the local show that he hosted now.

"It went well?" Maggie asked hopefully. It would be easier to tell Teddy her news if he'd gotten the promotion.

"Better than I expected," Teddy concurred. "You're looking at the new content producer of *Dial Soap's New York Radio Hour*."

Maggie's brow furrowed. "That's the show you anchor now. Why would you want to be the content producer? You were supposed to talk to Roger about hosting *Wheaties Radio Theater*."

Teddy picked up a pack of cigarettes and turned it over.

"Stan Metz is going to be the Wheaties host. I didn't want it anyway. It's too much pressure. This is much better. I'll be responsible for formatting the show and choosing the music between the breaks. If it goes well, Roger will give me national radio programs, *Sunburst Soap Talent Scouts* and *Imperial Margarine's Spooky Hour*."

Maggie played with her napkin. At least Teddy had been the star of the show; now he would be working behind the scenes. And it couldn't pay as much as being the host.

"I asked to be the content producer, and Roger agreed with me," Teddy said, noticing her disappointed expression. "Being on the air was stressful. Sometimes after a commercial, I missed my cue and I could never catch up. That's why I'm giving up smoking." He placed the pack on the table. "I don't need these anymore. I'm going to be as happy at work as when I was a kid delivering newspapers on my bicycle."

Teddy did look more relaxed. His eyes sparkled. The worry lines around his mouth had softened. Perhaps it was what he needed. The nighttime sweats would ease, and he would have the energy to come to terms with whatever haunted him about his past.

"If that's what you want, then of course I'm happy," she said carefully.

Teddy glanced at her expectantly. "You said earlier that you had news too."

Maggie's cheeks turned red. She was tempted to tell him something else—her neighbor's cat had kittens and her neighbor offered her one, or one of the listeners on the show sent her two tickets to *Peter Pan* on Broadway. But they were supposed to go to lunch with Tommy at the Waldorf. She couldn't put it off.

"I had a visitor on the set." Her voice was hesitant. "Tommy Fischer from Deluxe Baking Company."

"Sponsors belong behind their desks, not disrupting things at the studio." Teddy frowned. "Did you know that my father used to bring me into Manhattan when I was a kid, and none of those buildings—the Chrysler Building and the Empire State Building—existed? Now they're filled with companies like Deluxe and Dial that run our lives at home and at work."

"Tommy was very nice," she corrected. "He had a proposition."

Maggie told him about *The Maggie Lane Baking Show*.

"I probably shouldn't take it. I've never smoothed frosting on a cake or separated the yolks from the whites in an egg. And I really should wear my glasses to answer viewers' letters on the air," she said hurriedly. "If the ratings are low, I'll get fired. Then I won't be able to afford my apartment, and I may have to leave New York . . ."

Teddy put his hand out to stop her.

"Of course you should take it," he cut in gently. He kissed her. "They wouldn't have offered it to you if they didn't think you'd be a success."

Maggie let herself breathe a sigh of relief. All afternoon she had been thinking about having her own television show. It was beyond her wildest dreams, but she knew she could do it if she got the chance.

"And you wouldn't mind?"

"Mind?" Teddy repeated, puzzled.

She took a bite of chicken chow mein. "I'd be working longer hours, so we might not go out to dinner as often. On the weekends,

I should read recipe books instead of spending the whole day at museums."

"My workday will be shorter. I'll cook," Teddy said. "We'll drive up to my parents' place and get those pots and pans my mother keeps pressing on me. On the weekends we can read recipe books together."

"There's one other thing," Maggie said. Her voice choked up. Teddy was being so supportive, and she reflected on how lucky she was to have him. "Tommy wants me to give advice about running a household. He thinks I'm married. He asked us to lunch tomorrow at the Waldorf."

Teddy didn't say anything. He made a big production of arranging egg rolls on his plate.

"Then we'll get married. I'll call my mother," he said, without looking at her. "Father Darcy can probably marry us tomorrow." He glanced at his watch. "I'll call in sick at work, and we'll drive up this evening. He'll perform the ceremony in my parents' living room. We'll be back in New York by lunchtime."

Maggie's heart hammered. She had never heard a wilder idea. Even if her parents couldn't afford to host a wedding reception, they would want to be present at the ceremony. And she loved them. She didn't want to get married without them. Teddy's mother, Patty, had been hinting for months that she couldn't wait to throw Teddy and Maggie an engagement party.

Yet part of her was excited at the prospect of being married to Teddy. She would finally stop worrying whether she was making a mistake whenever she turned him down. And he was being so thoughtful, it made her less apprehensive about taking such a big step.

"We'll send your parents train tickets during the summer and treat them to a weekend in New York," Teddy said when she voiced her concerns. "And my mother can throw us a party when we return from our honeymoon. She'll be thrilled to introduce everyone at the country club to her new daughter-in-law, the host of *The Maggie Lane Baking Show*."

Maggie reached for her water glass.

"There won't be time for a honeymoon," she protested. "Tommy will want me to start immediately."

"You're the show's star. Tommy can wait. Every bride deserves a honeymoon." He reached into his pocket and took out a brochure. "Four nights at the Pines Resort in the Poconos. There's dancing every night, and the honeymoon suite has a view of the mountains."

The brochure was well worn, as if it had been in Teddy's pocket for ages.

"Where did you get this?" she asked. The resort resembled a long log cabin. The lobby had red carpeting and timbered ceilings and a stone fireplace. The dining room overlooked a flower garden, and there was a ballroom with round tables arranged around a dance floor.

"I couldn't ask you to marry me without planning a honeymoon," he answered. "It's close enough to New York that we won't waste time traveling. And they get big-name entertainment. Bob Hope performed last month."

Teddy looked so hopeful. Maggie had never felt so touched.

"It looks lovely." She folded it and handed it back.

"We can go next weekend." Teddy took her hand. "Maggie, from the moment we met, I knew you were the woman for me. You're bright and beautiful, and you make me want to be a better man. If you say yes, I promise I'll spend the rest of my life making you happy."

Maggie glanced around to see if any of the diners were watching. Teddy had proposed so many times before, each time it had been easy to say no. But this time, all her doubts—Teddy's black moods, her own past that he knew nothing about—disappeared. Teddy was proving that he was there for her. Even though she kept saying no, he hadn't changed his mind. It finally had all become clear to her. He loved her and she loved him. She had to believe in him if they were going to have a future. She couldn't think of a reason to turn him down. And she didn't want to. She was ready to be his wife.

Tears came to her eyes, and she blinked them away.

"Yes, I'll marry you."

Teddy leaned forward and kissed her. It was a warm, deep kiss.

"We'll go home and get the ring, and we can both pack an overnight bag," he said when they were done eating. "I'll ask my mother to order a wedding cake from the bakery, and we'll need some champagne for the wedding breakfast. Alice can make eggs Benedict, and my father will give a toast. I'll call the florist and order a bridal bouquet, and a boutonniere for my tuxedo."

Maggie had never seen Teddy in so much control. He seemed different from his usual self. She wondered whether he had been like that during the war, confidently making lists and giving orders. She was reminded that there were parts of him that she didn't know.

Suddenly, her hands felt clammy. It was all happening so fast. She tried to think of something to say. "Are you sure we're not rushing this? Your father won't have time to prepare a speech, and where will we find witnesses? I might not be able to get hold of my parents. They're probably already in bed. In the morning they'll be out before . . ."

Teddy kissed her. He placed a ten-dollar bill on the table and took her hand.

"What are you doing? You can't leave that much money, and you forgot the food for Edna and Mrs. Silverman," Maggie said.

"The waiter needs the extra tip. His wife is having a baby. I'll have Ruby's delivery boy bring the takeout to Edna and Mrs. Silverman." He led her outside and flagged down a taxi. "I forgot the most important thing. You'll see when we get there."

In the cab, Teddy leaned forward and whispered into the driver's ear. The taxi pulled into traffic, narrowly missing a bus. Maggie watched the sidewalk fly by, until the cab finally stopped in front of Macy's.

Teddy took a twenty from his wallet and handed it to Maggie.

"This should be enough. If it isn't, ask the saleswoman to put it on my mother's account." He glanced at his watch. "The store closes in twenty minutes. I'll wait here."

"What am I buying?" Maggie asked.

Her nervousness returned about what they were doing. Her stomach felt queasy, and she clutched the money in her hand. At the same time, she couldn't stop her mounting excitement.

Teddy's smile was as bright and broad as the marquees on Broadway. "Your wedding dress, of course. Don't worry, I won't see it. I already told the taxi driver to lay it down carefully in the trunk."

～

They drove Teddy's Buick Roadmaster to his parents' house in the hamlet of Rye. Rye was a mix of bucolic farms and white clapboard houses built on the sites of the old gilded mansions of upstate New York. Teddy's parents moved there in the 1920s, when the Bronx River Parkway made it easy for executives to commute to New York. His father worked for an insurance agency in Manhattan, and his mother was head of the local women's club. She belonged to a bridge group and a sewing circle. Teddy had adored his childhood. He often talked about afternoons spent in the Rye library and playing baseball in the town park. Being able to walk for miles without seeing anything but cows, eating ice cream sundaes at the corner drugstore.

His mother greeted them at the front door. Patty was pretty, with brown eyes and shoulder-length blond hair. She wore a V-neck circle dress. A strand of pearls hung around her neck, and she wore a heart-shaped silver watch.

"This is a lovely surprise," she gushed to Maggie. "I sent Harry out to buy champagne."

"You didn't have to do that." Maggie followed Patty into the living room. The room was stylishly furnished with a striped sofa and matching love seat. A wooden console held a television and radio. The floor was covered with a floral rug, and glass vases on the end tables held roses from the garden.

"Of course I did." Patty sat on the sofa and motioned for Maggie to sit beside her. "It's not every day that my son gets engaged and married."

The whole drive up to Rye, Maggie grew more anxious and wondered whether they were making a mistake. She would have to give up her studio apartment and move into Teddy's one bedroom. Teddy's place didn't have enough wall space, and she'd have to store her pictures and books. And she hated leaving her neighborhood. She'd miss her neighbor's cat, and she'd have to find a new laundry and nail salon.

"It is sudden. I told Teddy we should wait," Maggie wavered. "I know you want to throw us an engagement party, and I haven't been able to tell my parents. I tried calling them, but they're visiting my aunt. Perhaps it would be better to hold the wedding during the summer."

"Nonsense." Patty shook her head. "Teddy told me all about *The Maggie Lane Baking Show*, and I agree. Single career girls in New York don't know their way around a kitchen. It will be much nicer for your viewers if you're married." She eyed Maggie cautiously. "It's soon to think about it, but you should consider moving to Rye. The sweetest house became available on Elm Street, two bedrooms and a home office. Harry and I discussed it, and we'd be happy to help with a down payment. Imagine how handy it would be when the children come if Harry and I are down the street."

The last thing Maggie wanted was to move out of New York. As soon as she was hired, she planned on looking for an apartment that she and Teddy loved. Even if it took months to save up enough money, living in a Park Avenue duplex or in one of those wonderful prewar buildings on Riverside Drive was what she wanted most in the world. She couldn't remember when she'd first heard of street names like Park Avenue and Fifth Avenue and Lexington Avenue. It might have been in a movie she had seen, or a book that she had read. They conjured up images of buildings with striped awnings, and doormen in red-and-gold uniforms. It was all the opposite of the farm where she grew up, and she wouldn't rest until she owned an apartment.

But she liked Patty, and she didn't want to hurt her feelings.

"We're not ready to buy a house," Maggie said. "I don't even have the job, and I might be a complete failure."

"You need to have confidence in yourself." Patty squeezed her hand. "Father Darcy will be here soon to go over the ceremony. Why don't we go upstairs? You can get settled in your room."

Maggie glanced around for Teddy, but he was outside taking their bags from the car. She didn't have a choice but to follow Patty upstairs to the bedrooms.

"This will be your last time in the upstairs guest room," Patty said when they reached the end of the corridor. "On your next visit, you and Teddy will be married, and you'll sleep together in the downstairs suite."

Patty left, and Maggie set her handbag on the bed. She pulled off her gloves and walked to the window. The back of the house looked out on a field. A cobblestone path led down to Patty's rose garden, and there was a lawn area with a shaded pergola.

Rye was so different from New York. At this hour, if she stood at her apartment window she'd see the congested street below, with cars honking and yellow cabs lingering at the curb. Here, the only sound was the crickets in the fields, and instead of car headlights, a tapestry of stars stretched across the sky.

She could imagine living in Rye or White Plains or any of the other towns in Westchester County with as much difficulty as moving back to her parents' farm. Thankfully, Teddy felt the same. He often said that living in New York was like taking out a new identity card. Once you became a New Yorker, you could never go back to being someone else.

She had forgotten about their wedding night until Patty mentioned the guest suite. Now, a feeling of unease overcame her. Teddy knew she wasn't a virgin. She had waited as long as she could when they started dating, but eventually she had to tell him. He would have found out the first time they made love. He hadn't asked for details, and she hadn't given him any. So many times she started to tell him about Jake, but something always stopped her.

She and Teddy had been together for two years. There had been other women in his life before they met, but he never talked about them. Maggie was happy about that. It made her feel less guilty not talking about Jake and her own past.

Could she share a bed with Teddy every night without ever mentioning Jake? And what about Teddy's nightmares from the war? Maggie almost never slept over at Teddy's apartment, but when she had, he tossed and turned and often woke up bathed in sweat. Sometimes he even talked in his sleep. She'd be jerked awake by Teddy mumbling names of places she'd never heard of. French names she guessed were villages in France. A few times in the beginning, she'd asked him about them. Each time, he either made light of it and say she was imagining things, or a brooding expression would come over his face and he'd stalk out of the room. Eventually she had decided not to mention it again. He would confide in her when he was ready.

If only there was someone she could talk to. Between her work and Teddy, there hadn't been time to make friendships in New York. And her parents had such a happy marriage on the farm. It wouldn't be something her mother would understand.

There were good things about being married. She'd never be lonely. And she did love Teddy. He was everything she wanted. He was kind to others, like the residents in his apartment building. And he went out of his way to do nice things for her. Once when she ran out of her favorite lipstick and the drugstore didn't carry it anymore, he wrote to the cosmetics company and asked where he could buy it. The company sent back a thank-you letter for being a loyal customer, accompanied by two tubes of lipstick. Teddy had been so proud of himself. He loved to make her happy. But marriage seemed so complicated. They would have to discuss having children. She couldn't imagine having them for years, especially with her new career. But what if Teddy wanted them sooner?

"There you are." Teddy entered the room. He placed Maggie's overnight bag on the bed. "My father just got back from shopping. A bottle of champagne and some caviar are waiting in the living room."

"He bought caviar too?" Maggie said, feeling slightly guilty. Teddy's parents were being so sweet. She should be more enthusiastic.

Teddy grinned. "My mother called ahead and asked for everything she wanted. There's also crackers and a box of chocolate eclairs."

"Your mother is being so kind," Maggie replied.

"I heard her on the phone, telling everyone that her daughter-in-law-to-be is the star of a television show. She can't wait to introduce you to her sewing circle," Teddy said. "Father Darcy is here. He's going to go over the ceremony and ask us the important questions."

Maggie looked up from unfolding the clothes in her bag.

"What kind of questions?"

"The ones he always asks a couple before they get married. When did they fall in love, whether they've been engaged or married before. If there's anything stopping them from being legally wed."

A chill passed through Maggie. She glanced down at her overnight bag so Teddy couldn't see her expression.

"He sounds intimidating," she said with a half smile.

Teddy gave a little laugh. "Don't worry about Father Darcy. He's a pushover for a pretty, intelligent woman."

"Of course I'm not worried." Maggie tried to think of something to say. "It's just been a long day. I have a bit of a headache. I'm ready for bed."

Teddy wrapped his arms around her.

"Then I'll tell Father Darcy to keep it brief. The most important thing is that my bride gets a good night's sleep." He kissed her. "Tomorrow is our wedding day."

Chapter Three

The next morning, Maggie woke up early. She lay in bed gazing at the mist that had settled over the fields. In a few hours she'd be married. From now on, everything she did would include Teddy. She wouldn't be able to come home after a long day at the studio and head straight for the bath. Instead, she and Teddy would call before they left work and ask what the other wanted to do for dinner. Even if she was tired, if Teddy wanted to go out, she would go with him. And never again could she lather her face with cold cream and sit on the sofa with a bowl of cereal and a magazine.

She told herself that most couples got married eventually, and they were happy. But she was only twenty-four. She wasn't ready for a life of checking the pot roast in the oven and making sure the laundry put enough starch in Teddy's shirts. He was supportive of her career, but what if that changed? And when would Teddy figure out what he wanted to do that would make him happy? Surely he didn't see himself as a content producer forever, when he was so talented as an on-air presenter. Even if he wasn't ambitious, he was intelligent. And he liked nice things. His clothes and everything in his apartment were good quality.

She padded downstairs to the kitchen and made a pot of coffee. When Teddy woke up, she'd say that she'd tell Tommy the truth at lunch. She and Teddy were engaged, but they weren't going to get married soon. Starring in her new baking show would occupy her time, and Teddy had a new job too.

Teddy would be disappointed, but he loved her. He would understand. They'd go back to being the way they were except with a sapphire-and-diamond engagement ring on her finger.

Maggie took her coffee into the living room, and streamers hung from the ceiling. A banner over the fireplace read CONGRATULATIONS MR. AND MRS. TEDDY BUCKLEY. The table had been set with champagne glasses. There was a cake knife and a small stack of dessert plates.

Teddy had been so sweet the previous evening. He told Father Darcy that Maggie was tired, and the priest didn't ask them any questions. He just showed them where to stand for the vows and instructed Teddy when to kiss the bride. After Father Darcy left, Maggie and Teddy sat on the sofa, and she fell asleep against his shoulder. He picked her up and carried her upstairs to the guest room.

She took a sip of the hot coffee and tried to quell her anxiety. It was normal to have wedding-day nerves, and everything had all happened so quickly. She barely had time to recognize that in a few hours they were getting married. And now there were more reasons to go through with it. Teddy's parents were counting on the wedding happening. It would be wrong to disappoint them when they were so enthusiastic. She promised Teddy she'd marry him today, and she wouldn't go back on her word. She resolved to stop flip-flopping about her decision. Instead, she took the coffee cup upstairs and began to get ready. If she was going to get married, she wanted to be a bride that Teddy and his parents and she, herself, would be proud of.

An hour later, she stood at the top of the staircase in her wedding dress. She had fallen in love with the dress as soon as she saw it at Macy's. It was ribbed silk with a tea-length full skirt and sweetheart neckline. The cap sleeves had lace appliques, and gold and silver threads were woven in the hem. She paired it with kitten heels and a short lace veil.

Father Darcy stood in front of the fireplace, his cheeks pink from the glass of champagne he drank when he arrived. Teddy stood beside him, and when Maggie saw him—wonderfully handsome in his tuxedo, with his hair freshly brushed and his cheeks smooth with aftershave—something warmed inside her. He glanced up at her with an expression of such love and expectancy that everything she had been worrying about—*The Maggie Lane Baking Show*, finding the perfect apartment, Jake and the past—faded away. All she knew was that she couldn't wait to stand beside him.

When she reached the bottom of the stairs, the piano music started and Harry took her arm. She met Teddy in front of the fireplace, and Father Darcy read a psalm. Harry handed Teddy the rings, and she and Teddy exchanged vows. Then Teddy kissed her and everyone clapped, and it was a blur of popping champagne and colored confetti and the smell of eggs Benedict and wheat toast.

Later, when the cake had been cut and she and Teddy slow-danced around the living room, Maggie had never felt so happy. Though not everything had run smoothly. There had been the moment when Father Darcy asked if anyone knew a reason for the wedding not to continue, and her heart had hammered.

But no one noticed. And moments later, they slipped the rings on each other's fingers, and Teddy had kissed her. She could still taste his kiss—sweet and minty from toothpaste. Tonight was their wedding night, and they would spend it at Teddy's apartment. All she had to do was get through lunch at the Waldorf with Tommy, and then she could take a hot bath and relax.

"You're very quiet," Teddy said. They had just turned onto Park Avenue and pulled up in front of the Waldorf Hotel. Maggie had changed out of her wedding dress and wore a dove-gray two-piece suit. A pair of gloves was folded in her lap, and the new alligator-skin purse Teddy's mother gave her as a wedding present was by her side.

"I was thinking about the morning." Maggie turned to Teddy. "It couldn't have been more perfect."

Teddy grinned. "Except for the part where Father Darcy drank too much champagne and forgot your name during his toast."

Teddy's father had stepped in and finished the priest's toast. Everyone laughed, and Teddy's mother passed around slices of wedding cake. The cake was a traditional fruitcake with white icing and sugared rose petals for decorations.

"Your parents were lovely. Your mother didn't need to give me a wedding present," Maggie said, stroking her new handbag.

The bag was from B. Altman department store in White Plains. It would be perfect to have on *The Maggie Lane Baking Show*. It was the kind of handbag that sophisticated housewives wore, usually coordinated with gloves and matching pumps.

"She bought it for your birthday, but she wanted to give it to you today," Teddy said.

The buzz of champagne was wearing off, and Maggie felt emotional.

"I didn't know it would be so easy," she admitted. "Getting married seemed so difficult."

Teddy turned off the engine. He took her hand.

"I knew from our first date that we'd end up together," he said confidently. "Do you remember we spent an hour talking about our favorite museums in New York? You said the Met was the best because art expands your view of the world. I argued there was nothing better than the Natural History Museum because it teaches you science and history. We finally agreed that each were important, and the next weekend we visited both."

The Natural History Museum was on the Upper West Side. Afterward they walked around the leafy neighborhood and peered up at the apartment buildings. Teddy had been so engaging to talk to. He loved inventing stories about the residents of the different buildings. When she confessed that she'd always dreamed of owning an apartment in Manhattan, he listened without questioning how she was going to achieve her goal. For the first time in ages, Maggie had felt that anything was possible.

Now they were married, and she was going to be the star of *The Maggie Lane Baking Show*. She imagined walking into a real estate office with Teddy and asking to see an apartment on Park Avenue. The agent would hand them the keys, and they would walk in and admire the high ceilings and the views of Central Park and know immediately it was right for them.

She really did love Teddy. He loved New York as much as she did, and they were going to have a wonderful life. She didn't want to go into the marriage with any secrets. They had half an hour before they were meeting Tommy for lunch. This was the time to tell Teddy about her past. Then she could be truly happy, and there would be nothing to worry about again.

"There's something I want to . . ." she began.

Teddy glanced down at his watch. "I almost forgot. I promised Roger I'd call as soon as we got back to New York. There's a question about the music for this afternoon's show."

"Of course." Maggie hid her disappointment that she had missed her chance. She'd have to bring up the subject after lunch. "While you do that, I'll use the Waldorf's powder room and freshen up."

Tommy was already sitting at a table when Maggie entered the Waldorf's dining room. She'd never eaten there before. It was very grand, with tall marble columns and potted palm trees. Framed murals hung on the walls, and rounded windows were covered with velvet drapes.

Tommy jumped up. "Maggie, it's good to see you. I'm glad you came."

Maggie realized how nervous she was.

She wished Teddy hadn't gone to make a phone call. For the past day, all she'd thought about was the wedding and *The Maggie Lane Baking Show*. What if Tommy reconsidered and didn't offer her the job?

"I said I'd come," she reminded him with a smile. "And I don't know anyone who would pass up lunch at the Waldorf."

Teddy appeared at the entrance. He looked very handsome. Before they left Rye, he had changed from his tuxedo into a navy suit and fedora.

He took off his hat and joined them at the table.

"Teddy Buckley." He held out his hand. "My wife has told me all about you."

"I'm afraid I don't know anything about you." Tommy shook his hand. "There was nothing in Maggie's file at CBS on her personal life."

Maggie was about to say something, but Teddy spoke first.

"Well, you can be the first to congratulate us." He slid into the booth next to Maggie. "I've been asking her to marry me for months. We finally were married this morning at my parents' house. You're looking at the new Mr. and Mrs. Teddy Buckley."

Maggie blushed and proceeded to tell Tommy about the wedding breakfast at her new in-laws' house in Rye.

"That's the kind of story the show's audience will love," Tommy said when she finished. "Our studies have shown that since the war, the age of women getting married has dropped. Many couples have to pay for the weddings themselves. We can do a segment featuring a menu for a home wedding. The cake will be a Deluxe Baking Company dessert, of course."

Maggie thought that was a good idea. She would ask Patty for the recipe for eggs Benedict. And she'd find out where Patty bought the sugared rose petals for decorations.

Tommy ordered oysters Rockefeller for the table as appetizers. Tommy and Teddy both had the beef stroganoff as an entrée, and Maggie asked for veal cutlets with green beans. They talked about the format of the show and Maggie's celebrity guests.

Tommy turned to Teddy. "Tell me about yourself. There's something about your voice that sounds familiar."

Teddy picked up his water glass. He said he hosted *New York Radio Hour* on CBS. Before that he was the voice of Pathé News during the war.

Tommy beamed with recognition. "I used to listen to the broadcast with my parents every night. I have bad vision, so the draft board wouldn't take me. I envied you in a way. You were in the middle of the action, but you didn't have to fight."

Teddy reached for the packet of cigarettes that Tommy had placed on the table. "Do you mind if I have one?"

"Go ahead." Tommy took a lighter from his pocket. "The most moving segments were from that village in France. What was the name? I can't remember."

Maggie had never seen Teddy's face turn so white. His hand trembled as he held the cigarette.

"Oradour-sur-Glane." Teddy's voice was tight. "I was traveling in a British Army jeep. It was a coincidence that we were staying nearby." He inhaled. "We were too late, of course. The Germans killed everyone in the village—643 innocent men, women, and children. You can't imagine what it was like. An entire population gone. Nothing left in the village except a few empty prams and the balls the old French men used to play boules on the lawn."

Maggie's ears pricked up. Teddy had never mentioned Oradour-sur-Glane to her. She could tell from his anguished tone how it must have affected him. If only he shared his experiences during the war with her, she could help him. It wasn't the time to talk about it in front of Tommy, and she didn't want to make Teddy uncomfortable. She tried to think of a way to change the subject.

"You did an excellent job of reporting," Tommy continued before she could say anything. "I'm surprised you're not doing national news now. You could be like Edward Murrow on the radio, or become a news anchor on television."

In the last few years, CBS and NBC had started evening news programs sponsored by R. J. Reynolds Tobacco Company. Maggie wasn't usually home in time to watch them, but she often walked past an appliance store from the subway and saw the news anchors on the television sets in the window.

"Teddy is happy doing local radio," Maggie said to Tommy. "In fact, he's just been named the show's content producer."

Tommy set his napkin on the table.

"Well, you might change your mind. Television is the future," Tommy offered. "Let's talk about *The Maggie Lane Baking Show*. We're confident that Deluxe Baking Company's customers are going to fall in love with Maggie."

Teddy stubbed out the cigarette. His cheeks were still pale, and he looked queasy.

"Of course they will. I fell in love with her the first time we met. She's irresistible." He kissed Maggie on the cheek. "She will be a natural in front of the camera."

Tommy took a pile of papers from his briefcase. "Now, if we're all in agreement, let's look at the paperwork."

The first few pages detailed the salary and bonus structure. Maggie's mouth fell open. She was going to earn three times her current salary with two weeks' paid vacation. There were health benefits and a pension plan.

Tommy noticed her expression. "Deluxe Baking Company takes care of our employees. We're like a family. Why don't you take the packet home and look over it together. You can sign everything and bring it to CBS television studios in the morning. I'll give you a tour and introduce you to everyone on the show."

Maggie let out her breath. It really was happening. She was going to be the star of her own baking show.

"There are a few more papers to sign." Tommy was going through his briefcase. He handed her a paper. "A noncompete, and the morality clause."

Maggie held the paper. "A morality clause?"

"They're very common. I'm surprised you didn't sign one at CBS," Tommy said. "It's particularly important for the show. Maggie Lane is going to be America's girl next door. There can't be any skeletons in our star's past."

The paper shook under her fingers. Her stomach dropped, and a feeling of foreboding overwhelmed her. Tommy and Teddy were both looking at her expectantly.

"I'll sign everything and have it back to you tomorrow."

Tommy snapped shut his briefcase. He turned from Maggie to Teddy.

"Then why don't we order a bottle of champagne and dessert to celebrate!"

The thought of more champagne made Maggie's head spin. "Teddy and I have had enough champagne and cake for one day," she said firmly. "Thank you, it's been a wonderful lunch."

~

It was evening, and Maggie sat in Teddy's bedroom. His apartment was furnished in the latest style. There was a step-down living room with chocolate-brown leather sofas and a little writing desk next to the window. A cocktail cart was placed next to the fireplace, and one wall was taken up by a bookshelf. The hallway led to the bedroom. On the other side of the hall was a bathroom with mirrored walls and a kitchenette outfitted with the latest appliances.

Maggie glanced over the papers that Tommy had given her. If she signed the morality clause, she could never tell Teddy about her past. She would be asking him to hide something too. If she didn't sign it, she wouldn't get the job. Teddy was as excited about it as she was. She heard him telling the parking attendant at the Waldorf that his new bride was going to be a television star.

She reached for the small box she had brought over from her apartment. It contained the business cards of Realtors she had collected over the years. Each one represented an apartment she had fallen in love with—a one bedroom on the Upper East Side a few blocks from the Metropolitan Museum of Art. A flat in one of the co-op buildings on Madison Avenue with a doorman who would walk your dog. And a gorgeous top-floor apartment opposite Central Park with a second bedroom that had been converted into an indoor solarium.

She and Teddy would start looking for a place of their own to buy. When they found one, they would furnish it with pieces they loved. One of those teak dining table sets from Denmark that was all the rage. The living room would have art deco–style furniture and a combined television/radio console. And they'd bring over Teddy's cocktail cart and his collection of books.

Maybe Teddy would even let his mother buy some things for the apartment. It would make Patty happy, and Maggie wouldn't feel guilty about not moving to Rye. If they could afford a two bedroom, or a one bedroom plus a small office, Maggie could invite her mother to stay. It would be fun to show her New York.

There was no reason not to sign the papers. It wasn't as if she was going to become a famous movie star like Betty Grable or Lana Turner, with her face splashed all over magazines. She was the host of a television baking show.

She scribbled her name on the printed line and tucked the papers into her purse. Then she went to take a bath.

Chapter Four

CBS television studios was on Madison Avenue in Midtown. Maggie arrived at 9:00 a.m., when the lobby was bustling with activity. Executives in pin-striped suits and fedoras carried leather briefcases. Secretaries wore dirndl skirts and blouses with cap sleeves. Maggie had dressed carefully in a floral dress with a wasp waist and full skirt. She wore a pillbox hat and carried her alligator-skin handbag.

When she gave her name to the security guard and he handed her a badge and directed her to the elevators, she couldn't stop pinching herself. She pushed the button for the fourth floor, and Tommy's assistant, Marjorie, was waiting at the elevator bank. It all seemed too exciting to be real. The reception area with art deco furniture and photos of famous television personalities on the walls. The glassed offices with views of the Empire State Building and Rockefeller Center.

Tommy was delayed in a meeting, so Marjorie gave Maggie the tour. There were four soundstages, where different television shows were being filmed. She showed Maggie the sound booths where music for the shows was mixed and the coffee stations where Maggie could get fresh coffee and pastries. The most thrilling part was seeing the set for *The Maggie Lane Baking Show*. The construction had just begun, but the pantry was installed, and there was a bay window where she could put cake trays to cool and a round table where she would sit and answer letters from viewers.

Marjorie apologized that she had to get back to her desk, and Maggie wandered around alone. A hallway was lined with dressing rooms. Maggie recognized the names of the stars of some of her favorite programs. Two of the doors didn't have name plaques. She wondered if one of them was hers.

She knocked tentatively on one of the doors without a plaque and poked her head in.

A young woman about her age was standing in front of a mirror. Her dark hair was cut in layers above her shoulders. She had a pretty, heart-shaped face and almond-shaped brown eyes.

"Excuse me, there was no name on the door," Maggie said.

The woman turned around. "Please come in. I'm Dolly Meyers. They haven't gotten around to putting up my name plaque yet."

Maggie recognized her. Dolly played the female lead in a half-hour weekly show called *Fair Game*. The male lead was a sports reporter, and Dolly played his on again/off again girlfriend who was a sports reporter for a competing newspaper.

"I watch *Fair Game* whenever I'm home," Maggie said. "You're a wonderful actress."

Dolly picked up her hairbrush and pulled it through her hair. "I was supposed to play a secretary at the rival newspaper, but the viewers wrote in and wanted to see more of me on the air. It was my idea to make my character the competing reporter. The writers thought it wasn't believable that a woman knew anything about sports."

"I'm Maggie Lane," Maggie introduced herself.

Dolly beamed. "You're going to be the star of *The Maggie Lane Baking Show*."

"I'm so nervous. I've never been on television before besides a few commercials," Maggie confided. "I had my own radio show."

"I appeared in commercials when I was a kid, but my dream was to be a television actress," Dolly replied. "I'm lucky to have my role. Every week, I wait for the ratings to come out. If they go down and the show is canceled, I don't know what I'd do."

"I'm sure that won't happen. It's one of my favorite programs," Maggie said diplomatically.

"I am grateful to have my job," Dolly acknowledged. "I'll be twenty-four next month, and I haven't had much luck with men. Most men want wives with perfect figures and no thoughts in their head except how to fix a martini and keep their slippers warm in the evenings."

"You have a beautiful figure," Maggie commented. Dolly was right—most men didn't care what a woman was thinking. And they didn't want a wife who worked outside the home. It made her grateful to have Teddy. He listened to her when she talked. And he cared about her career.

Dolly wore a pencil skirt that accentuated her rounded hips. A scarf was tied around her neck, and she wore a poplin blouse with a wide belt.

"I'm happy with my looks." Dolly walked over to the dressing table and picked up a bottle of colored tablets. "These have helped. You should get some. They give you enough energy to stand on your feet on the set all day and still go out to dinner and dancing at night."

"What are they?" Maggie asked.

"My mother's doctor prescribed them to her. They used them during the war to keep the soldiers alert. They're harmless. The only difference is instead of craving a burger and fries at lunch, I'm happy with a salad and piece of chicken."

Maggie shook her head. She didn't trust pills, and she would never give up burgers and fries.

"I've talked too much already." Dolly placed them on the dressing table. "Trust me, you'll do wonderfully on the show. Perhaps we can get a drink after work sometime."

Maggie said she'd like that. She felt an instant connection with her new colleague. Dolly was the costar of a popular television program, but she had her own doubts and insecurities. And it would be wonderful to have a female friend at the studio. She walked back to the reception area. Tommy was waiting beside the desk.

"Maggie, I'm sorry I was delayed," he greeted her. "Come into my office, and we'll go over the show."

Maggie followed him into a large office with floor-to-ceiling windows. There was an oak desk and two leather desk chairs.

"I enjoyed lunch yesterday." Tommy sat behind the desk. "You and Teddy make a perfect couple. Now let's go over the format. Each segment will begin with you holding the box of whatever dessert you'll be baking—Deluxe Baking Company pineapple upside-down cake, or Deluxe Baking Company strawberry shortcake. Then while the cake is in the oven, you'll read some letters on the air." He took a piece of paper from the drawer. "Our writers created these samples, but they're the kind of questions you'll receive."

Maggie scanned the paper. How to make the fluffiest pancakes. How to get a chocolate stain out of a blouse. How to sleep in separate beds and keep your husband interested in the bedroom.

She'd never made pancakes. And she didn't have any idea how to get rid of food stains. She took everything to the laundry. The strangest question was the last one. Did viewers really expect her to respond on the air to questions about the bedroom?

Tommy noticed her expression. "Remember, Maggie Lane is going to be America's girl next door. Pretend you're inviting your best friend over for coffee and cake while you discuss your husbands and families."

"Yes, of course." Maggie tried to hide her embarrassment. She'd never had a best friend. And she couldn't imagine talking about sex. But she couldn't let Tommy see that she was nervous.

"You'll get the hang of it in no time," he assured her. "I'll take you over to wardrobe. That reminds me, Elizabeth Bennett from *TV Guide* magazine is coming to interview you tomorrow."

"So soon." Maggie ignored the lump in her throat. "I haven't even had my first day on the set."

"She'll just ask some background questions. Where did you grow up, when did you start baking."

Maggie nodded in agreement. She'd make up a few stories about growing up on the farm. How her mother used fresh cream from the cows and apples from their apple tree to make the most delicious apple Brown Betties. Elizabeth wouldn't ask anything more than that. Why should she? Maggie wasn't famous.

The woman in the wardrobe department showed her the racks of dresses she could choose from for each show. There were separates in a dozen colors, swing dresses with full skirts, and a whole rack devoted to cardigans in summer fabrics. In the hair and makeup department, a man named Mack teased her hair and tried different powders and lipsticks on her face.

By the time she left, it was past lunchtime. Somehow it seemed too ordinary to sit in a diner with a sandwich and a soda when she'd floated through the past few hours. She decided to pick up her favorite Chinese takeout and sit in Central Park instead.

First, she had to stop at the jewelry store. Her wedding band was too big and kept slipping off. She gave the gold band to the clerk and waited while he went to the back. An antique ring behind a glass case caught her eye. She peered through the case more closely.

It couldn't be the same ring. Her eyes were playing tricks on her. When the salesclerk returned, she'd ask him to take it out of the case, just to make sure. Her legs felt wobbly, and she sat down in a chair and waited.

She remembered the last day of Jake's leave. They had met only eight days earlier, but he was so easy to be with, she felt like she had known him forever.

～

Jake's ship was supposed to leave in the second week of February 1944. But it needed repairs, so he and Maggie had an extra six days together. It seemed such an unexpected gift, like the New York weather that had suddenly turned pleasant—pale blue skies instead of gray clouds, temperatures in the fifties instead of dipping into the low forties. They decided they couldn't waste it and spent almost every minute together.

Jake loved to walk, so they took the subway to the Lower East Side and strolled all the way uptown. They stopped at the New York Public Library to sit by the fireplace in the reading room and at Rockefeller Center to drink hot chocolate and watch the ice-skaters.

One day, they took the train upstate and wandered around the mansions along the Hudson River. Jake told her about growing up in Ohio and how when he came to New York he felt like an explorer who'd discovered a new continent. Maggie slipped her hand into his pocket to keep warm and answered that she felt exactly the same.

They talked about his desire to become a heart surgeon when he got out of the navy, and how Maggie still didn't know what she wanted to do. The one thing she was sure of was that she wasn't going to leave New York. It was everything she had hoped it would be.

Jake was leaving the next day, and Maggie had planned a special evening. She was going to surprise him with reservations at Keens Steakhouse on Herald Square. Every Tuesday night they had a special for servicemen where the entrées were half price. The restaurant was part of New York history, and its mutton chops were supposed to be delicious. She spent all morning deciding what to wear and how to do her hair. Usually, those things didn't matter to her, but she wanted Jake to remember her sitting across from him in the candlelight, looking lovely.

In the morning, the temp agency called and said she got her first television commercial. It didn't pay much because the camera wouldn't see her face—only her legs dancing on top of a Westinghouse washing machine. But it was still exciting, and it would buy a good bottle of wine at dinner.

The telephone rang as she was about to go out and buy flowers for the apartment. If Jake came over after dinner, she wanted the space to look warm and inviting.

"It's Jake." His voice came over the line. "I have a special dinner planned. Meet me on the corner of West Broadway and Park Place at five o'clock."

Jake said he would have picked Maggie up, but he had to take care of some things first.

"Where are we going?" Maggie asked.

"I'm not going to tell you, but it's a wonderful surprise."

Maggie hung up, feeling oddly deflated. She didn't have the heart to tell him she already made dinner reservations elsewhere. It was Jake's last night before he went back to the South Pacific. They should spend it any way he wanted.

Jake was waiting for her when she arrived. He looked very handsome in his uniform. Maggie wore her best outfit—a two-piece wool suit with padded shoulders that she usually reserved for job interviews. She had borrowed a fur-lined stole from a neighbor and wore a velvet ribbon in her hair.

"These are for you." Jake handed her a bunch of lilies. He took her hand and led her down Broadway. They stopped in front of Woolworth's department store.

Maggie wondered whether Jake needed to buy some aftershave or a pair of socks. But instead of going to the men's department, he led her to the lunch counter. It was busy with shoppers having a cup of tea before they got on the subway.

"What are we doing here?" she asked.

He sat on a stool and motioned for her to sit beside him.

"We're having dinner."

Maggie didn't understand. Jake wasn't poor. He had given her small presents all week—a box of Hershey's chocolates, another book from the Strand. He could afford a more expensive final dinner than at the lunch counter at Woolworth's. She loved Woolworth's. She shopped there for her makeup and stockings. And the lunch counter's milkshakes were the best she tasted. But she had wanted their last dinner together to be somewhere romantic. A restaurant where they could sit for hours, gazing at each other by candlelight, so that she could remember the evening after Jake was gone.

"Let me order for you," Jake said.

Maggie felt overdressed in her suit and fur-lined stole. And she wasn't in the mood for the sometimes greasy food at Woolworth's. She had been picturing Keens's juicy mutton chops with a side of vegetables. But she hadn't seen Jake so animated. His blue eyes sparkled, and he kept shifting on his stool.

Jake ordered pea soup to start and a turkey sandwich to share. This time the sandwich felt heavy in Maggie's stomach. Perhaps she and Jake were more different than she thought. It took all her effort to chew and concentrate on what he was saying.

They talked about what time Jake was leaving the next day and where the ship would dock in the South Pacific. Maggie kept wanting to tell him about the commercial, but every time she started, he signaled the counter clerk for more ketchup or mustard.

Finally, the plates were cleared. The clerk brought them dessert menus.

"We don't need a menu." Jake handed it back. "Maggie and I are going to share a banana split."

"I don't want dessert," Maggie replied.

Jake's brow furrowed. "You must have dessert. Woolworth's banana split is the best in New York."

All the frustration bubbled up inside her. She waved at the empty plates behind the counter. "I didn't want the pea soup or the turkey sandwich. I made reservations at Keens Steakhouse. It was going to be a romantic dinner with a bottle of red wine and candlelight. I was going to say how much I'll miss you and that this has been the best week of my life." She gulped for air. "This morning, I got my first television commercial. It's not much money, but if I get more, I could have a real career. When the temp agency called me, I was so excited. The more I thought about it, it wasn't about the commercial itself, it was that I had someone to share it with." She thought of how much she had grown to care about Jake in a short time, and her eyes grew moist. She had never felt this way before. "But you obviously don't have the same feelings. To you, I'm just a girl you spent your leave with. Someone who doesn't rate anything more special than a bunch of flowers and a turkey sandwich at Woolworth's."

Before Jake could answer, the clerk set the banana split in front of them.

"If I was you, I'd be careful eating the glazed cherries," the clerk said to Maggie. "Especially the one on the right."

Maggie hunched forward on the stool. She shouldn't have lost her temper. Maybe the Woolworth's lunch counter reminded Jake of his hometown in Ohio. Or he was anxious about going back to the war and wanted to get their evening over early so he could be alone.

"I'm sorry," she said. "It was a nice dinner, and you're probably tired. Why don't we . . ."

"I'm not tired," Jake cut in. "I picked Woolworth's because it reminded me of the day my life changed forever." He took Maggie's hand. "Being with you during this week made me remember why I joined the navy in the first place. Life can be wonderful if you're with the right person, and all those soldiers out there, and the civilians that get hurt in the crossfire, should get to experience the same thing—meeting someone out of the blue and falling in love."

Maggie's eyes widened, and she let out a gasp. She couldn't believe what Jake was saying. He did have deep feelings for her, just as she had for him.

"Did you say you were falling in love with me?"

Jake nodded. He held her hand more tightly and pointed at the dessert dish. "If you don't believe me, look at the banana split."

Maggie's gaze drifted to the dessert. Instead of three glazed cherries, there were two cherries and a ruby-and-diamond ring.

Jake picked up the ring.

"I didn't realize how you feel about Woolworth's. You must think this is the cheesiest marriage proposal. But my parents taught me that sometimes being cheesy is good. It means your heart is so full." He wiped the ring and held it in his palm. "I asked my commander, and I can get a special marriage license. We'll be married in the morning before the ship leaves. I love you, and I promise that when the war is over, our lives will be filled with happiness."

Maggie practically glowed at Jake's words. He was in love with her. He wanted to marry her. Then reality hit. For a moment, she had forgotten about the war. How could they plan a future when Jake was leaving the next day? They were two children writing the end of a fairy tale. And what if something happened to him and it was her fault? It was the thing she dreaded most, and she couldn't get it out of her mind. He might become distracted thinking about her when he was in battle instead of focusing on what was going on around him. She wasn't usually superstitious, but she had heard stories about soldiers not looking up from the letters they were writing to their fiancées and being blown up by a grenade. If anything like that happened to Jake she could never forgive herself. The whole scenario put her on edge. Yet she couldn't live without him. He was the best thing that had happened to her.

The clock above the lunch counter said it was 6:00 p.m.

"Where did you get this ring?" she asked.

Jake seemed surprised by her question.

"At a jewelry store in the Diamond District," he answered.

"You have to take me there now," she said urgently.

Jake paid for their meal and they walked outside. A taxi took them to a storefront on Forty-Seventh Street. The sign above the door read EDELMAN JEWELERS. The door was locked, but the light was on.

Maggie knocked on the glass. A middle-aged man unlocked the door. He had a narrow build and dark, thinning hair.

"I'm sorry. I'm closed," he said. "You can come back in the morning."

"Please, it's very important. It will just take a minute," Maggie replied.

The man looked from her to Jake quizzically. He shrugged and allowed them to come inside.

"Jake bought this ring and we need to return it," Maggie said.

Jake took the ring out of his pocket, puzzled.

"I'm sorry. We don't accept returns on engagement rings," the man said.

"You have to," Maggie urged. "I can't accept it. It would put Jake in danger."

The man said he didn't understand.

Maggie explained that Jake was returning to the South Pacific the next day. If she accepted his marriage proposal, he might spend all his time thinking about her and not stay alert. If she turned him down, he might get so despondent he'd put himself in danger.

She tried to quell her confusion. It felt like she was on a Ferris wheel at the fair and couldn't get off. Her thoughts refused to settle down. She knew she was grasping at something that was almost impossible. How was Jake supposed to forget that he asked her to marry him? But she had to make him see it her way. Everything about Jake going back to the war was frightening. She couldn't make it worse.

"So you see the only thing to do is pretend the proposal never happened," she addressed Jake and the jeweler. "I'm in love with Jake. I want him to be safe."

"That's the craziest thing I ever heard," Jake said.

"I fought in the First World War. She has a point," the man cut in. "I was engaged to my wife, Ethel. Once, I narrowly missed being struck by a mortar round because I was reading one of her letters."

Maggie became even more determined. "If you won't refund the ring, I'll pay for it myself. But I can't keep it. You have to take it back until after the war."

The jeweler opened the cash register and took out a hundred-dollar bill. He handed it to Jake.

"I'll take back the ring. God willing, it will be here when you return."

Maggie and Jake walked back onto the street. Maggie felt strangely empty, as if she had left something important behind.

"Do you really feel that way, or were you just letting me down easy?" Jake asked.

Maggie looked up at Jake under the light of the streetlamp. His eyes crinkled at the corners. He looked so handsome. She felt so much love for him, it was like a large wave threatening to knock her over. It would have been so easy to say yes to his proposal and spend the next months planning their lives together. Never again would she feel so alone. But the voice in her head telling her not to wouldn't go away.

"I'll write to you once a month. That way you'll know that I care about you, but you won't be expecting my letters every day," she suggested.

He nodded slowly. "I'll do the same. The next time I propose it will be at the Carlyle Hotel, after a three-course dinner and dancing."

"We could dance now." She waved up at the streetlamp. Her voice was shaky, and there was a lump in her throat. More than anything, she wanted to press herself against his chest. If only she could stop time and the moment would never end.

Jake took her in his arms. He hummed "I Love You" by Bing Crosby, and they danced on the sidewalk.

Maggie lifted her face up to his. He kissed her and she kissed him back. It was a long, warm kiss, and his arms tightened around her.

"I love you," Jake whispered.

"I love you too," Maggie answered.

Her pulse raced, and she was afraid that she would run back to the jeweler and ask for the ring. It took all her willpower to step away.

"I should go. I have to be on the set early tomorrow morning."

Jake flagged down a taxi. When they reached her apartment, he offered to walk her to the door, but she shook her head.

"I'll see you when you get back," she said.

Then she watched the taxi drive away, and her heart broke.

~

The salesclerk brought out her wedding band. She slipped it on her finger, and it fit perfectly. It wouldn't fall off again.

"Could I see the ring in the case?" Maggie pointed at the ruby-and-diamond ring.

He took it out of the case and handed it to her. It wasn't Jake's ring. The band was platinum instead of white gold.

"Thank you." She handed it back.

She walked onto the street. She'd get pizza for her and Teddy. They'd eat it in Central Park together, and she'd tell him about how she was going to get her very own dressing room.

She loved Teddy. If it was a different kind of love than she had for Jake, that made sense. She was older, and so much had happened. But she would never have married Teddy if she hadn't believed in their love for each other. All she had to do was relax, and they would have a bright future together.

Chapter Five

Maggie spent the next two weeks in rehearsals. Mack, in hair and makeup, experimented with hair styles. He tried the victory roll, which had been popular after the war, and the new sleek style inspired by the latest fashion silhouettes, which created a bun from Maggie's back hair and a fuller pompadour on her forehead. They finally agreed on keeping Maggie's hair in its natural layers. Mack cut it shorter so it hugged her chin and accentuated her eyes.

In wardrobe, she was given an array of clothes. The pencil skirt, which she would wear with kitten heels and a strand of pearls around her neck. Swing dresses with white collars and cap sleeves for most of the shows. And a glamorous Dior "Bar Suit" from his 1947 collection for when she had celebrity guests.

In the evenings she practiced recipes in Teddy's kitchenette. Teddy read the directions on the cake box out loud while she cracked eggs and sifted flour. Afterward, they'd eat dinner in the dining alcove and then curl up in front of the television and watch Arthur Godfrey's variety hour.

Maggie couldn't remember why she had been anxious about getting married. Teddy was being so sweet. He called a few times a day to tell her he was thinking of her, and whenever she arrived home at night after he did, jazz music was playing on the phonograph and he had made a pitcher of gin fizzes.

They made love almost every night, and it was different from the times they'd made love before they were married. Maggie felt closer to Teddy. She wasn't afraid to ask him to place his hand in a certain spot or brush her breasts so that her whole body felt alive. Afterward, when Teddy snored beside her, she didn't have to decide between calling a taxi or waking up early to go home and change her clothes. Instead, she could do what she loved most—drink a glass of water and stand by the window and watch the traffic on the street below.

There were a few times when he woke up in the middle of the night with the night sweats. The second time it happened, she was determined to do something about it. They were married, and she couldn't let it go on forever.

She waited until morning and brought him breakfast in bed. Fresh coffee, scrambled eggs on toast, with half a sliced orange.

"What's this?" he asked. It was a Wednesday morning, and they both had to be at work in two hours.

"The coffee will make you alert, and the protein in the eggs gives you energy." She sat on the bed. "I thought you'd need them, since you hardly slept last night."

Teddy eyed the breakfast tray. He turned to Maggie. "What do you mean that I hardly slept?"

Maggie explained that Teddy had tossed and turned all night. When she glanced over at him during the night, his pillow was damp and his cheeks had a sheen.

"I'm not used to sleeping with you every night. The bed is warmer. We don't need so many blankets," he replied.

Maggie knew that wasn't true. She tried to be gentle. "You even talked in your sleep, but I couldn't make out what you said."

"I've always talked in my sleep. Ask my mother. She used to read *Winnie-the-Pooh* to me before bed. During the night I'd mumble about Eeyore and Piglet. It doesn't mean anything." Teddy's face took on a stubborn expression.

"Night sweats can't be normal. I've read about soldiers who come home from the war and—"

Before she could finish, Teddy interrupted. "I was a newscaster. I spent most of the war reporting from a studio in London. If I disturb you, I can sleep in the study."

Maggie bit her lip. They had been married for only two weeks; it was the last thing she wanted him to do. This had gone all wrong. She had to fix it.

She leaned forward and kissed him. "I never want to sleep anywhere but beside you. I just thought you might be hungry."

Teddy sat up against the headboard. The smile came back into his eyes, and his tone became lighter.

"I'd rather spend any extra time in the mornings making love to you than having breakfast in bed." He ate a bite of eggs on toast. "But the eggs are delicious, and it was thoughtful of you to make them."

Maggie hadn't mentioned the night sweats again. Whatever was troubling Teddy, helping him would have to wait until they had been married for longer.

Today was the first day of filming. When she arrived at the studio, there was a note from Dolly accompanied by a small bowl of fruit and a vase of roses from Tommy. Even Teddy's mother sent a gift: a copy of the article about Maggie in *TV Times* magazine in a silver frame. Maggie placed it on the dressing table next to her wedding photo.

Tommy poked his head in. "Maggie, you're here."

"I couldn't sleep. I got here early," Maggie admitted, checking her hair and makeup in the mirror.

"Today will be easy. The main goal is to show viewers around the kitchen and let them get to know you."

Maggie had spent the previous evening memorizing the show's script. She hadn't told Tommy that she wore reading glasses, and she still wasn't comfortable with her new contacts.

"I'm as ready as I'll ever be." She gave her hair one last touch-up.

Even though she had rehearsed all week, stepping onto the stage with the cameras whirring felt completely different. She stood at the kitchen counter, with the bright lights trained on her, and could feel her heart thumping.

"By the way, we made a few last-minute changes to the script," Tommy said. "The latest version is on the cue cards."

Cue cards held all the words that the actor had to say.

"Cue cards?" Maggie repeated. She hadn't wanted to use them. She worried that she wouldn't be able to read them from far away.

"There are only a few minor changes," Tommy said.

Before Maggie could protest, the red light on the camera flashed and they started filming.

She squinted at the cue cards.

"Good morning, ladies," she began. "Don't you love mornings? All we have to do is give our husbands breakfast and make sure they don't forget their briefcases, then we can go about our day. I'm training my husband, Teddy, to only want coffee and toast in the morning. Otherwise, I'm spending my time with my hands submerged in dish soap instead of doing what I love: drinking my first cup of coffee and choosing which Deluxe Baking Company dessert I'm going to make for dinner."

Tommy gave her a thumbs-up from where he stood in the corner, and Maggie let herself relax. The words on the cue cards were big enough to read.

She gave viewers a tour of the pantry, which was stocked with Deluxe Baking Company cake boxes and jars of frosting. The cameras did a slow pan of the kitchen table and chairs, where Maggie would answer viewers' letters.

She rested her arms on the counter, the way she had rehearsed, and read the last paragraph.

"This morning, we're going to make a granny cake. Before we do, I want to thank you for tuning into *The Maggie Lane Baking Show*. I'll let you in on a little secret. Women say they want a career, but the folks at Deluxe Baking Company know that isn't always true. What makes a woman happy is the look on her family's faces when she sets down a Deluxe Baking Company pumpkin chiffon pie. Women love to be in the kitchen, especially when it's a beautifully outfitted kitchen like *The Maggie Lane Baking Show* kitchen."

Maggie frowned under the lights. None of that had been in the original script.

The director yelled cut and told everyone to take a break.

Tommy came over to her. "That was fantastic."

"The last paragraph was a surprise," she ventured. "I know quite a few women who have careers. All the women I worked with at CBS Radio, and my friend Dolly."

"Most of them are secretaries and are waiting for a man to put a ring on their finger," Tommy said confidently. "Deluxe Baking Company has done their research. Women today want to be housewives, and you're going to show them how good they have it."

Maggie wanted to argue, but she needed the job. It wasn't her place to challenge the script.

The rest of the show went smoothly. The granny cake was easy to make—all she had to do was mix canned peaches and pineapple into a bowl with flour and eggs and baking soda. Then the cake went into the oven and baked for forty minutes. After it cooled, she covered it with a layer of coconut frosting. At the end of the show, Maggie sat at the kitchen table with a cake plate and a cup of coffee. The camera zoomed in on her enjoying a slice of cake, and she looked up and gave the camera a little wave.

Teddy was waiting outside the studio when she finished filming.

"This is a surprise. I didn't know you'd be here," she greeted him.

"They didn't need me on the radio show this afternoon." Teddy took her arm.

Maggie was exhausted. All she wanted to do was go home and take a bath. And she wondered why Teddy had the afternoon off. It wasn't a good sign if the radio show didn't need him. But he led her up Madison

Avenue. They walked around the Upper East Side until they ended up on Fifth Avenue and stopped in front of a prewar apartment building. It had a striped awning and a doorman in a blue uniform.

"What are we doing here?" Maggie asked.

"You'll see," Teddy said.

He gave the doorman a dollar bill and walked inside. The lobby had mirrored walls and a small gold settee. There were two potted plants and a marble-topped table.

The old-fashioned grill elevator opened at the third floor. Teddy crossed the hall and took a key out of his pocket. Maggie followed him inside and her eyes widened. The apartment was beautiful—high ceilings with crown molding. The walls were covered with velvet wallpaper, and there was a fireplace with a marble mantel. A hallway led to a bathroom and a bedroom with parquet floors and a small balcony. It was unfurnished except for a card table and a couple of folding chairs in the kitchen.

"You haven't explained why we're here." Maggie glanced around in awe at the pastel-colored steel cabinets and white dual sink.

Teddy took a paper bag from the counter. He opened cartons of Chinese takeout and arranged them on the card table.

"We're celebrating your first day as the star of *The Maggie Lane Baking Show*." He handed her a pair of chopsticks.

"What are we doing in this apartment?" Maggie waved around the kitchen.

The Realtor was a close friend of Teddy's mother. The apartment was her listing. The key was theirs for the afternoon.

"You did all this for me?" Maggie noticed the vase of flowers next to the window.

"My mother made the introduction," Teddy admitted. "All I had to do was pick up the key and buy the takeout and flowers."

"But why? We can't afford to buy an apartment on Fifth Avenue. Even if we could, your mother wants us to move to Rye." It was the kind of apartment she dreamed of. She imagined holding dinner parties in the hexagon-shaped dining room, standing on the balcony at night, looking up at the sky.

Teddy wrapped garlic noodles around his chopstick. "We can't afford it now, but someday we might. I love my mother, but we get to choose where we live. That's what marriage is about."

Tears filled Maggie's eyes. She told herself she was just overwrought from the day's taping. But it was more than that. Teddy was so good and loving, she had to stop doubting him. Even with his night sweats, and whatever troubles from his past that he refused to share, he loved her and was always there for her. But the changes that Tommy had made to the end of the show were still troubling her. She set down her chopsticks and told Teddy about the last paragraph of the script.

"How can I give viewers the wrong message every week?" she said when she finished.

"It may not be wrong for the women who are watching," Teddy reasoned. "They enjoy being housewives."

Maggie would know that she wasn't being honest. When she decided to move to New York, she had been determined to find a career that she loved. She couldn't imagine staying home all day, cooking and cleaning. Having a career was vital to her happiness.

"Perhaps when you answer viewers' letters, you can encourage women to find things they enjoy outside of the home," Teddy ventured.

He had a point. She could suggest they start a charity, or get a part-time job. There would still be time in their day to bake a Deluxe Baking Company dessert, but they'd have something of their own.

"What if Tommy doesn't approve?" Maggie asked.

Teddy said it wasn't something she had to do immediately. First, she had to settle in on the show.

Maggie leaned forward and kissed Teddy.

"You understand people. You should be more than the content producer. You should produce the radio show," she said before she could stop herself.

They finished the takeout and talked about driving up to Rye the upcoming weekend and visiting his parents.

Tommy had suggested that Teddy be a guest on *The Maggie Lane Baking Show*. Maggie wanted to mention it, but something held her back. Teddy had been so happy and relaxed since he'd stopped being the host of *New York Radio Hour*, she didn't want to do anything to upset him. She was beginning to realize that she was the one who wanted more for him. In the short time they'd been married, she was learning that the important thing was to accept how the other person felt. It would be difficult, but she had to stop herself from pushing him to do things he didn't want to do.

After they had cleaned up and taken one last look around the apartment, Teddy went to return the key and Maggie walked home. She had been so anxious about the job, but now she felt happy. She loved the new feeling of anticipation of waiting to be called on the set, and the moment when the lights on the camera flashed and she was on the air. And she couldn't get over the delight of having her very own television kitchen.

When she arrived home, she tidied up the living room and entered Teddy's dressing room. A few shirts were strewn on the floor. She picked up a shirt and noticed a half-empty pack of cigarettes. Teddy hadn't smoked since their lunch with Tommy. Why was there a pack of cigarettes underneath his clothes? She crouched down and found an ashtray and a notebook.

The notebook was open on a page pasted with several photos. The first was of a church in a village. The caption under the photo read "Oradour-sur-Glane, June 1944. Lady Arabella Cousins, Teddy, Ian."

The photo was of two men and a woman standing in a village square. The man in the middle was Teddy.

She remembered Tommy asking Teddy about the German massacre of the village of Oradour-sur-Glane at the end of the war. She looked more closely at the photo. The woman couldn't have been more than twenty. She was very beautiful—blond hair, large blue eyes, and a trim figure in her uniform.

Who was she, and who was the soldier standing on the other side of Teddy? A shiver ran through her. This was the first time that she had seen a photo of Teddy during the war, except for a few framed photographs at his parents' house. Those had been the typical wartime photos sent home so that his parents didn't worry about him. Teddy smiling in his uniform at the bar at the Savoy, before he was loaned to Pathé News by the army. Teddy posing in front of the Tower of London, holding a bag of fish and chips. The photos could almost have been of Teddy on holiday instead of him being in Europe in the middle of the war.

This photograph was of a village in France that Maggie knew no longer existed. Everyone in the village had been murdered by the Germans. When Tommy asked Teddy about it, Teddy only said he had gone there in a jeep. He never mentioned he was with anyone else. Especially someone as beautiful as the girl in the photo.

She closed the notebook and left the cigarettes and ashtray where they were. Whatever the photo meant to him, it was obvious that Teddy didn't want her to know anything about it. If only she could ask him. Then she recalled how upset he had become when she mentioned his night sweats. She'd have to leave it for now.

Chapter Six

The Maggie Lane Baking Show had been on the air for two months, and it was a success. Every week the stack of letters from viewers increased. Housewives started calling the switchboard at CBS and asking to speak to Maggie. A telephone was installed in her dressing room, and a commercial for the show featured Maggie waiting to get her hair done with the phone pressed to her ear.

Learning her way around the kitchen was easier than she had expected. The General Electric dual range and oven was simple to use, and it was handy having two ovens. When a celebrity guest appeared on the show, they could bake two desserts at the same time. Maggie adored the Kelvinator refrigerator. It was a new model and roomier than the Frigidaire in Teddy's apartment. The Kelvinator had shelves inside the door for egg cartons and a temperature control so that the food tasted fresh.

Maggie became good at whisking flour and butter in the electric mixing bowl while talking to the camera at the same time. And she learned to check the edges of the cake so that it was done but still moist when she pulled it out of the oven. Sometimes when she took home a Deluxe Baking Company devil's food cake, Teddy joked that if the show ended, she could get a job as a pastry chef.

There was an article about her in *Ladies' Home Journal*, and she was named one of "Four Women to Watch on Television" in *Good Housekeeping*, along with Dolly, Gracie Allen, and Betty White.

Teddy's mother's bridge circle took the train into New York to have lunch with Maggie. The lunch was held at Tavern on the Green, and Patty presented Maggie with a Hermès scarf and a badge that made her an honorary member of their group.

Maggie and Dolly had become good friends. They often grabbed lunch together in CBS's cafeteria, though Maggie noticed that Dolly usually picked at her sandwich and left all the croutons on her side salad. When Maggie commented on it, Dolly shrugged and said she ate a big breakfast. Once, Maggie walked into the powder room after lunch and saw Dolly swallowing a handful of colored pills. She didn't say anything, but she worried that her friend was taking more pills than she had before.

This evening, Dolly had invited Maggie over for dinner to meet her parents. Teddy was helping one of his friends move, so Maggie had the night to herself.

Dolly lived with her parents in a townhouse on the Upper East Side. She greeted Maggie at the door, wearing a puff-sleeve blouse and pleated skirt. Her hair was teased into a bouffant, and she wore a pearl necklace.

"My mother is getting ready, and my father is running an errand." Dolly led her into the living room.

The room was decorated with expensive, tasteful furniture. There was a sectional sofa and two side tables with art deco lamps. The television cabinet held the latest RCA model. A Lalique vase was filled with flowers, and gold-framed paintings hung on the walls.

Dolly motioned for Maggie to sit on the sofa.

"I know I should get my own place and have the single girl in New York experience." Dolly crossed her legs. "But I could never afford anything as nice. Besides, my mother is my best friend. When I'm not working, we do almost everything together. Shopping at Henri Bendel, visiting galleries, seeing Broadway shows."

"This place is lovely. I wouldn't want to move either," Maggie agreed.

"After dinner, I'll show you my bedroom," Dolly said. "When my brother got married, we turned his room into my own suite. My parents are sweet. They don't want me to leave until I get married." She sighed. "If I ever get married. One more year and at twenty-five I'll be officially on the shelf."

Maggie was surprised that Dolly felt that way. Dolly had a career that most young women only dreamed about. And she must have plenty of dates. She was practically famous.

"You'll get married, if you want to," Maggie assured her. "You're beautiful and intelligent, and you're the star of a television program."

"Being on television doesn't help with men in real life. They want a wife who stays home and cooks. And I'm not like you, I'm not naturally beautiful," Dolly said.

Lately the show's producers wanted Dolly's character to be sexier. She was given a new wardrobe and encouraged to have facials to make her skin smooth and special hair products so her dark hair would have an extra shine.

"Now they want me to have a tiny waist like Elizabeth Taylor," Dolly said. "I told them that's impossible. I'd never be able to eat a steak or a baked potato with sour cream again."

"You're perfect the way you are," Maggie said. "A lot of actresses have voluptuous figures. Look at Lana Turner."

"There is a guy I'm interested in." Dolly fiddled with her necklace. "That's what I want to talk to you about. I thought if we have a double date, he'll be impressed with you and Teddy, and I'll have a chance."

Maggie was about to answer when Dolly's mother entered the living room. She was in her late forties. She had Dolly's dark hair and brown eyes.

"I'm Ruth, Dolly's mother," she greeted Maggie. "Dolly told me all about you, and I've watched your show, of course."

Maggie stood up and shook Ruth's hand. "It's nice to meet you."

"Please sit down." Ruth sat opposite them on the sofa. "It's wonderful for Dolly to have a friend her own age. Most of the girls she grew up with are married with families." She turned to Dolly. "Sometimes, I think I'm being selfish not setting her up with young men. But then who would go with me to the fashion sample sales?" She gave a little smile. "Bernie and I have been married for thirty years and I love him, but there's nothing like having a daughter."

For a moment, Maggie missed her own mother. How wonderful it was for Dolly and Ruth to share this time in their lives. Then she imagined her mother shopping in one of the department stores on Fifth Avenue or having afternoon tea at the Carlyle and the fantasy dissolved. She couldn't imagine her parents moving to New York. Even though their lives could be difficult, her mother and father loved the farm. And Maggie never could go back there. She wanted to stay in New York forever.

They talked about *The Maggie Lane Baking Show* and living on the Upper East Side.

"When Bernie and I got married, we lived on Fourteenth Street near Union Square," Ruth said. "I used to ride the subway to the Upper East Side and pace up and down the streets, dreaming of being one of those women who walk out of their apartments into a taxi that's waiting to take them wherever they want to go," she continued. "I pinch myself all the time that my life turned out so well. A wonderful husband, two lovely children. Not to mention a successful shoe business and a daughter who's on television. So what if Dolly had to change her name? Every Jewish actor has a stage name. And I never liked Meyerowitz. I was born Ruth Levine."

Maggie glanced from Ruth to Dolly in surprise. Dolly never mentioned that she was Jewish. Ruth noticed her expression.

"I guess Dolly didn't tell you," Ruth said curiously. "Bernie's parents emigrated from Germany in the 1920s. Bernie and his father opened Meyerowitz shoe stores. The new salon is on Fifth Avenue. Ten thousand square feet between Forty-Ninth Street and Fiftieth Street. Next year, we're opening a store in Palm Beach."

Maggie had browsed in Meyerowitz Shoes many times. It was three floors of gorgeous shoes, with gloves and belts and matching purses. The shoes were displayed on glass cubes, and there were velvet settees where customers could relax when they got tired. Maggie had never bought anything. The shoes were too expensive.

"I should have told you," Dolly said as if she could read Maggie's mind. "Anytime you want, you can have a discount on shoes and accessories."

The door opened and a man of about fifty entered. He was barely taller than Dolly, with brown hair and very blue eyes.

"You must be Maggie Lane." He held out his hand. "I'm Bernie Meyerowitz, Dolly's father."

Maggie shook hands and said it was nice to meet him.

"Ruth and Dolly make me watch the show every week." He beamed. "The Deluxe Baking Company peach cobbler is my favorite dessert. But tonight is Shabbat dinner, so we have a kugel from the bakery." He held up his package. "Come, it's time to light the candles."

Maggie didn't know any Jewish families, and she had never been to a Shabbat dinner. There were several Jewish neighborhoods in New York, but she'd never visited any of them, and she didn't shop at any of the clothing stores in the Garment District, which was predominately run by Jews. She didn't know what to expect.

The dining table was formally set with gold-rimmed china and crystal wineglasses. Dolly's father lit the candles and led the table in two hymns. He poured four glasses of a sweet red wine, and they each took a few sips. After that, Maggie followed Dolly and her parents into the kitchen to wash their hands before they each ate a bite of challah.

The challah wasn't like any bread that Maggie had tasted. It was sweet and fluffy, and warm straight from the oven.

They returned to the dining room and the meal was served. Matzo ball soup followed by a chicken dish and side plates of roasted vegetables. Maggie hadn't seen Dolly look so comfortable. The conversation flowed easily, and instead of picking at her food, Dolly ate everything on her plate.

"Dolly hasn't invited a friend to a Shabbat meal since high school," Ruth said when Bernie went into the kitchen to get the dessert. "I can understand. Sometimes, it's easier not to tell the world that you're Jewish. It's better to keep it between family and people you love and trust." She looked at Dolly knowingly. "We've never been a completely traditional household. Bernie does the cooking because his matzo ball soup is better than mine. I worked at the shoe store with Bernie for years; now I teach calisthenics at a senior citizen center. And instead of encouraging Dolly to attend college, we supported her dream of going into television." She gave Dolly's hand a squeeze. "The important thing is to be happy."

Dolly tried to hide her embarrassment.

"My mother gives the best advice. One day, when I'm a big star, I'll get her a talk show," she said fondly.

After dinner, Maggie and Dolly went upstairs to Dolly's bedroom suite. Double doors led into a study furnished with a low pink sofa and matching armchair. There was a bookshelf and a small desk. An arch led to the bedroom, with a queen-size bed, dressing table, and balcony with views of Central Park. The bathroom had two walls of mirrors and the kind of plush white robes found in luxury hotels.

"My parents spoil me, but they also taught me to work hard and give back to the community." Dolly noticed the awe in Maggie's expression. "My father never gets home from work before dinnertime, and he donates to many Jewish charities. And my mother gives classes at the Jewish senior citizen center at no charge."

"Why didn't you tell me you were Jewish?" Maggie sat on the sofa in the study.

"I couldn't tell you when we first met. It's not something I share with anyone. Then I wanted to tell you once we became friends, but I didn't know how. The easiest way was to show you by inviting you here tonight," Dolly answered truthfully. "Please, you mustn't tell anyone.

No one at the studio knows. They wouldn't have hired me. Can you imagine the lead actor's character falling in love with a Jewish girl? The television audience wouldn't approve."

Maggie started to protest that it wouldn't make any difference to the producers if Dolly was Jewish. But Dolly had a point. Tommy had wanted Maggie to be married because the star of *The Maggie Lane Baking Show* was supposed to be a housewife.

Dolly told Maggie about Alan, the young man she had started seeing. He was from Cleveland, and he was a new writer on the show. They only had a few cocktail dates, but he was sweet and funny.

"He wants to pick me up at home and take me to dinner," Dolly said. "What if he and my parents start talking and he realizes I'm Jewish? He probably never met a Jewish girl in Cleveland. He won't ask me out again."

Maggie said if Alan liked her, he would keep seeing her. She was surprised that any man would think about Dolly differently just because she was Jewish. She hadn't experienced anything like that in her own life. She'd read about anti-Semitism of course, and she knew it existed. But if Alan really liked Dolly, the fact that she was Jewish shouldn't matter to him.

"Not if he's considering marriage," Dolly countered. "And I do like him. I thought if we went on a double date, we could get to know each other better before he finds out I'm Jewish."

They went back downstairs, and Maggie thanked Dolly's parents for dinner.

An hour later, she sat in her living room, going through a stack of viewers' letters. She received so many letters, she read them at home so she could choose which ones to read on the air.

There was a letter from a viewer asking whether a Deluxe Baking Company pound cake should be kept in the fridge overnight. A question about whether to use condensed milk or whole cream in a German chocolate cake and what was the best dessert for a child's birthday party.

One viewer wanted to know how Maggie stayed so trim, and another asked whether too much sugar could give her a headache.

Maggie set them in a pile and sat back against the cushions. She was tired from working all day and then having Shabbat dinner at Dolly's parents' house. She wanted to sit quietly for a while and think about what was bothering her. Then she would answer the viewers who counted on her for advice.

She hadn't said anything to Teddy about the photos in the notebook that she had found almost two months earlier, but they still troubled her. The more she helped viewers by answering their letters, and the closer she became to Dolly and listened to Dolly's problems, the more she was determined to help Teddy get rid of whatever demons from the war still troubled him.

All her instincts told her that the night sweats, the talking in his sleep, were connected to the little village in northern France. She had even looked up Oradour-sur-Glane in the encyclopedia, but she could find only a couple of paragraphs about what occurred. The Germans had surprised the villagers, and there had been no resistance. She had searched for more information but couldn't find anything. There had been so many similar stories during the war, the encyclopedia couldn't include all of them.

Teddy wouldn't be home for a while. She walked to his dressing room and took out the notebook. There were a few blank pages, and in the back a manila envelope was stuck to the cover. She slipped her hand inside and took out a stack of photographs.

The photos were of Teddy, with the two people in the first photograph. She remembered their names, Lady Arabella and Ian.

She spread them on the bed. A few were of just Teddy. Him looking handsome in a tuxedo, a scarf draped around his neck. The caption underneath read "Claridge's Hotel, London. 1944." There was a photograph of Teddy in front of a microphone in a studio, with Pathé News scrawled across the wall. Most of the other photos were of Teddy and

Arabella and Ian. Ian was taller than Teddy. He had light-colored hair and a lean build. Maggie thought he was handsome too.

But it was the photos of Arabella that interested her most. She counted six in the stack. Arabella wearing an evening gown that seemed too sophisticated for a young woman. It had a plunging neckline and slit skirt. A fur cape was draped around her shoulders, and she wore a diamond necklace. There was another photograph of Arabella in her Wrens uniform of a double-breasted navy jacket and matching skirt with a shirt and tie, digging in a garden, with a stone mansion in the background. Two photos were of Arabella curled up in front of a fireplace and petting a large dog. There was another one of her and Ian and Teddy in a restaurant booth, with a bottle of champagne and a plate of oysters. None of those photos had captions, except the dates. They were all taken from 1943 to 1944.

Maggie set the photos aside. So Teddy had known Arabella and Ian for a while during the war, and they did things together. How did they meet, and how did they end up traveling to Oradour-sur-Glane together?

She felt guilty to be snooping through Teddy's personal things. It wasn't like her, but she wanted to help him. And she hadn't expected to find a whole batch of photos. She slipped them back in the envelope without looking at the ones she hadn't taken out.

She went back into the living room. She should be ashamed of herself. What would she do if Teddy found out about Jake? But this was different. She hadn't meant to be snooping. The notebook had been on the floor in the dressing room when she'd first found it. She poured another cup of tea and waited for Teddy to come home.

Chapter Seven

It was the following Saturday night, and Maggie and Teddy were meeting Dolly and Alan for dinner at Delmonico's. Maggie entered the small space off the bedroom that Teddy used as a dressing room. He wore a navy suit. A yellow handkerchief was folded in his breast pocket.

"That's a beautiful suit," Maggie said admiringly. "Was your mother in New York?"

Every time Patty visited, she brought a gift. A vase or kitchen bowl for the apartment, a shirt for Teddy, and a pair of gloves or a scarf for Maggie. Maggie encouraged Teddy to accept them. Patty had good taste, and it made her feel needed. Since the wedding, Teddy had become more relaxed. He still wouldn't take financial help from his parents, but he was all right with accepting small items that he and Maggie could enjoy.

Teddy finished adjusting his tie. He turned around.

"I bought the suit at Macy's. I opened a charge card in both our names."

Maggie's eyes widened in surprise. Neither of them had a charge card before. Maggie believed you shouldn't buy something you couldn't pay for, and Teddy agreed.

"Do we need a charge card?" she asked.

"You're the star of a television program," Teddy answered. "Your viewers expect you to dress a certain way. It wouldn't look good if your husband stands beside you in a threadbare suit."

Maggie was about to say that Teddy was a wonderful dresser. But his suits were a little worn, and on his reduced salary he hadn't bought any new ones.

"I could have given you the money for a suit," Maggie offered.

"I'm not to the point where I accept handouts from my wife." Teddy's voice was tight. "Besides, everyone has a charge card these days. I'm thinking of getting a Diners Club card. Then we can charge things anywhere we want."

There had been an article about the new Diners Club card in the *New York Times*. The article called it a credit card, and it could be used at restaurants and hotels.

"I'd rather pay for our meals." Maggie turned and folded Teddy's shirts so he wouldn't see her anxious expression.

Maggie liked nice things as much as Teddy. At the same time, she loved seeing her bank account grow. It meant that soon they could start looking for an apartment.

They would have to discuss it later. When they arrived at Delmonico's, Dolly and Alan were waiting in a booth. Dolly wore a pencil skirt and leather pumps. Alan was tall and thin. He had light-brown hair and wore round glasses.

"It's wonderful to meet you. Dolly has spoken so much about you," Alan greeted them.

They ordered jumbo prawns as appetizers and rib eye steak with tortellini as a main course. The only time that Dolly seemed uncomfortable was when the waiter set down their plates. She took a large bite of the tortellini and then reached for her water glass. The rest of the meal she spent pushing the pasta around her plate and drinking glasses of water.

"I grew up in Cleveland. My father is a doctor. My parents talked about me attending medical school for as long as I can remember," Alan said, eating a slice of Delmonico's bread dipped in melted butter. "Every night after dinner, we used to listen to radio shows. I loved the comedy hours like Abbott and Costello. My parents liked detective series, *The*

Adventures of Sam Spade and Sherlock Holmes. I became obsessed with writing for the radio. After they'd gone to bed, I'd stay awake for hours, writing scripts.

"After the war, I convinced my parents to let me get a job in radio in New York. They agreed to give it a year. If it doesn't work out, I'll finish medical school and take over my father's practice.

"When I arrived here and discovered there were jobs writing comedy for television, not just radio, I was like a boy who discovered you could get paid for watching the Yankees play baseball at Yankee Stadium."

Maggie and Teddy laughed, and Dolly gazed at Alan admiringly.

"I call my parents every Sunday and describe my life," Alan finished. "They've never left Cleveland. They were high school sweethearts, and they live in the same suburb where they grew up."

They talked about Alan's family coming to visit and Maggie and Teddy going to see Maggie's parents in Pennsylvania. Maggie didn't miss the farm, but she did miss her parents. They almost never came to New York. There were always animals to be fed or some new farm equipment that had to be paid for. And she had a feeling that they weren't comfortable in the city. She had stopped encouraging them to visit. She didn't want them to do something they weren't eager to do.

A woman holding a book approached their booth.

"I'm sorry to interrupt," she said. "You're Maggie Lane. My name is Agatha. I was having dinner with my friend and noticed you. You'll never believe it, but I bought the Deluxe Baking Company recipe book this afternoon. I wonder if you'd sign it."

Maggie blushed and took the book.

"I never miss an episode," Agatha gushed. "You saved my life on my father's birthday. I forgot to bake a cake. I found the recipe for a No Bake Lemon Cheesecake, and he loved it."

Maggie handed the book back.

"I'm glad you enjoy the show."

Agatha waved at her friend to join her.

"Could my friend take a photograph?" she asked. "Our friends back in Michigan won't believe I met you."

Agatha slid into the booth next to Maggie. She turned to Teddy.

"Do you mind if it's just me and Maggie in the picture?"

Teddy pretended to straighten his tie, but Maggie could tell he was embarrassed. He moved out of the frame, and the woman snapped the camera.

"I can't tell you how much this means to me," Agatha thanked Maggie. "Every morning, my friends know not to call me until *The Maggie Lane Baking Show* is over. It's the best part of my day."

During dessert, another small group of women approached the table and asked for Maggie's autograph. *The Maggie Lane Baking Show* was in its third month on the air, and this had happened to Maggie only a couple of times before. But the women had seen the first woman approach Maggie and wanted to do the same thing. Teddy joked that Maggie was going to become a tourist attraction. She noticed him asking Alan for a cigarette. He took only a few puffs before he stubbed it into the ashtray, but it still made her uncomfortable. It had been so important to Teddy when he stopped being on the radio that he also gave up smoking. Why had he started again now?

After dinner, they walked onto the street together.

"This has been a wonderful evening," Alan said enthusiastically. "Maybe we could take a drive some weekend. I haven't been outside of Manhattan yet. I heard that the area upstate is great for exploring."

"That's a good idea," Teddy agreed. "In fact, Maggie and I are thinking about buying a new car. It would be great to take it for a spin in the countryside."

Maggie glanced at Teddy in surprise. They hadn't talked about buying a car. They didn't need a car in New York, and Teddy's old Ford was adequate for when they visited his parents in Rye.

She waited until they got home before she said anything.

"Alan was nice," Teddy said, taking off his suit jacket. "I can see why Dolly likes him."

Maggie ignored what he was saying. "What did you mean about the car?"

"Just what I said. I visited a Chrysler dealership the other day. They have a new-model Town & Country. Leather soft top and wood paneling. It's a beauty."

Maggie replied that they rarely went away on the weekends, except to visit his parents. There was so much to do and explore in New York. New cars were expensive.

"I love New York. But it would be good for us to get some fresh country air now and then," Teddy said. "I know how much money you make. We can afford it."

Teddy was right. Maggie could write a check for a new car with the money in her bank account. But she felt like she was looking through a telescope, and her dream of buying a Park Avenue apartment was moving farther away.

At the same time, she wanted Teddy to be happy.

"I suppose we could look in the showroom," she said uncertainly.

Teddy kissed her. "Good. I'll call Hank, the salesman, and make an appointment for next Saturday." He started unbuttoning her blouse. "Now, I'm tired of talking, and I'm tired of smiling at tourists we don't know. Let's go to bed."

Teddy leaned forward and kissed her breasts. Maggie felt the light headiness as if her body wasn't part of her. She pushed her hips against him, breathing in his cologne. His hands moved down her thighs, and she had the familiar tugging sensation between her legs. Then his mouth was on hers, and his arms were around her, and there was no time to think. There was only the pounding in her head as they lay down together, then the swift uptake when Teddy entered her.

Teddy's breathing came faster. She tried to match his movements, but it was difficult to concentrate. She finally caught his rhythm, and her body tipped higher. He gave the little shout that signaled the end of their lovemaking. She waited for her own release, but it didn't happen. Then he let out one more groan and collapsed on the bed.

For once, after he fell asleep, Maggie didn't feel like standing at the window and gazing down at the street. She wanted to stay tucked in his arms. As if she was afraid that something might separate them.

~

On Monday morning, Maggie sat in her dressing room waiting for Mack to do her makeup. She and Teddy had spent Sunday afternoon walking in Central Park. In the evening they saw the film *Little Women* at the Roxy Theatre. Afterward, they picked up Chinese takeout and watched *The Milton Berle Show* on television.

Maggie knew how lucky she was to be married to Teddy. They both liked the same movies and foods. And they were perfectly content spending an evening at home, curled up on the sofa. Yet she couldn't help the uneasy feeling that had settled over her. Teddy was smoking again, when he had been adamant about giving it up. And he wanted new clothes and a car, when those things had never really interested him.

He said he wasn't ambitious for himself, and yet he had become irritable at dinner when those tourists asked Maggie to be in a photograph. She told herself that her fame was new to both of them, and it would become easier over time. But what if it didn't? Teddy was a man, and he was quite proud. What if he started resenting the attention Maggie was receiving?

There was a knock. Instead of Mack, it was Tommy.

"I have good news." Tommy entered the room. "You'll never guess this week's celebrity guest. It's Katharine Hepburn."

Maggie's mouth dropped open.

Katharine Hepburn was one of the most famous actresses in America. She won an Academy Award when she was only twenty-six, and she starred with Cary Grant and Jimmy Stewart in one of Maggie and Teddy's favorite movies, *The Philadelphia Story*.

"Katharine lives part-time at her farm in Connecticut, and she watches your show every morning. Her one request is that you make the Deluxe Baking Company chocolate brownie together. That's her favorite recipe."

Tommy riffled through his notes.

"*Life* magazine wants to do a piece on how a Pennsylvania farm girl is becoming the most trusted woman on television. The White House is going to include a Deluxe Baking Company dessert at the next state dinner."

"You heard from the White House?" Maggie repeated in astonishment.

"President Truman's wife, Bess, tried the recipe for Deluxe Baking Company sweet cream cake and loved it."

Tommy reeled off more numbers, but Maggie wasn't listening. She kept thinking how Teddy behaved at dinner on Saturday night. What if the show caused things to change between them?

A brochure for the Chrysler Town & Country car sat on the dressing table. Tommy picked it up.

"Are you and Teddy getting a new car?"

Maggie flinched. "Teddy wants one, so I said I'd go to the showroom."

"But you don't want one?" Tommy asked, noticing her concerned expression.

She didn't want to appear ungrateful. "I'm paid well, so we can afford it. It's just that we hardly use a car, and I'm saving for an apartment."

She felt somehow as if she was being disloyal to Teddy, but it felt good to put her feelings into words.

Tommy folded his arms. "I've seen this happen before, when one half of a couple becomes famous. It's only going to get worse. My advice is to buy the car."

Maggie was surprised. "I don't want a new car. We're married. We're supposed to make these decisions together."

"Perhaps you're right. But as your boss, I have to put the show first," Tommy said. "A new car seems a small price to pay to keep your husband happy, when Deluxe intends to make you the most recognizable female face on television."

Maggie admitted that she hadn't thought of it that way.

Tommy stood up. "I have to go. Remember the morality clause that you signed. The worst thing for the show would be if you and Teddy got divorced."

"Of course we're not getting divorced. Teddy and I love each other."

Tommy smiled. "That's what I like to hear. Let me know when you buy the car. I'll send a bottle of champagne to your apartment so you can celebrate."

The day's taping went smoothly.

Maggie started the show the way she always did—by greeting viewers and giving them a tour of the kitchen. She usually held up some new gadget—a Bakelite cake breaker, perfect for delicate chiffon cakes, that gently pulled apart pieces of cake instead of pressing down and crushing it. Or a General Electric dishwasher, which fit on the kitchen counter and was perfect for small apartments.

The segment had been Maggie's idea, and the producers loved it. Each episode was fresh and interesting, and the manufacturers paid for product placement.

Another of her ideas for the show was to read an article out loud from the *New York Times*. Deluxe Baking Company had been against it. Studies showed that housewives only read women's magazines and the romance novels one found at the supermarket checkout. But viewers wrote in and gushed that the articles gave them something to talk about with their husbands at dinner.

Then came the segment when Maggie baked a Deluxe Baking Company dessert. Sometimes she had on a celebrity guest. While they spread frosting on a carrot cake, they chatted about the celebrity's latest book or movie. Other times, Maggie baked alone while talking animatedly to the camera. The television audience seemed to enjoy those programs the best. One viewer wrote in and said that she could see movie stars anytime she went to the cinema. The best thing about *The Maggie Lane Baking Show* was watching a television star who knew what it was like to be a housewife.

At the end of today's show, Maggie sat at the table with a slice of raisin cake and a cup of coffee. She unfolded a letter and read into the camera.

> Dear Maggie Lane,
>
> I'm twenty-three and a stewardess for Pan Am. I love seeing new places and helping passengers on the plane. On a longer flight, I serve each passenger a hot dinner, make sure he has enough blankets and pillows, and adjust the seat so he can sleep. There are even shaving kits on the plane. Before we land, I pass out warm hand towels.
>
> I've always dreamed of being a stewardess. But there are two things wrong with the job. The first is the weight limit. My weight has never been a problem, but lately when I get home from a trip, my boyfriend treats me to fancy dinners and I've put on a few pounds. I've tried to tell him that if I eat any more steaks I'll lose my job, but he doesn't listen. So far, the girdle I wear at work hides it, but if I gain any more weight, I might get fired. The other problem is that stewardesses aren't allowed to be married. My boyfriend and I have only been dating a few months, and he's not going to propose soon. But he's afraid to get serious because he's worried that I love my career and won't want to be a housewife.
>
> Betsy Carmichael

Maggie put down the letter and smiled into the camera. "Dear Betsy, being a stewardess sounds like a dream job, and you should enjoy the opportunity to travel and meet new people. Don't fault your boyfriend for buying you nice meals. Instead, substitute heavy main courses for something healthy—a fresh salad, or a piece of fish with vegetables. You can ask him to order the same for himself; he'll feel healthier too. After the meal, suggest you take a walk—nothing is more romantic than a moonlight stroll after dinner.

"As for your boyfriend proposing, tell him that you can save money for your future together by working now. Open your own bank account, and when you get married and stop working, you'll be able to contribute to the household expenses.

"Love and marriage are about compromise. If you and your boyfriend truly love each other, you'll work it out."

Maggie paused before speaking her closing lines. "That's all for today. Remember, we at Deluxe Baking Company are always here for you. Tune in to tomorrow's show to make a JELL-O aspic salad."

Maggie went back to her dressing room and changed into a pair of slacks and a sweater. She thought about Betsy's letter and Tommy's advice to buy the new car.

Before she could change her mind, she picked up the phone and dialed Teddy's number at work.

"I decided we shouldn't go to the dealership next Saturday," she said when Teddy answered.

His tone was slightly belligerent. "I already told Hank we would be there. He's coming in especially to meet with us."

"What if the model you like is gone by the weekend?" she continued in a rush. "I'm getting off work early. We could go today instead."

The line went quiet. Maggie wondered whether Teddy had hung up.

"Are you sure?" he asked finally.

"Completely sure. What's the point of working if we don't use the money to buy something we enjoy? You're right. I couldn't breathe if

I had to live anywhere but New York. But sometimes inhaling fresh country air is just what we need."

"I love you, Maggie," Teddy said matter-of-factly. "I'll finish here and meet you at the studio in an hour."

Maggie held the phone tightly. "I love you too. I'll be waiting outside."

Chapter Eight

Maggie and Teddy had owned the new car for four weeks. On the first weekend, they invited Dolly and Alan and drove up the Taconic Parkway to the Hudson Valley. They stopped to buy apples from a fruit stand, went souvenir shopping in Rhinebeck, and finished the afternoon by taking a tour of the Gilded Age mansions along the Hudson River.

The following week it rained almost every day, and instead of Maggie getting soaked taking the subway to work or spending a fortune on taxis, Teddy insisted on driving her.

Teddy found a parking garage near his office, and he loved surprising her at lunchtime. She'd run outside to get a sandwich and find him sitting in the Chrysler with the motor purring and people walking by and admiring the car.

Instead of arriving home at different times, he often waited in the car for her after work, and they'd take a drive before picking up Chinese takeout and going back to the apartment. Teddy was at his most relaxed when he was behind the steering wheel. He'd hum to the latest Perry Como song on the radio while Maggie navigated.

Tommy had been right—the new car was an easy way to keep Teddy happy. Maggie could concentrate on building her savings. She kept her bankbook tucked in her purse. Every Friday when she deposited her check, she couldn't wait to add up the credit column. In another month, she would start looking for an apartment.

They were driving up to Rye this weekend for Teddy's father's birthday. Maggie had stopped at Macy's to buy a present, and now she was late for work. She stepped off the sidewalk without looking. Suddenly, there was the sound of honking, then the screeching of brakes. She had just enough time to avoid the approaching car before she fell and landed on the pavement.

A man rushed out of the car and crouched down beside her.

"Good God, I thought I'd killed you. Are you all right?"

Maggie's heart was pounding. She glanced up. The man was in his fifties. He had straight brown hair and wore a suit and tie.

"It was my fault. I wasn't looking."

"It doesn't matter whose fault it was if you'd been hit," the man said. "Let me help you up."

Maggie took his arm. There was a tear in her skirt, and the heel of one of her pumps was broken.

He appraised her. "You're a bit of a mess. Why don't I drive you somewhere? Do you live near here?"

If Maggie went home, she'd be even later to the studio. It would be better to borrow a dress from the wardrobe department.

"I work nearby," she replied. "You could drop me there."

He opened the car door for her. "It's the least I can do. I don't usually go around running over young women." He held out his hand. "I'm Malcolm Walsh."

"Maggie Lane." Maggie stepped into the car.

He slipped into the driver's side and turned to her.

"You have that baking show. My wife watches it every day," he said. "Now I feel even worse. I almost ran over her favorite television star."

"I'm hardly a star, and it wasn't your fault. I stepped in front of the car."

Malcolm gave a little chuckle. "Not on purpose, I hope."

"Of course not." Maggie shook her head. "I wasn't looking. I was thinking about something else."

Malcolm turned onto Madison Avenue and stopped in front of CBS. He handed her his card.

"We're all guilty of that sometimes. Here's my card. Maybe you could send my wife a signed recipe book. She'd be grateful to me forever."

Maggie watched him drive away. It was only when she slipped the card in her purse that she realized her hands were shaking. Instead of going into the studio, she entered the coffee shop next door.

She needed to calm down before anyone saw her. She ordered black coffee and stared out the window. If the car had stopped a moment later, she might have been run over. She recalled the time six years earlier when she had slipped in the rain and her future changed forever.

~

It was April 1944, and Jake had been gone for two months. Everyone said it had been the wettest spring in New York for years. Every day, Maggie woke up to rain drumming on the windows. There was a puddle in the kitchen where there was a leak in the ceiling, and the whole apartment had a damp, musty smell.

The television commercial hadn't led to steady work. She was still relying on the temp agency for her income. On the days when she didn't have a job, she was tempted to stay in bed. It was cheaper to lay under the covers rather than go out and want to sit in a coffee shop with a bowl of soup to keep warm. But she forced herself to get dressed and walk up and down Midtown, looking for a job. But all the secretarial positions and salesclerk jobs were filled.

She would find something. Other young women made it in New York, and so could she. She needed to give herself time.

If only Jake were there. They had known each other for only ten days before he shipped out. She had half hoped that she hadn't been in love with him and would forget him. But her feelings only grew stronger. She'd see a new building going up and want to tell him about it, or read something in the newspaper and tear it out to send to him. She started volunteering at the animal shelter on weekends because he mentioned he loved dogs, and every now and then she walked through the men's department at Woolworth's to sample the cologne that she had bought him.

He had written to her twice, and she wrote back as promised. He didn't say much about the war other than it was very hot in the tropics, and though a diet of pineapple and papaya and mango sounded delicious, he'd give anything for a cheeseburger and a milkshake. He ended every letter by saying that he was in love with her and that one day soon he would appear on her doorstep.

Jake had the first day of his next leave all planned out—breakfast at the greasiest diner they could find so he could fill up on bacon and eggs and toast, followed by a rowboat ride in Central Park because it was the kind of thing tourists did, and a returning serviceman deserved to be a tourist for the day. Next was the most important stop—Tiffany's on Fifth Avenue. The first engagement ring had been inexpensive, but that wasn't going to happen again. He was saving a portion of his pay so they could walk in and Maggie could have any ring she wanted.

Maggie smiled at this, not because she wanted an expensive diamond ring but because when she read it, she could see Jake beside her, handsome and confident in his uniform, eagerly asking the saleswoman to show them the biggest, shiniest rings in the glass case.

This morning, Maggie was more hopeful than she had been in days. The temp agency called and said Westinghouse was casting a new commercial. She was to report to the studio at 9:00 a.m.

When she left her apartment, it was raining so hard she could barely see the sidewalk. The subway was crowded, and a few minutes before her stop it came to a screeching halt. She waited with the other passengers, her stomach dropping further as the clock ticked closer to nine. Finally, the train started moving and reached her station.

She emerged from the subway and strode to the traffic light on Fifty-Second Street. As she was about to cross, a bus pulled close to the curb. She darted around the bus, but her shoe slipped on the wet leaves. She could see the approaching cars, but there was nothing she could do. She fell hard onto the pavement, and then everything went black.

When she came to, a small crowd had gathered around her.

A man of about thirty crouched above her. He wore a raincoat and a fedora.

"You're awake," he said. "I was about to call an ambulance."

"An ambulance?" Maggie repeated, alarmed. "I'm fine. I slipped."

"You're not fine. You've been lying here for fifteen minutes." He waved at the people standing nearby. "Look around if you don't believe me."

Maggie struggled to sit up. Her head pounded, and she lay back on the sidewalk.

"Thank you, you can tell everyone I'm all right." She flinched at a sudden pain in her ankle. "If you would help me up, I'd appreciate it. I'm late for an appointment."

The other spectators wondered off, but the man stayed with her. He gave her his arm, and she gingerly stood up.

"You see," she said triumphantly. "Just a few bruises and a rip in my stockings."

"And a possible concussion. Head injuries can be dangerous," the man said. "You're not going anywhere until a doctor checks you out."

Maggie wanted to tell the man she didn't need a doctor. But standing up made the throbbing in her head worse. Her hands were shaky, and there was a numb feeling in her throat.

"If I miss the appointment, I won't get the job," she said. "I promise I'll go to the emergency room as soon as I'm done."

The man studied her quizzically.

"I'll drive you to your appointment and wait for you. Then we'll go to the emergency room together."

Maggie was about to protest that she didn't even know him and he must have better things to do. But the studio seemed so far away. She couldn't imagine walking the few blocks to get there.

She sat huddled against the seat of his late-model Buick, feeling lucky not to have gotten badly hurt. Then she closed her eyes for a moment. When she opened them, the car seemed to spin. She leaned back against the seat and felt herself slipping into some sort of crevice. Her eyes closed and she fainted.

This time, when she opened her eyes she was lying in a strange bed. At first she thought it was a hospital room, but it was too elegant. The room had a high ceiling with crown molding. The walls were papered in a bamboo print, and on the opposite wall was a framed mirror. A bookshelf took up one wall, and in the corner was an armchair and matching ottoman.

The man who had rescued her was sitting in a chair next to the bed. Maggie blinked. "Where am I?"

"In the guest room of my apartment," the man said. "I'm Charles Grey. I'd offer to shake hands, but the doctor said no sudden movements." He took two pills out of a bottle and handed them to her with a glass of water.

"Take two of these aspirin. They'll help with the headache. Then get more sleep."

No matter how much her head hurt or how dry her throat was, she couldn't be in a strange man's apartment.

"You've been kind, but I have an apartment. If you drive me there, I'll sleep it off and you can get back to your day."

Charles shook his head. "Besides the concussion, you have a sprained ankle. The doctor gave strict instructions not to move you for forty-eight hours. I'll go to your apartment and get your things," he offered. "Be a good patient and rest. We'll talk more when you wake up this afternoon."

Maggie was in too much pain and too groggy to argue. She took the pills and did what he said. When she woke up, the clock on the bedside table said it was 5:00 p.m. Outside the window, the rain had stopped. Mist rose from the sidewalk, and she could see the outline of trees.

There was a knock, then the door opened.

Charles had changed into a cashmere sweater and slacks. Without his fedora, Maggie noticed that his hair was very blond. He had green eyes and a square jaw.

He carried a tray. There was a bowl of soup and bread rolls with butter.

"You're awake." He set the tray on the bedside table. "I hope you weren't thinking about getting up. The doctor said no weight on that foot for a few days."

Maggie blushed. "I was going to look outside. I don't even know where you live."

"Apartment 2B, 910 Fifth Avenue," he said. "I took the apartment for the view of Central Park. It's too misty to see the park today. So I suggest you be a good patient and have a bowl of soup. My housekeeper, Ellen, prepared it. She took an immediate liking to you when I brought over your things. You have the same taste in books."

Maggie thought about the small collection of books she kept on her bedside table. They had all been recommended by Jake. Her eyes flew open wider. What would Jake say when she wrote that she got stranded at a strange man's apartment?

"Did I say something wrong?" Charles noticed her expression. "Since you're going to stay here for a while, I thought you'd want your books. They'd be the first thing I'd want to have with me."

Maggie replied that she couldn't stay there. She'd call the temp agency in the morning and tell them what happened. As soon as she was allowed to move, she'd go home and get back to work.

"We'll talk about your employment later," Charles said. "You're certainly not going back to the apartment. I wrote a letter giving your notice and left it in the landlord's mailbox. He's lucky you're not going to sue him."

Charles said the place was uninhabitable. The thermometer read forty-five degrees with the heater on, and the leak in the kitchen was causing mold.

"I don't notice the temperature when I wear my coat inside, and the leak is recent. There probably isn't any mold."

"There will be soon," Charles replied. "The place needs insulating. I can only imagine how hot it gets during the summer."

Maggie had been worried what it would be like in the summer. But she was lucky to have been able to afford anything in Manhattan.

"Well, I can't stay here," Maggie said, flustered. The thought of going back there and managing by herself was overwhelming, but she had to do something. "I'll get a hotel room until I find a new place."

Charles's eyebrows shot up. "Your bankbook happened to be open when I collected your things. I couldn't help but notice the amount in the credit column. No offense, but you couldn't afford the cheapest hotel in New York. You're going to stay here until you're better. Before you say that's not possible, Ellen lives in the room between mine and yours. Even if she didn't, I don't have time for women. I'm a playwright, and my next play is due to my producer in two months."

Charles had written two successful Broadway plays and was working on the third. The down payment for the apartment came from a trust from his grandmother, but everything else—the late-model car, the live-in housekeeper, the expensive suit and cashmere sweater—was paid for with the proceeds from his plays.

Maggie didn't have any other options. She was too wonderfully warm and comfortable to argue.

"You don't know me. Why are you doing this?" she asked.

"I was born and raised in New York. New Yorkers have a reputation for not caring about other people. I want to change that." He gave a small smile. "And I told you I'm a playwright. What could make a better story than saving a damsel in distress?"

~

Maggie sat in the coffee shop next to the CBS studios and finished her coffee. That had all happened so long ago. What if she had gone around the bus and not slipped? Everything in her life would have turned out differently.

Back then, she never would have dreamed that she'd have her own television show and that she'd be married to Teddy. She loved Teddy. They made each other very happy. She adored their dinners at Ruby Foo's, when they talked about their day. And she loved feeding the ducks in Central Park. They'd laugh about which duck was the greediest. Teddy was her best friend as well as her husband and lover.

If only there was a way to tell him about Jake and Charles and everything that happened.

She paid for her coffee and stood up to leave.

Chapter Nine

A few weeks later, Maggie sat in her dressing room after the day's taping. A stack of letters lay on the dressing table, next to her bobby pins and tray of face creams.

After each show, she answered a few of the letters that there wasn't time to feature on the air. Tommy had suggested using a form letter from *The Maggie Lane Baking Show* thanking the viewer for her letter and hoping that she'd continue watching. Maggie pictured a housewife, sitting at her kitchen table and pouring her worries onto the paper, and knew it wasn't enough. A personal letter from Maggie was a much better idea.

~

She picked up a letter from a woman named Meryl Brown and began to read.

> Dear Maggie Lane,
> When I first started watching your show, the other women in the Chicago suburb where I live wondered why I wanted to watch a show about a housewife in New York. So, one day I hosted a viewing party. I baked a Deluxe Baking Company sour cream coffee cake and we crowded around the television. You'll be

happy to know that now all the women tune in to your show every day. Once a month, one woman in the neighborhood hosts a viewing party in her home, and we've started a recipe club using Deluxe Baking Company recipes.

I've painted a pretty picture of my life, but truthfully, most of the time I'm unhappy. Dan and I have been married for five years, and we've been unable to have a baby. I didn't mind at first. I worked as a secretary at a firm in Chicago and enjoyed it. But after Dan received a promotion and a raise, he made me quit my job and stay home. Now he travels every week, and I'm often alone. The women in my neighborhood are nice, but most of them have small children so they spend their days at the park. I've talked to Dan about going back to work until I get pregnant, or even after we have the baby, but he won't hear of it.

Recently a friend told me about a secretarial opening at my old firm. I'm tempted to take it without telling Dan—he's away so much he might not find out. I know it's wrong to keep secrets in a marriage, but if I spend one more day reading movie magazines and deciding what color to paint my nails, I will go mad.

Sincerely,

Meryl Brown

Maggie turned the paper over thoughtfully. She should reply that being a housewife could be fulfilling if Meryl kept the right attitude. Meryl could start each day by heating up the Deluxe Baking Company pastry she baked the night before. A Deluxe Baking Company French breakfast puff was the perfect treat to give Dan as he rushed out the door to catch his train.

After that, Meryl could watch an episode of the new type of television show called a soap opera. Maggie, personally, was a fan of *Hawkin Falls*. Then it would be time for a trip to the supermarket armed with a shopping list for the night's dinner. Maggie believed in buying fresh fruit and vegetables every day, along with a chicken or a thick steak from the meat counter. Then, of course, there was choosing the dessert. Most supermarkets in major cities had a large selection of Deluxe Baking Company cake mixes. The Extra Moist Yellow and White Cake was one of Maggie's favorites.

By the time Meryl returned from the market, it would be time to start dinner. She could finish her afternoon with a warm bath, then put on her prettiest dress, mix a pitcher of martinis, and wait for Dan to come home.

On the days that he traveled, Meryl could treat herself by eating dinner in front of the television or inviting over one of her friends. Meryl was lucky to be able to stay at home and be a housewife. Maggie and everyone at Deluxe Baking Company wanted to help her get the most out of her day.

Every time Maggie started to write the first paragraph, she crossed it out.

Meryl had enjoyed being a secretary. Why should she lead a life that she didn't like just because she was married?

> Dear Meryl,
> First, I want to thank you for watching *The Maggie Lane Baking Show*. My viewers are so important to me, and I take every letter very seriously.
> You mustn't lie to your husband about taking a job. Lies can do irreversible harm to a marriage. Instead, tell Dan gently that you're lonely and bored and want to go back to work.
> Dan probably feels that if you earn money too, he won't be the breadwinner in the family. Point out to

him the things you'll be able to afford—two vacations a year instead of one, a new set of golf clubs for him and a sewing machine for you. Get him on your side and make the decision for you to go back to work together.

Husbands can be stubborn and proud. But if you don't try to get what you want, you'll remain unhappy. Please write back and tell me how it works out.

Best,

Maggie Lane

She read it over, wondering what Tommy would say if he saw it. It didn't matter—she had to be honest with her viewers or they'd stop watching. And she wasn't saying anything bad about being a housewife, she was just giving Meryl some options. If only she could be as open and honest in her own marriage. She couldn't just think about herself. She had to consider how telling Teddy about her past would affect the Deluxe Baking Company. She could ruin everything that she and Teddy were working toward.

Before she could second-guess herself, she slipped the letter in an envelope.

Dolly peeked her head in. She wore a polka-dot dress with a boat neckline and carried a pair of white gloves.

"You're all dressed up," Maggie acknowledged.

"I have a doctor's appointment," Dolly said. "I wanted to see if you'd come with me. I need your opinion."

Maggie asked if it was anything serious.

"I'm not sick, but it is serious." Dolly turned to the mirror. "I'm thinking of getting a nose job."

Dolly's nose was a bit long, and it had the tiniest bump, but it wasn't anything Maggie would notice.

"Before you say I have a perfectly fine nose, it's fine for Dolly Meyerowitz, shoe heiress, but it's not fine for Dolly Meyers, the actress,"

Dolly said as if she could read her thoughts. "It's going to be hard enough getting acting roles as I get older. If I have to compete with actresses with perfect snub noses, I'll be out of work. Besides, Alan's parents are coming to New York soon."

"You want to surprise Alan with a new nose?" Maggie asked in disbelief.

"Men don't notice those things, but his mother will," Dolly replied. "Our first meeting will go better if I have the kind of petite nose she'd like to see on her grandchildren."

Maggie said that nose jobs must cost a fortune. And Dolly was one of the most popular young actresses on television.

"That can change at any minute. Television audiences are fickle. If a bright new actress appears on the cover of *TV Times* magazine with a smaller nose and trimmer figure, I could be television history."

"It's not right." Maggie picked up Meryl's letter. "Every day I receive letters from women who would be happy if they were allowed to be themselves instead of always trying to please other people. You don't need surgery to make Alan and his family like you. And you should be judged on your acting talents."

"Alan didn't ask me to get a nose job. He doesn't know I'm thinking about it." Dolly played with her gloves. "You don't know what it's like to grow up Jewish. I'm falling in love with Alan. I don't want to miss out on being happy because his mother doesn't approve of me."

Maggie wanted to say there was no reason to think Alan's parents wouldn't like her. But Dolly could be stubborn. There was no use arguing with her.

The plastic surgeon's office was in a tall office building on Lexington Avenue. Dolly and Maggie were led to a room with teak furniture and diplomas on the walls. Family photographs were displayed on the desk, and there was a sideboard with a pitcher of water.

A slim man entered the room. He was in his fifties, with dark hair and blue eyes. "I'm Dr. Abel. Which one of you pretty young women is Dolly Meyers?"

Dolly raised her hand. "I am."

Dr. Abel shook hands and motioned for them to sit in the chairs facing the desk.

He explained that rhinoplasty, as it was called in the medical field, had advanced since the war. It had been used extensively on injured servicemen, and recently Hollywood actors and actresses, like Dean Martin and Carmen Miranda, were getting nose jobs.

"The studios keep it secretive, of course, but it's becoming popular."

"Dolly has a lovely nose," Maggie piped in. "It suits her face."

Dr. Abel studied Dolly closely.

"It's a good nose, but it has imperfections," he answered. "A little smoothing on top and a tiny bit off the end would make a big improvement."

Dolly shot Maggie a triumphant look. She asked the cost and how long it would take for her to recover.

"The surgery is fairly easy. The biggest risk is the anesthesia. Whenever a patient goes under, there can be complications. On the other hand, anesthesia has also become much safer since the war."

Dr. Abel examined Dolly thoroughly and talked through the fees and timetable for the surgery.

"Take home the reading material and then contact my scheduling nurse," he finished. "Any surgery is scary, but you'll be glad you had it done. Looks are so important for young, professional women."

They left the doctor's office and walked a few blocks to a diner.

"I don't think you should do this," Maggie said, when they were sitting at the counter. "The show's producer never said you needed a nose job, and how will you explain it to Alan? At least talk to him about it first."

"That's because my makeup artist spends ages shading my nose." Dolly picked up the menu. "I can't tell Alan. I'll say I'm visiting an aunt in another state."

Maggie couldn't help feeling frustrated. "The doctor admitted there are risks. Patients have been known to die from the anesthesia. And for what? Alan might like your nose; he likes everything about you."

"He likes my nose because he doesn't know it's a Jewish nose." Dolly's brow furrowed. "He'd like it more if it was a bit smaller."

Maggie wanted to say that Dolly shouldn't keep secrets from Alan, but she had her own secrets. She had never told anyone about Jake.

"You can't just erase your religion," Maggie said instead.

"No, but I can make it more difficult for people to notice," Dolly countered. "What if Alan and I attend a dinner party and one of the guests doesn't like me because I'm Jewish?" She looked at Maggie sharply. "Before you say I'm crazy, it happened to my parents. This may be America in 1950 and not Germany during the war, but some things don't change."

Maggie was silent. She'd never heard Dolly speak so passionately about something.

"I'm sorry," Maggie said finally. "I had no idea."

Dolly gave herself a little shake.

"Of course you didn't. You're my best friend, and I'm grateful to have you. Let's talk about something else. When are you going to start looking for an apartment?"

They talked about the real estate listings Maggie had seen in the newspaper. She had torn out the advertisement for a two bedroom on a leafy street on the Upper East Side. They couldn't afford it yet, but in another couple of months they would.

The waiter set down their order. Maggie had a BLT on toast and ice tea. Dolly had only asked for a Coca-Cola.

"Since when do you drink Coke?" Maggie frowned. "And why aren't you having any lunch?"

"Alan introduced me to it. All the writers drink Coke. It keeps them awake when they have a late-night writing session." Dolly took a sip. "I'm not hungry. I had a big breakfast."

The last time that Maggie had been in Dolly's dressing room, she noticed the boxes of crackers and jar of peanut butter were missing. Instead, there was only instant coffee and a new mini fridge where Dolly kept her sodas.

She set half her sandwich on a napkin and handed it to Dolly.

"Eat this. It's bacon, lettuce, and tomato. You won't have to worry about dinner later."

Dolly looked from the sandwich to Maggie as if she was trying to find a way to avoid it.

"All right, I'll eat it if it makes you happy." Dolly kept her voice light. "I have to use the powder room first."

Maggie waited until Dolly disappeared into the powder room. Then she slid off the stool and followed her.

Dolly was standing at the sink, holding a handful of pills. She quickly swallowed them and turned to Maggie.

"I'm sorry. I didn't mean to get angry," Dolly said. "Please don't start on me about the pills. I've been tired lately. I've been working ten hours on the set and then going out with Alan at night."

"The answer is to get more sleep, not to rely on those things," Maggie said.

Dolly's face turned hot. "Everything is easy for you. You're the star of your own baking show, and you have Teddy. I could be replaced next week, and the television audience will fall in love with the new actress. That's how TV shows work. Alan is my last chance at finding love. If he doesn't share my feelings, I'll never find anyone else."

Maggie felt terribly guilty. She hated making Dolly upset, but she couldn't watch her best friend do things that were bad for her. Eating the right foods was important, and the more pills Dolly took, the more she would become dependent on them. Maggie only wanted to help her.

Before Maggie could answer, Dolly strode back to the diner counter. She ate a bite of the sandwich and glared at Maggie. "Are you satisfied?"

"I care about you." Maggie's voice was low. "I want you to be happy."

Dolly took a few dollar bills from her purse. "I'm sorry. I drank too much instant coffee this morning. It always puts me on edge. I should go. I'll see you later."

After Dolly left, Maggie sat and finished her ice tea. Dolly had left the rest of her sandwich on the plate. Maggie wondered how she could make Dolly see the truth. It wasn't the instant coffee that made Dolly anxious. It was the coffee on top of the soda, and the pills, and the lack of food and sleep.

Maggie paid and walked outside. It was late afternoon. She'd pick up some things for dinner and go home. It was rare that she left work early. Maybe she'd get home before Teddy. They could go for an evening stroll, and she'd voice her concerns about Dolly.

She was about to enter the butcher when she saw Teddy's mother walking down the street. Patty was dressed in a skirt and blouse and matching jacket.

"Patty." Maggie stopped her. "It's nice to see you. Teddy didn't say you were in New York."

Patty's face took on a guilty expression. "Teddy doesn't know I'm here."

Patty always announced her visits to the city. Maybe she was sick and came to Manhattan to see a doctor.

"There's nothing wrong, but I wanted to keep it private," she said. "Why don't we walk together? I want to show you something."

They turned onto Fifty-Seventh Street and entered an art gallery. Large paintings, splashed with bold colors, covered the walls. There were a few ottomans where buyers could sit and a desk stacked with brochures.

"I didn't know you were interested in modern art," Maggie said. They stood in front of a painting of a woman wearing a floppy hat and laden with packages. In one hand she carried bunches of flowers; in the other, a shopping bag with a loaf of bread peeking out.

"This is my favorite," Patty said. "It's inspired by Virginia Woolf's novel *Mrs. Dalloway*."

Maggie had read the book. It was about a wife who never had enough hours in her day, trying to get ready for a dinner party.

Maggie searched the canvas for the artist's signature. "It's very good. Who's the artist?"

Patty pulled at her gloves. "I am. Though I use my middle name. I don't want anyone to know."

Patty had painted when she was young, but she stopped when she and Harry got married. She never thought she'd take it up again, but one day she entered an artist supply store and bought canvases and paints and brushes. She kept them in the storeroom above the garage and painted while Harry was at work.

"Most of the galleries in New York are in Greenwich Village, and they're full of young bohemians," Patty said. "But the owner here is lovely, and he was interested in my paintings. He's already sold three pieces, and he has a potential buyer for *Mrs. Dalloway*."

"That's wonderful. Harry and Teddy will be so proud."

"You see, I can't tell Harry. We'd never be invited to a dinner party again. Wives in Rye aren't artists." Patty shook her head. "I need something to fill my day, and I enjoy it. When I'm standing in front of the easel, I feel as if I'm twenty."

They walked outside and sat at a table in a restaurant. Patty ordered coffee for both of them.

"Funnily enough, I got the idea from watching your television show." Patty stirred cream into her coffee. "I haven't thought about what makes me happy since Teddy and his sister were born. Maggie Lane made me see that there's more to life than fluffing cushions and creating floral arrangements."

Maggie said she didn't understand. The point of the show was about being the perfect housewife.

"I see it differently," Patty argued. "It's more about doing something that you never thought you could do. Before I started watching the show, I bought all my cakes from the bakery. One day, I was bored and baked a Deluxe Baking Company triple berry cheesecake. It was fun to bake, and Harry loved it. After that, I went into New York and bought the art supplies. At my age, it's difficult to change my routine. You gave me the courage to try new things."

Maggie didn't know what to say. She had never looked at the show that way. She was pleased that Patty had branched out to try new things. It made her consider her own life. Were there hobbies that she wanted to try? She had always wanted to take singing lessons but never had the opportunity. There hadn't been enough money before she was married, and it wasn't the kind of thing a housewife did. Maybe she'd mention it to Teddy. She could take a lesson every now and then while he was playing squash.

Patty sipped her coffee. "Now, I need advice on what to do if Harry finds out."

"Hang one of your paintings in the entry before your next dinner party," Maggie suggested. "When someone asks who painted it, admit that you did. Everyone will be impressed, and Harry will be pleased." She smiled knowingly. "Men like having a talented wife, as long as you give him some of the credit."

Patty squeezed Maggie's hand.

"I knew you'd have the answer. I'm so glad I ran into you." She reached into her purse. "Here's Teddy's cigarette lighter. He forgot it when he came to Rye last Monday."

Maggie's good mood disappeared. Teddy didn't have days off during the week. And she hadn't seen him smoke since their dinner with Dolly and Alan a month ago.

"I didn't know that Teddy was in Rye." She stirred her coffee.

"I'm surprised he didn't tell you." Patty shrugged. "We had a lovely afternoon. He took me for a drive in the new car."

Maggie picked up the lighter. Patty's words disturbed her. She didn't know how to answer. Instead, she changed the subject.

"Does Teddy ever talk about Oradour-sur-Glane?" she asked.

"What's that?"

Maggie said it was a village in France where there was a German massacre during the war.

"We don't talk about the war. I never listened to a single one of Teddy's programs." Patty looked slightly guilty. "Harry used to get frustrated since I wouldn't allow him to listen to them either." Her eyes grew larger. "What would I have done if a bomb fell during a segment? I feel terrible about it now. Everyone says Teddy was so good on the radio. But I'm his mother, I didn't care about that. All I wanted was for him to be safe."

Maggie wished she could tell Patty about the photographs she had found in the notebook and ask whether Teddy ever talked about Arabella and Ian. Patty would think that Maggie had been snooping, and she'd be right. Maggie still hadn't mentioned the notebook to Teddy. The more she thought about it, the more she realized she couldn't without him being angry with her.

She hated keeping secrets in their marriage, but she didn't know what else to do. Teddy's night sweats hadn't stopped, and there was nothing she could do about them.

Maggie and Patty talked about how much Westchester County had grown. The local country clubs had built swimming pools and tennis courts to attract young families. White Plains had two department stores, and Rye was getting a new supermarket.

"I should go. I can't miss the train." Patty took a five-dollar bill from her purse. "Thank you for the advice. Tomorrow morning, I'm going to call the gallery and say I've changed my mind about selling *The Hours*. Then I'm going to hang it in the entry before Saturday night's cocktail party."

Chapter Ten

The following Sunday morning, Maggie sat in the living room of their apartment. Teddy was playing squash with a friend. After his match, Maggie and Teddy were going to spend the afternoon viewing a new exhibit at the Metropolitan Museum of Art.

Maggie was glad to have some time alone. She hadn't mentioned to Teddy that she had seen his mother or that Maggie had his cigarette lighter. Teddy had been so warm and loving lately—calling in a favor from a friend so they could attend a taping of one of their favorite television shows, *The Lone Ranger*. Afterward they were going to have dinner with Clayton Moore, the show's star, and use Teddy's new Diners Club card.

She didn't want to upset him. But there had to be a reason why he took off work and why he was smoking again. She wondered more and more lately if *The Maggie Lane Baking Show* was to blame. The more successful the show became, and the more Maggie was stopped in the street for her autograph, the wider the gulf in their careers became obvious. Even if Teddy didn't want fame for himself, it couldn't be easy for him to watch Maggie become so well known.

It didn't help that he still tossed and turned all night and woke up drenched in sweat. Maggie never mentioned it. With their lives becoming more complicated, she was afraid of upsetting Teddy even more. Once, they had been watching a television show set at a country estate in the English countryside. She had asked if he had ever visited one of those elegant country houses when he was in London during the war. She hoped that he might mention Arabella and Ian, but he had gone to the kitchen for a glass of milk and ignored her question.

Had Teddy been in love with Arabella? She was beautiful, and he had been young and alone, so far from home. Who was Ian, and how did the three of them end up in France together? There was no reason for Teddy to hide it from her. It had all happened years ago. But she had never told him anything about Jake.

She wanted to help him, but she didn't know how. Right now, it would have to wait.

She had to get ready and meet Teddy at the Met.

Maggie's favorite thing about the Metropolitan Museum was the building itself. It was a huge Beaux-Arts structure on Fifth Avenue between Eightieth and Eighty-Fourth Streets. Entrance was free, so ever since Maggie arrived in New York, she had loved wandering through the exhibits. Vast halls of Greek and Egyptian artifacts. European paintings and early-twentieth-century photographs, and whole sections of fashions through the ages. Teddy loved it too. It was better than the cinema, where one could get restless sitting for too long, and every time they came, there was something different to see.

But today, Maggie wasn't in the mood to stand among hordes of tourists. She had the sensation that Teddy was slipping away from her. She wanted to be alone with him, somewhere quiet, where she could remind herself how much they loved each other.

Teddy was waiting for Maggie on the steps when she arrived. He looked handsome in his squash clothes—a knit V-neck sweater and white cotton slacks.

"There you are. I thought you'd forgotten." Teddy waved at his brochure. "We should see the Asian art exhibit first. There's already a line out the door."

"It's a beautiful day, and I feel like walking," Maggie said. "Why don't we go across to Central Park first?"

Teddy glanced at Maggie in surprise. They had been looking forward to seeing the new exhibit all week.

They crossed the street and strolled around the lake. Maggie began to feel calmer. She was with Teddy in the city that she loved. Everything she had been worrying about—Dolly's pills, Teddy's cigarettes, the photographs of Teddy and Arabella and Ian—faded with the bright colors and scents of the flowers.

"This is what I needed. I've been spending too much time in the studio," she said when they were sitting on a bench.

"That's what happens when you become America's sweetheart." Teddy's voice was casual.

Maggie looked at him sharply. "What do you mean by that?"

"It's nothing." Teddy shrugged. "You were the talk of the squash court today."

A woman had begged Teddy to be his squash partner for a doubles match. Teddy had refused. The woman was young and pretty, and he thought Maggie wouldn't approve. It turned out she wanted to be his partner so she could get Maggie's autograph.

"Here's her name and address." He handed Maggie a slip of paper.

Maggie opened her handbag. It tipped over, and the contents fell onto the bench.

Teddy picked them up. "What's this doing here?"

It was Teddy's cigarette lighter.

Maggie explained that she had run into his mother, and Patty had given it to her.

"You saw my mother and didn't tell me, and now you're keeping my cigarette lighter?" Teddy's brow furrowed.

"You're twisting things. That's not how it happened."

"It seems to me it is," Teddy declared. "Why didn't you tell me you saw her, and why didn't you give me the lighter right away?"

Maggie tried to think of an answer. Anything she said meant that she didn't trust Teddy.

"Why did you go to Rye without telling me?" she demanded. "And why are you smoking again when you gave it up?"

Teddy replied that there was nothing wrong with smoking.

"You should know, with all the television we watch," he snapped. "The cigarette commercials all show doctors who say it's harmless."

"I thought we liked watching television," she replied. "Doctors aren't always right. The cigarettes make you cough. And look at Dolly. Her mother's doctor prescribed those pills. She says that they're not addictive, but every time I see her, she's taking more."

Teddy stood up and began pacing.

"If you must know, I went to Rye because I had a disagreement with my boss. He didn't like the music I selected and insisted I take the afternoon off." He shoved his hands in his pockets. "And it isn't always easy being Maggie Lane's husband. Last week, I ate at a restaurant with Alan and paid for the meal with my Diners Club card. The waitress recognized me from some movie magazine. When she saw the card, she asked me why it said Teddy Buckley and not Teddy Lane. I had to explain that even though we were married, you use a different name on television."

Maggie hadn't thought about that. When Tommy first approached her about doing the television show, she and Teddy hadn't been married. Maggie Lane was the name she had used on her radio program.

"I put up with it because I love you and we're a team," he continued. "If you can't trust me enough to tell me that my mother is in town, or that she gave you something of mine, then our marriage is in trouble."

"I would hardly call your situation 'putting up with it.'" Maggie was angry now. What did Teddy have to complain about? Their lives had become filled with all the things that he enjoyed since she took the job. "*The Maggie Lane Baking Show* paid for the new car, not to mention the charge cards." She waved at his athletic clothes. "You wouldn't have joined the squash club without my increased salary. Do you think it's easy working such long hours? This is the first Sunday afternoon I haven't spent answering readers' letters in weeks."

"Instead, I forced you to go to the Metropolitan Museum," he fumed. "At least the exhibition was free, so we didn't waste your money on that." He returned to the bench. "I don't feel like looking at Asian art anymore. I'm going back to the squash club. If it's all right, I'll pick up Chinese takeout for dinner. It will be nice to stay home instead of letting our food get cold at a restaurant because you're signing autographs. Why don't you call ahead to Ruby Foo's? You're Maggie Lane. When the hostess hears your voice on the line, she's bound to include an extra portion of wontons."

Teddy stormed off and Maggie sat on the bench, holding his silver lighter. Her stomach rose to her throat, and there was a pounding in her ears. How many times had she given the advice that the most important thing in a relationship was communication? She hadn't asked Teddy about the photographs of him and Arabella and Ian. What if bringing up something in his past upset him even more? She always thought that he would tell her about the war when he was ready.

But after thinking about the photos, she wanted to learn more about Oradour-sur-Glane and what Teddy had witnessed. When had they arrived, and did he meet any of the villagers? Is that what kept him up at night, and why wouldn't he talk about it?

She wanted to be angry at Teddy. He had encouraged her to become a television star. But she felt sorry for him. It couldn't be easy if everyone he met wanted to know Maggie. And Teddy could get so much more out of his own career, if only he came to terms with whatever it was in his past that haunted him.

She was tempted to rush after him and say that she loved him and they'd solve whatever problems they encountered together. Something stopped her. Teddy had never been so angry. If she tried to appease him and nothing in their lives changed, next time it could be worse.

They needed the television show to support their lifestyle. And there were so many things she loved about being Maggie Lane.

Answering letters from readers and knowing she was improving their lives. Tommy's praise when he showed her the ratings numbers. The satisfaction of standing on the set, the smell of a delicious chocolate dessert baking in the oven, and imagining her viewers sitting happily in front of their television sets.

Instead of following Teddy, she dragged herself back to the museum. She did a few loops around the Asian art exhibit and then walked home. For once, she didn't feel like strolling down Seventy-First Street and dreaming of which townhouse she wanted to buy. The thought of sitting in a diner by herself and having a milkshake or a piece of pie was unappealing.

Teddy wasn't home when she let herself into the apartment. She curled up on the sofa with a magazine. She must have dozed off for a couple of hours. When her eyes opened, the sky was turning pink with the sunset.

A key turned in the lock. Teddy stood in front of her. He was holding a birdcage with a sheet thrown over it.

"This is for you." He set it on the coffee table.

Maggie took off the sheet. Inside the cage were two green birds with orange faces.

"They're lovebirds." Teddy sat on the sofa. "Do you know how hard it is to find an open pet store on a Sunday? I had to take the subway to Queens. A friend knew of a shop that sold lovebirds."

Maggie had never felt so touched. Her mouth opened, but no words came out.

"You can buy yourself clothes or jewelry. I wanted to give you something to show how much I love you," he continued. "The pet store owner swore that lovebirds make the perfect pets for an apartment."

Teddy was sorry for everything he'd said earlier. It wasn't Maggie's fault that strangers wanted to meet her. It meant that she was good at her job, and he was proud of her.

Maggie listened to Teddy, and her eyes misted over. Teddy was never afraid to show his feelings, and he wasn't afraid to apologize first.

The lovebirds were such a unique and thoughtful gift, it made her love him even more.

"I could do something else," she offered. "Or maybe you'd like to try something different, and we can focus on your career."

"I'm happy with my job, and I like my wife being the star of *The Maggie Lane Baking Show*." He leaned forward and kissed her.

Maggie kissed him back. His lips were warm, and he tasted of mint toothpaste. He wrapped his arms around her, and she felt the hardness of his chest.

He stood up and took her hand.

"Let's go to bed," he whispered.

Chapter Eleven

The next month passed happily. Maggie named the lovebirds Humphrey Bogart and Lauren Bacall after two of her favorite movie stars. Teddy and his boss got along better, and Teddy was made content producer for two more local radio shows. *The Maggie Lane Baking Show* grew even more successful. Maggie was nominated for the most prestigious award in television. It was called a Peabody Award, and she had been nominated as best host of a daytime television program.

Not everything was perfect. Maggie received an angry letter from a man named Ed, saying that her advice to his wife, Moira, practically ruined their marriage. Maggie had encouraged Moira to get a job that she enjoyed outside the home. Now, there was never a pitcher of cocktails and a nicely set dining table waiting for him. Moira bought meals from the frozen section in the supermarket, and they ate on trays in front of the television.

Maggie wrote back that she and her husband, Teddy, ate dinner while watching television all the time. The trick was to find a program they both enjoyed, then they'd always have something to talk about. The best part about eating from a tray was there was less washing up to do. That extra time could be spent together in the bedroom. Maggie included a no-bake recipe for Deluxe Baking Company pineapple upside-down cake. Moira could make the cake in a few minutes when she got home from work.

Two weeks later, Ed wrote another letter saying Maggie's latest advice had improved their communication and their sex life. He was grateful and invited Maggie and Teddy to dinner the next time they were in Philadelphia.

Another viewer named Lois wrote and said she took Maggie's advice to be honest in her marriage and admitted a flirtation to her husband. Her husband responded by filing for divorce. Lois was so angry at Maggie, she stopped watching the show. But a few weeks later she discovered that her husband had been having an affair for ages. He'd been looking for a reason to divorce her. She was glad to be rid of him and had already been asked out by an attractive man she met at the gas station.

Maggie sent Lois two tickets to a Broadway musical and a recipe for a Deluxe banana bread. Lois and her new boyfriend could bake it together.

~

It was Saturday morning, and Maggie had an appointment with a Realtor. She hadn't told Teddy. He played in a weekly squash tournament, and she didn't want to interrupt his time on the court. First, she'd find a few apartments she liked, then she would ask him to accompany her.

The Realtor's name was Nancy. She was in her midforties with a Veronica Lake peek-a-boo hairdo. The first apartment was in a co-op building on Madison Avenue between Seventy-Second and Seventy-Third Streets. Nancy pointed out the double-glazed windows and art deco mirrors. There was a view of the park from the bedroom, and the kitchen had a butler's pantry.

"Of course, if you're thinking of starting a family soon, you'll want something bigger," Nancy twittered, standing in the living room.

"We only got married a few months ago," Maggie responded. "We won't be having children for ages."

"Newly married couples make that mistake all the time," Nancy said knowingly. "Babies come whenever they like. All of a sudden, the couple is stuck in what we call a one bedroom plus. The galley kitchen is too small to heat up baby bottles, and the second bedroom isn't big enough to hold a crib. So the baby sleeps in their bed. I don't know how many wives come to me, desperate to find something else."

Whenever Maggie imagined their new apartment, she pictured a small second bedroom that could be used as a home office or as a closet for Maggie and Teddy's clothes. Nancy had a point, though. Maggie didn't want to keep moving, and they wanted children eventually.

There was a bigger listing on Fifth Avenue she could show Maggie.

"You won't find a place in the neighborhood with better light," Nancy said when they entered the apartment. "The seller needs the cash, so the price per square foot is reduced."

Maggie fell in love with the parquet floors, the sunlight streaming through the floor-to-ceiling windows. It had an L-shaped dining room and a tile bathtub in the bathroom. But even if it was a good price, it was more than they could afford.

"There must be something else similar in the neighborhood," Maggie said.

"I do have something a bit farther up on Fifth Avenue. It's not on the market yet, but I can show it to you."

Maggie followed Nancy up Fifth Avenue. She recognized the block right away. Each apartment building had a doorman. In the middle of the block was a small park, with a bench and a rose garden.

"This is one of the best blocks on the Upper East Side," Nancy said. "Apartments almost never become available. You practically have to kill someone to live here."

There was a tightness in Maggie's chest, and she found it hard to swallow. She tried to think of something to say. "It's too far uptown. We both work in Midtown."

"That's nonsense. It's a perfect location. You're steps away from the park and the museums." Nancy took a key from her purse. "The apartment is on the ground floor. It will just take a moment to walk through it."

Nancy had been recommended by Dolly's mother. Maggie didn't want to offend her.

"Actually, I've been thinking. I really love the last apartment," Maggie said. "Why don't I go home and talk about it with my husband."

Nancy's expression brightened. She slipped the keys back in her purse.

"It is a more central location, and you can't beat the light in the living room," she agreed. "Call me tomorrow, and I can show it to both of you."

Maggie crossed the street and sat on a bench in Central Park. Her hands were shaking, and her knees felt wobbly. Charles's apartment had been on the same block. She remembered after her accident, when she was well enough to leave the building for the first time.

~

Maggie had been staying at Charles's apartment for three weeks. The first two weeks passed in a blur of long naps, punctuated by Ellen's home-cooked soups that Charles insisted Maggie eat to regain her strength. Maggie had worried that Charles would want to eat together. She hadn't known him long, and she didn't know what they would talk about. But he mostly left her alone. Her bedroom was lovely. Every day Ellen brought fresh flowers and replaced the towels in the bathroom with warm, fluffy towels straight out of the dryer.

Maggie wrote a letter to Jake telling him what happened. She was healing, and there was nothing to worry about. She would send her new address as soon as she found an apartment. In the meantime, he could write to the address on the return envelope. She wondered what Jake would think when he saw it was on Fifth Avenue.

Today she finally felt well enough to leave the apartment. She was going to the temp agency to see about a job. Her sprained ankle hurt when she walked on it, and she had frequent headaches from the concussion, but it didn't matter. She couldn't stay at Charles's apartment forever.

Charles had brought over her clothes, and they were hanging in the closet. She put on a polka-dot dress and a matching hat. She slipped on a pair of pumps and tucked gloves into her handbag.

The trees on Charles's block were perfectly manicured, and there was a bench and patches of flowers. The surrounding apartment buildings were in the Beaux-Arts style with striped awnings and doormen wearing uniforms and little caps. Women walked by dressed in the latest fashions, and nannies pushed strollers outfitted with pink and blue blankets.

Maggie wondered how much Charles's apartment cost to keep up and how he could afford it. He must have been even more successful than he had let on.

When she reached the temp agency, the waiting room was full of young women dressed similarly to Maggie. They all wore bright lipstick and looked determined to find a job. She waited nervously until the receptionist called her name.

"I heard about your accident," the woman said when Maggie entered her office. "I'm sorry you missed the audition with Westinghouse."

"I'm all better now." Maggie sat in a chair opposite her desk. "If they're casting another commercial, I'd love a chance."

"I'm sorry. They were so happy with the girl we sent, they're going to keep using her."

"Is there anything else I could audition for?" Maggie asked, trying to keep the desperation out of her voice.

The woman riffled through her notes. "At the moment, all we have are secretarial jobs. You weren't interested in those."

Maggie answered that she had changed her mind. She'd take anything that paid a decent salary.

"Your file doesn't mention your typing speed. You'd need to be able to take shorthand."

Maggie hadn't typed since a class she took in high school. It couldn't be that difficult. Charles had a typewriter; perhaps she could borrow it. And she could learn shorthand.

"I'll do anything. Please, I need a job."

The woman looked at her kindly. "I'll set up a few interviews for next week. That will give you time to refresh your skills."

Maggie thanked her and left. She had to do something to improve her chances at finding a job. She stopped at the Strand and bought a book on shorthand. It had been so long since she had been in the fresh air. It would have been lovely to sit in Central Park, or stroll past the department store windows on Fifth Avenue. But if she had any chance of finding a job, she had to go home and practice her typing.

When she arrived at the apartment, Ellen was out running errands and Charles wasn't home. Maggie took off her gloves and entered the living room. The typewriter sat on a desk next to the window. Maggie had asked Charles why he didn't write in the study. It seemed perfect with its tall bookshelves and sideboard set with bottles of scotch. Charles had laughed that all those books were intimidating, and it would be too easy when he felt stuck in his writing to fix himself a cocktail instead.

He preferred writing in the living room. The sound of Ellen's vacuuming was strangely soothing, and the view from the window—of a neighboring stoop with a cat—was interesting without being completely distracting.

Maggie could wait and ask Charles's permission to use the typewriter, but he might be gone all afternoon. She knew what he would say. That she didn't want to be a secretary. There was no hurry for her to get a job. She could stay at the apartment as long as she liked. But the sooner she found something, the sooner she could move and write to Jake with a permanent address.

Before she could talk herself out of it, she slipped paper into the typewriter. Then she opened a book and started to copy the page.

An hour later, the door opened. Charles entered the living room. Maggie jumped up hastily.

"What are you doing?" he asked.

Maggie explained about the visit to the temp agency.

"You should have told me. I would have driven you," Charles replied. "You shouldn't be walking on that ankle."

"My ankle is fine. I had to," Maggie said. "You've been kind, but I can't stay here forever."

"It hasn't even been a month," he reminded her.

Maggie toyed with the writing paper. "You hardly know me. I'm sure you want some privacy."

When Maggie moved in, she worried that she would feel uncomfortable around Charles. He was worldly and sophisticated, and she was a single young woman with little experience around men. Yet that had never been the case. He was often gone in the evenings. He always left wearing a well-cut suit or a blazer and slacks. She assumed he took different women to dinner and dancing. On the nights that he stayed home, he spent a lot of time in his study or went to bed early. He was always friendly yet slightly formal with her, so she felt completely at ease. It helped that Ellen lived there too. Maggie was almost never alone with Charles in the apartment.

"I told you I'm too busy to date seriously," he said as if he could read her thoughts. "Anyway, I'm not that kind of man. I would never bring a woman back to my apartment." He paced around the living room. "If you must get a job, be my secretary. I told you I'm stuck on this play. If someone else typed it for me, it would go faster. You can take over my correspondence. I'm terrible at answering letters."

"I couldn't do that," Maggie blurted out without thinking about it. He had already been so kind to her, she couldn't accept any more favors.

"Why not?" Charles warmed to his idea. "I'd pay you double what you'd make at an office, as well as room and board. Before you say that you can't accept charity or that I have ulterior motives, I do the same for Ellen. I believe in rewarding the people who make my life easier."

Charles made good points. If she was considering being a secretary, why shouldn't she work for him? Her typewriting skills probably weren't good enough to get a secretarial position in a busy office. At least with Charles, she could work at her own pace without fear of being fired.

But how would it feel to work for Charles and live in his apartment at the same time? It would mean that her living situation wasn't temporary. What would Jake say when she wrote and told him? And yet, it would be wonderful to save money for when she and Jake started their new life together.

"I'm not a fast typist, and I've never taken dictation in my life."

"You'll practice at night." Charles waved his hand. "Unless you go out on dates; then you can practice before breakfast. I follow a rigorous schedule. Three hours of writing in the morning, followed by an hour's lunch break. In the afternoon, I write again until dinnertime. I'm a fair boss, and it will be more interesting than typing out business memos."

Maggie could put aside the money she saved to find an apartment for her and Jake. The war couldn't last forever. Jake would return, and they'd get married.

"All right," she agreed. "I'll do it."

"Excellent." Charles beamed. He glanced at her as if he just got an idea. "We'll go to the 21 Club to celebrate."

The 21 Club was one of the most popular restaurants in Manhattan. All the Hollywood movie stars and celebrities ate there when they were in New York.

"That sounds lovely, but I can't," Maggie declined. "It's too expensive, and I don't have anything to wear."

"It will be my treat. Consider it a starting bonus. You need to get out of the apartment. You've been cooped up here for weeks," Charles said.

Maggie sighed dreamily. The thought of sitting in a restaurant, surrounded by women wearing elegant cocktail dresses and men in elegant dinner jackets, was too tempting to ignore.

"Thank you, I'd love to go." She nodded.

"Why don't we both go get dressed. You can wear one of the dresses I bought this afternoon," Charles said casually. "I asked Ellen to hang them in your closet."

Maggie frowned. "What do you mean?"

"When I brought your things over, I noticed you had very few dresses," he replied. "I picked up a few today at Lord & Taylor."

Maggie wanted to say that whatever Charles had bought he had to return. She couldn't accept gifts from him. But she was beginning to realize he did what he wanted, and she wouldn't be able to persuade him. She told herself that she was going to be working for him. She could accept the dresses as part of her first month's salary.

She entered her room and opened the closet.

One whole side was devoted to new dresses. There were day dresses with cinched waists and full skirts. Blouses and skirts with matching jackets.

She flipped through them and caught her breath.

The closet held one of the most beautiful evening gowns she had ever seen. It was off-the-shoulder yellow satin. A satin cape fell down the back of the dress, and the belt had a yellow bow. It must have cost a fortune. She could never wear it. But when she tried it on and saw her reflection in the mirror—the fabric made her skin glow and her hair look shinier—she couldn't take it off.

She picked up her hairbrush and noticed an envelope on the dressing table. It was addressed to her, in Jake's handwriting. She opened the envelope and unfolded the letter.

> Dear Maggie,
> We promised we'd only write to each other once a month, but I had to reply to your letter. I couldn't bear the thought of you being injured. I went straight to my commanding officer and asked to be sent home on compassionate leave. He wouldn't allow it. You weren't in danger, and we're not even married.

I'm glad that you are being taken care of. I admit,
I was surprised by the return address on the envelope.
I remember our walks down Fifth Avenue. The apart-
ment buildings looked so expensive.

I'm scheduled for another leave in a few months,
if the war isn't over before then.

Until then, I think about you every day.

All my love,

Jake

Maggie folded the envelope. She tried not to think about Jake,
sweltering at some naval base in the South Pacific.

She gave her hair one more brush, applied lipstick, and went into
the living room.

~

Now, sitting on the bench in Central Park, Maggie touched her hair,
as if she could go back in time. It was all so long ago. Everything in
her life was different. She had finally put the past behind her. She got
up and strolled along the path. Charles had moved away years ago, but
she couldn't buy an apartment on the same block where he had lived.
It brought back too many memories.

She'd let the Realtor show her and Teddy the other apartment. At
the same time she'd keep looking. The perfect apartment was waiting
for them. She just had to find it.

Chapter Twelve

The following Tuesday, Maggie sat in her dressing room going over the show notes. She had seen the apartment again with Teddy and loved it even more. The art deco mirror Teddy's parents gave them as a wedding present would look wonderful in the entry, and the little writing desk and cocktail cart fit perfectly in the living room.

But it was too expensive. There wouldn't be money to dine at nice restaurants or spend the weekend at quaint hotels in the Hudson Valley. Teddy knew how much Maggie wanted it, and he even offered to give up his squash club membership. Maggie refused. Teddy loved his squash matches, and there was plenty of time to find an apartment they could afford.

Dolly poked her head in. She wore a striped dress and a jacket with padded shoulders. Maggie noticed that Dolly's neck looked thinner and her cheekbones were sharper. At least Dolly hadn't gotten her nose job. Her mother had convinced her not to. She sat Dolly down and showed her photos of nose jobs that had gone wrong. Dolly conceded that she was content with her nose and that it suited her face.

"I brought you something." Dolly handed Maggie a shoebox.

Maggie opened it. Inside was a pair of Italian leather pumps. "They're beautiful, but what's the occasion?"

"I need a favor." Dolly sat on a chair next to the dressing table. "I need Teddy to teach me how to play squash."

Alan had recently joined a sports club. It had a swimming pool and tennis and squash courts.

"I learned to swim at a Jewish summer camp when I was a child," Dolly said. "But I've never played squash or tennis."

"Why don't you tell Alan?" Maggie asked.

"I don't want to embarrass him. It's probably one of those clubs where all the members were raised playing tennis at their weekend estates on Long Island," Dolly said.

Maggie frowned. "You mean, the other members are good at sports because they're not Jewish."

"Something like that," Dolly conceded.

"I'll ask Teddy. I'm sure he'd love to help," Maggie agreed. "You didn't have to give me a pair of shoes. You're my best friend. I would have done it anyway."

"It's always nice to receive gifts." Dolly fingered the charm bracelet on her wrist. "Alan gave me this bracelet last week. I asked what the occasion was, and he said it was the sixtieth day since we met. I've never heard anything so sweet."

Maggie had never seen a couple so in love. Whenever they went to dinner as a foursome, Dolly and Alan couldn't keep their eyes off each other. They had gotten into the habit of ordering their coffee the same way, and they often finished each other's sentences.

"Alan is going to propose soon," Maggie said confidently.

"I hope so. But he hasn't talked about marriage." Dolly suddenly had an idea. "Maybe Teddy can talk to him and see when he's going to propose. They spend so much time alone together, Alan would confide in him."

"What do you mean they spend time together?" Maggie's brow furrowed.

"Doesn't Teddy tell you? Ever since Teddy got his Diners Club card, he's always asking Alan to cocktails after work."

Maggie had been working late, so they often met for dinner at a restaurant. Teddy never mentioned that he had been out with Alan.

She hadn't seen any bills from Diners Club. She wondered if Teddy had been hiding them.

Maggie was probably imagining things, and she wasn't ready to share her worries with Dolly.

"I'll ask Teddy to teach you squash on one condition." She turned her attention to Dolly. "That you promise to eat a proper breakfast. You can't faint on the squash court."

Dolly squirmed uncomfortably. "I don't like breakfast. It makes me feel sluggish." She shrugged. "If it makes you happy, I'll eat a slice of toast with honey."

"It's a deal." Maggie smiled and held up the shoebox. "Thank you for the shoes. I'll wear them on today's show."

A little while later, Tommy entered the dressing room. He wore a dark suit and striped tie.

He set a stack of notes on the dressing table. "I stopped by the switchboard on my way here, and Jane gave me your messages. If the Maggie Lane show gets more popular, we're going to have to hire an extra switchboard operator."

The top message was from Nancy, the Realtor. Maggie read it quickly. If Maggie was serious about the apartment, she had to make an offer.

Tommy noticed her expression. "Is everything all right?"

Maggie returned the paper to the stack. "Teddy and I saw an apartment over the weekend that we loved. But another couple is interested in it."

"If your Realtor says that Maggie Lane wants to buy it, the sellers will be thrilled."

Maggie shook her head. "Don't be silly. I'm not a movie star."

"You're something better." Tommy perched on a chair. "That's what I came to tell you. You're being honored at this year's New York Botanical Garden gala, along with Eleanor Roosevelt and Jacquelyn Joy Mercer."

Maggie gasped in astonishment. "Did you say Eleanor Roosevelt?"

"According to the *Washington Post*, she's the most recognized woman in America today. You're number three, right after last year's Miss America, Jacquelyn Joy Mercer."

Maggie had seen Jacquelyn Mercer interviewed on television. She was the last winner who was allowed to enter the Miss America contest even though she was married. For this year's pageant, all the contestants had to be single.

"There must be some mistake," Maggie replied. "What about all the famous actresses and celebrities?"

Tommy had to have it wrong. Maggie could think of many actresses—Lauren Bacall and Ethel Barrymore and Katharine Hepburn—whose photos were on the cover of movie magazines. Or there was Margaret Chase Smith, who had just become the first woman to serve in both houses of Congress.

Tommy explained that women didn't care about politics, unless it was someone like Eleanor Roosevelt. Movie stars were well known, but not everyone had the time or money to attend the cinema.

"Television has changed everything," he finished. "You're in millions of homes while women are preparing school lunches and ironing their husbands' shirts. You're giving them advice on the most important aspects of their lives."

"I suppose I am," Maggie agreed slowly.

Sometimes it all seemed unreal, as if the star of *The Maggie Lane Baking Show* was someone else. She was still Maggie, worrying about whether she could afford to buy the apartment she wanted and whether her best friend was in trouble.

"You'll give a speech. Teddy will be with you, of course," Tommy continued. "I saw the photo of him and a friend having dinner at Keens. It's great if he eats at New York's finest restaurants, but you should accompany him."

Maggie's stomach did a little lurch. "What photo? I didn't see it."

"I have a copy of the *New York Post*. I'll ask my secretary to bring it to you," Tommy said. "You're getting so well known, Teddy is practically famous too."

Maggie wasn't listening. She was thinking about Teddy's new charge cards. It wasn't just the Diners Club card. He had also opened accounts at Lord & Taylor and Saks. They had agreed he should pay them from their joint bank account. She would have to check the bank statements.

~

When Maggie arrived home, Teddy was still out. She walked straight to the desk in the study where they kept their bankbooks. She flipped through the book for their joint account. The last entry was the payment of a utility bill.

She let out a sigh of relief.

Tommy had been mistaken. Teddy hadn't been using the charge cards. But then how were he and Alan eating at all those restaurants? She dug her hands deeper into the drawer. There was a brochure for the new car and a copy of Teddy's squash club membership. Underneath was a stack of envelopes. The top one was from Diners Club. Maggie opened it and stared in disbelief.

In less than a month, Teddy had spent $150. That was half the mortgage on a new apartment. She opened the next envelope and read through the bill from Macy's.

Three pairs of men's cashmere socks. Two bottles of shaving cream and cologne. Bally shoes from Saks and a squash racquet at Bloomingdale's. There was even a new charge card from Henri Bendel, but he hadn't charged anything to it yet.

Maggie sank onto the chair.

If Teddy wanted new things, why hadn't he discussed it with her first?

She read over the bills again. None of them were marked paid; two of them were thirty days overdue. That's why there wasn't any money missing from their joint account. Teddy had been running up bills all over New York without paying them.

Her stomach roiled and she strode into the bathroom. She splashed water on her face and glanced in the mirror. She would have to confront Teddy at dinner. There was no way around it.

The doorbell rang as she was getting dressed. Teddy's mother stood in the hallway.

"Patty!" Maggie exclaimed after she opened the door. "What are you doing here?"

"I hope I'm not disturbing you." Patty entered the apartment. "I was in Manhattan and thought I'd drop this off."

Patty set a large bag on the coffee table in the living room.

"I was surprised when Teddy called and asked for his baseball card collection," Patty said. "I haven't thought about it in years. He was so serious about it when he was young, and there were some valuable cards. A Babe Ruth and a Ty Cobb."

"Did he say why he wanted them?" Maggie asked, trying to keep her voice casual.

"He's donating a few cards to a charity auction." Patty beamed. "It's a wonderful idea since they're not doing any good gathering dust in the attic."

Maggie wondered if that was the real reason. What if he was looking for a way to pay off the charge cards without telling her? She went to the sideboard and poured a glass of water so that Patty couldn't see her expression.

"It was good of you to bring them. We could have picked them up the next time we were in Rye."

"It did seem odd that he was in a hurry, especially since you're coming up this weekend." Patty nodded. "That reminds me—tell him that the house on Walnut Street that he was asking about is two bedroom. It has a separate garage and a little studio."

Maggie's voice was sharp. "Teddy asked you about a house?"

Patty glanced at Maggie with concern. "Goodness, you and Teddy haven't been communicating. He called a week ago and asked about a house that just came on the market. I told him it was too small but I'd contact the Realtor anyway. I was surprised about that too. I thought you wanted to live in New York." She stopped, as if a thought just came to her. "Unless there's something you're both not telling me. Am I going to be a grandmother?"

Maggie stood up and paced around the living room. A tightness formed in her chest, and she found it hard to concentrate. Patty had to be mistaken. Teddy couldn't be looking at houses in Rye when they both loved New York.

"Not yet, but I promise you'll be the first to know." Maggie pulled herself together. "We've actually been looking at apartments in Manhattan. Maybe he was comparing prices."

Patty seemed embarrassed. "Of course. Why didn't I think of that?" she said hurriedly. "Well, I should go. I came to visit the gallery. They sold two more of my pieces."

Maggie was relieved to change the subject. "That's wonderful news."

"I did what you suggested and hung one of my paintings in the entry. Now half the women in the bridge circle want a painting."

"Anyone could see how talented you are," Maggie answered.

Patty fiddled with her gloves. "I hope this doesn't sound like a bossy mother-in-law, but be careful with your own life."

Maggie asked what she meant.

"When Teddy was a baby, every evening I listened to *The Palmolive Hour* on the radio. They had all kinds of celebrity guests, and their lives seemed so glamorous. I'd climb into bed, exhausted from a day of changing diapers and fixing baby bottles, and dream of a life where I attended elegant events wearing fur stoles and fancy dresses. Then I'd read in a magazine how a certain guest star was getting a divorce or had a drinking problem. I'd creep into Teddy's room and watch him sleeping and realize how lucky I was." She paused. "You and Teddy love each other. Don't let anything come between you."

After Patty left, Maggie sat on the sofa. None of what Patty said made sense. She and Teddy weren't planning on going to Rye this weekend, and Teddy wasn't involved in any charity event.

She wondered what other lies he had been telling his mother. When had the distance between her and Teddy begun? Was it when he opened the charge cards without telling her, or was it even before that? In the first months of *The Maggie Lane Baking Show*, when she had been so busy worrying about the ratings and Deluxe Baking Company's happiness with her, she had thought about little else. Had Teddy given her warnings signs that she ignored? His dinners with Alan, the cigarettes, the comments he made about Maggie's new fame. Were the cracks in their marriage her fault? Should she have handled Teddy more carefully?

For a moment, she longed for the time before she was the star of *The Maggie Lane Baking Show*, when their lives had been about the two of them. It had all been so much fun. Meeting Teddy after work and riding the subway together. Evenings spent eating takeout at his apartment because they didn't want to spend the money on restaurants. Teddy always fixed each of them a cocktail. Maggie would watch him standing at the cocktail cart with the ice shaker, his light-brown hair flopping over his forehead, his smile lighting up his eyes, and think he was the most handsome man in New York.

Now that Teddy worked less, he liked to eat out almost every night. Maggie enjoyed herself, but sometimes she was so tired after a long day on the set, she would have given anything to share a club sandwich at the coffee table in the living room.

Now there were the charge card bills. Even though she made a good salary, they'd never be able to afford the apartment they wanted if Teddy kept up his spending.

She roused herself from the sofa and went to brush her hair. Teddy was already waiting for her at Delmonico's. She'd talk to him about it over dinner.

When she walked downstairs, a town car was idling at the curb. The driver jumped out.

"Ms. Lane? I'm Edgar. I'll be driving you tonight."

Maggie glanced at him in surprise.

"There must be a mistake. I'm meeting my husband for dinner in the Financial District."

Edgar opened the rear car door.

"My instructions are to take you to the Carlyle Hotel." He glanced at his watch. "We better hurry. There's a bit of traffic, and you're expected at 7:45 p.m."

Maggie searched her memory to see if Tommy had said anything about a publicity event. Once, he had forgotten to tell Maggie about a CBS dinner at the Plaza Hotel. He assumed his secretary gave Maggie the details, but she had been sick and gone home early.

"I'm not dressed for the Carlyle." Maggie slid into the car. She was casually dressed in a skirt and matching blouse.

Edgar smiled back at her in the rearview mirror. "If you don't mind me saying so, you look lovely. My wife watches your show every morning. The homemade apple cake is her favorite. She was never good at baking before." He beamed. "Now, even my mother is impressed."

Maggie was silent for the rest of the drive. The car pulled up at the hotel entrance. A valet rushed over and opened her door.

A man in a gray uniform was waiting at the top of the steps. "Ms. Lane, it's an honor to have you with us tonight." He held out his hand. "I'm Stephen. Please, follow me."

Maggie followed him through the lobby. Other guests looked up and gave little smiles. She noticed a group of women pointing at her and whispering.

"Isn't the ballroom over there?" Maggie asked when they passed a huge space with crystal chandeliers.

"We're not going to the ballroom." Stephen continued down the hallway. "You'll be in the Carlyle Restaurant."

Maggie wondered whether it was a sponsor dinner or something to do with the upcoming Botanical Garden gala. She wished she had time to go to the powder room and refresh her makeup, but it was already eight o'clock.

Stephen stopped at the entrance to the restaurant. It was decorated in silver and gray tones. Silver bread carts were lined up near the kitchen. A marble fireplace took up one wall, and a huge gray urn filled with white roses stood in the center of the room.

Maggie searched the tables for Tommy. Her eyes stopped at a round table in the corner. Dolly and Alan sat next to each other. Teddy was staring expectantly at the entrance.

When he saw her, he jumped up and strode across the room. He had never looked so handsome. He wore a pin-striped suit over a crisp white shirt.

"Maggie, you're here." He took her hand. "I was afraid Edgar messed up and you weren't coming."

Teddy led her to the table. Each place setting had porcelain plates and crystal champagne flutes. On her plate was a large box with the familiar Henri Bendel brown and white stripes.

"I don't understand. What am I doing here?" she asked.

Tommy had called Teddy and told him that Maggie was going to be honored at the Botanical Garden gala. She was the third-most-recognized woman in America.

"Tommy made the reservation and ordered the car," he said eagerly. He took her hand. "I'm so proud of you. I had to do something to celebrate."

The waiter poured glasses of champagne, and Teddy made a toast to his beautiful, talented wife. Dolly and Alan gave her a bottle of her favorite perfume, and the chef himself brought out the appetizer—salmon and caviar puffs on melba toast.

For the main course, Teddy and Alan had filet mignon. Maggie ordered the veal cutlets and Dolly ate a seafood salad. For dessert there was a selection of small cakes, inspired by Deluxe recipes.

Teddy pushed the gift box in front of her.

"Open this. I hope you like it."

Maggie untied the bow and took out a red leather handbag. It had a gold lock with a key. It was the kind of expensive handbag women who lived on Park Avenue carried.

Teddy opened it and showed her the silk lining and matching change purse.

He looked at her, and there were worry lines on his forehead.

"If you don't like it, we can return it and choose another one together."

Maggie's mind went to the Henri Bendel charge card she found in the desk drawer.

It was the most beautiful handbag she'd ever seen, but it must have been expensive.

"I love it, but I can't keep it. We couldn't possibly afford it," she blurted out.

Teddy leaned forward and kissed her. He smelled of a new cologne.

"Price doesn't matter as long as you like it." He squeezed her hand. "You're Maggie Lane. You deserve the best of everything."

Chapter Thirteen

The next morning, Maggie sat at the kitchen table, stirring sugar into her coffee. Tommy had left a message, telling her not to come to the studio until noon. She should take the morning off and finish celebrating.

Except Maggie didn't feel like celebrating. She had a pounding headache. Teddy had tossed and turned all night, and she barely slept. She had been hoping to talk to him at breakfast, but by the time she had gone to the bathroom and put on her robe, he was gone.

Dinner at the Carlyle Hotel had been wonderful. After she opened her presents, they shared another bottle of champagne, and Teddy asked her to dance. Harry James was the bandleader, and he played his biggest hits, "Velvet Moon," and "Trumpet Blues," and "You Made Me Love You (I Didn't Want to Do It)." Teddy swept her around the dance floor. When the last song ended, everyone clapped. A dozen women crowded around their table, asking for her autograph. For once, Maggie turned them away. She explained it was a special night for her and her husband and their close friends. The women understood and smiled appreciatively.

It was only when the check arrived, and Teddy took out his Diners Club card, that Maggie realized Deluxe Baking Company wasn't paying for dinner. The evening had been Teddy's idea. Tommy merely gave Teddy the name of the car service.

After that, Maggie felt so ill she swallowed three spoonfuls of Pepto-Bismol and two aspirin before she went to bed. Neither of them helped.

All she could think about was how much Teddy had spent on the town car, the champagne and caviar, and the thick steaks they all had as entrées. Then there was the handbag from Henri Bendel. On the way home, she asked how much it cost, but Teddy squeezed her hand and said that one never discusses the price of a gift.

Now, she sipped her coffee. At 9:00 a.m., she would call Nancy, the Realtor, and say the other couple could have the apartment. It would be ages before they paid off the charge cards and could afford a down payment.

After work, she would confront Teddy about the unpaid bills. She knew he loved her. He had been so sweet last night at dinner. He asked if she enjoyed each course, and he made sure the red wine was full bodied the way she liked it. He wouldn't let her see the bill, and he patiently waited when the coat check girl asked for Maggie's autograph. She still loved him with a physical longing. Her heart swelled when she looked at him. He was the same Teddy she had wanted to date all those years ago. He was good looking and kind to others. When he held her in his arms on the dance floor, she didn't want to be anywhere else. The money and fame from *The Maggie Lane Baking Show* were new to both of them. It was easy to get off track. Together, they would make a plan for the future.

But now more than ever, she needed to know what still troubled him. Perhaps there was something in Teddy's past that could derail everything they were working toward. It was important that she knew about his time during the war and whatever it was that kept him up at night, but she couldn't ask him again. She had tried so many times before.

Suddenly she had an idea. She didn't have to be at the studio for three hours. She poured the coffee down the sink and went to get dressed.

An hour later, she stood at the reference desk at the New York Public Library. Maggie loved the library. It was located in a Beaux-Arts building on Fifth Avenue in Midtown. Just walking through the arched lobby with its marble busts and mosaic ceiling made Maggie feel excited.

"Can I help you?" the librarian asked.

Maggie explained that she was looking for any information about a village in northern France during World War II.

"Oradour-sur-Glane?" The librarian scribbled on a piece of paper. "It was a terrible tragedy, especially since it happened after D-Day. The war was practically over."

"The massacre was after D-Day?" Maggie repeated. She had known that Teddy had reported from France earlier in the war. But he never told her that he was there after the invasion in Normandy.

The librarian nodded. "I watched a news program about it a few years ago. The villagers were completely unprepared. There hadn't been any fighting nearby for a while. The Germans hopped out of the trucks with their rifles. They remained until everyone in the village was dead. The only survivors were a couple who owned a vineyard just outside the village. They were interviewed on the show. They had let some Americans stay the night in their barn. If the Americans had stayed in the village, they would have been dead too." The librarian toyed with her pencil. "It was an interesting program. I'm glad I watched it."

After Maggie thanked the librarian for giving her the paper so she could do more research, she walked the few blocks to the studio. The librarian said that some Americans had stayed the night in the couple's barn. Could it have been Teddy and Arabella and Ian? What if Teddy felt guilty that they had survived? That would explain the night sweats.

The more she learned about it, the more she wanted to know. Why had Teddy been driving the jeep, and wouldn't he have been eager to return to England and do the broadcast?

She felt as if she was on the edge of discovering something important. It made her feel more hopeful than she had been in days. Teddy had been through something terrible, and he had managed to carry on. He could be so brave. If only he would let her help him, their marriage would make him stronger.

She pictured Teddy's face the previous evening when she'd entered the Carlyle Restaurant, his loving expression when she opened the box from Henri Bendel. Of course being the star of her own television show gave him insecurities. She had to be patient, and they would work through it together. That's what love and marriage were about.

Everything was going to be all right, and she had nothing to worry about.

When she arrived at the studio, Tommy was waiting in her dressing room.

"Thank you for giving me the morning off," she greeted him.

"There's something we need to talk about," he replied. His brow was furrowed. He was hunched over a stack of papers.

Maggie's mind went to the worst things that could happen. The show's ratings had dropped. They'd never be able to pay off the charge cards. She'd have to stop looking for apartments. They might have to move into something smaller.

"I know we had trouble with last week's guest," she said awkwardly.

Frank Sinatra had been the celebrity guest. When Tommy suggested it, Maggie thought it was a wonderful idea. He was one of the most famous singers in the world, and she loved his songs, "I'll Never Smile Again" and "All This and Heaven Too." But he wouldn't wear the Deluxe Baking Company apron, and when she asked him to stir the devil's food cake mix, he said men didn't use kitchen utensils, that's why he had a wife and a maid.

Maggie's viewers wrote furious letters saying just because Frank Sinatra had a beautiful voice didn't mean he was better than the women in his life. A few viewers even gave his albums to the Salvation Army and refused to buy his new one.

"Frank Sinatra has the golden touch. We got some nasty mail, but the ratings were terrific." Tommy shrugged. "It's something more serious."

He handed Maggie a letter.

The paper had a lawyer's letterhead. It said that Maggie Lane told the lawyer's client, Agnes Byrd, to serve Deluxe peanut butter brownies at her daughter Gladys's birthday party, even though Maggie knew the girl was allergic to peanut butter. Gladys ended up spending her birthday at the doctor's office.

"I had my secretary look up the correspondence," Tommy said. "On June 4, Agnes wrote and asked what she should serve at her seven-year-old daughter's birthday party. You responded on June 20 with a list of birthday desserts, including peanut butter brownies." He handed Maggie two pieces of paper. "Agnes mentioned her daughter's allergies in the last paragraph of her letter. Gladys is also allergic to pecans and strawberries."

Maggie remembered Agnes's letter. She was going to suggest her favorite birthday dessert recipe, Deluxe strawberry shortcake, until she read that Gladys was allergic to strawberries. How had she missed that Gladys was allergic to peanut butter too?

"The doctor said that Gladys was fine. Agnes is suing for mental distress because Gladys had to send her friends home."

"Mental distress?" Maggie repeated, puzzled.

Tommy handed her another piece of paper. "Additionally, Agnes sent the bill for Charlie the Clown who had been scheduled to perform, plus the supermarket receipt for the sandwiches and sodas that weren't consumed.

"Our accounting department is issuing Agnes a check for the money spent on the party. If we respond to the mental distress claim, other viewers can follow suit."

A viewer could blame Maggie if her sex life didn't improve, after Maggie suggested the viewer and her husband share a Deluxe fudge cake before bed. Or she could be sued by a viewer's husband for undue influence over his wife if there was no longer a pitcher of Tom Collins waiting for him when he arrived home.

Maggie understood, but she still felt terrible. It must have been frightening for Agnes and Gladys.

"There must be something I can do," she said. "I could bring them presents. A pair of lizard-skin pumps and a matching handbag from the Meyerowitz's shoe store for Agnes. A Magic 8 Ball and a game of Cootie for Gladys. And I could bring a birthday cake—vanilla with rainbow icing. It would be like having a mini birthday party," Maggie suggested.

Tommy shook his head.

"Can you imagine what the newspapers would say if they got hold of the story? 'Maggie Lane tries to buy off seven-year-old girl who she put in the hospital on her birthday.'"

Maggie let out a long sigh.

"I suppose you're right," she agreed.

"Deluxe Baking Company's attorney will make the lawsuit go away with a firm letter." Tommy closed the subject. "Let's talk about the Botanical Garden fundraiser. We've hired a speechwriter. You'll be speaking after Miss America. It's a perfect opportunity for a new designer to provide the dress. Claire McCardell has been dying to show you her new line."

Maggie would have liked to write her own speech. At least Claire McCardell was a woman, but she would have preferred to wear one of her own dresses. The New Look Dior that she adored, or her Chanel cocktail dress. But this wasn't the time to argue with Tommy.

"That sounds fine," she agreed. "I'd love to see Claire's designs."

"Good. I'll schedule an appointment." He stood up. "Don't worry about Agnes. That's what we pay the legal department to do. Just keep on being Maggie Lane, the star of *The Maggie Lane Baking Show*."

Maggie spent the rest of the afternoon working on notes for the show. At the end of the day, she went home and let herself into the apartment. She was reading a magazine in the living room when Teddy arrived home. He was surprised to see her.

"I thought you'd still be on the set." He entered the living room. "I was going to call and suggest I pick up Chinese from Ruby Foo's. There's an interesting documentary on television." He loosened his tie. "Or if you feel like going out, we can get steak and baked potatoes at Keens."

Maggie glanced up at Teddy. She was reminded of how good looking he was. His brown eyes were warm, and his chest was broad under his suit jacket.

"We've eaten takeout four days this week." She set aside the magazine. "I thought we could cook tonight."

Teddy's eyes widened. "Neither of us cook."

"That's not true." She fiddled with the sofa cushion. "You make delicious scrambled eggs."

"I can whip up an egg breakfast. I don't know a thing about dinner."

"Then we should learn. I'll buy some cookbooks at the Strand."

Teddy sat beside her on the sofa. "You never wanted to cook before. What's this about?"

Maggie wished Teddy wasn't sitting so close to her. He was so handsome in his navy suit, and his body was so familiar. She never stopped wanting him physically. And how many times had he wrapped his arms around her when she was scared or unhappy, or let her bury herself in his chest? It made it hard to stay angry at him.

"All married couples cook. Getting takeout and eating at restaurants gets expensive."

Then it all came out. She thought dinner at the Carlyle Restaurant had been paid for by Tommy until Teddy took out his Diners Club card. Teddy's mother bringing his baseball card collection, and mentioning that he planned on going up to Rye without telling Maggie. The drawer full of unpaid charge card bills and the new charge card from Henri Bendel.

"You didn't refuse the handbag from Bendel," Teddy said icily when she finished. "In fact, you loved it."

Maggie's face flushed. "Of course I loved it, but that doesn't mean we can afford it. It will take months to pay off those cards. We'll never be able to buy an apartment."

"The cards only make a small dent in your salary. Tommy said it's important that Maggie Lane is seen in the best restaurants. It's good for your image."

Maggie was going to tell him about Agnes's letter and the lawsuit, but Teddy kept talking.

"I've had the baseball cards since I was a kid. I can do whatever I want with them." He stood up and poured a glass of water from the pitcher on the sideboard. "And since when do I have to ask permission to visit my parents? If you don't want to come, that's fine."

Maggie had never felt so miserable. She wanted to ask him about Oradour-sur-Glane and why he never mentioned Arabella and Ian, when they had obviously been through something so traumatic together. To tell him about Jake and her fear that her own past could come out and ruin everything. The strain of being the star of *The Maggie Lane Baking Show*, and knowing that if she was fired everything they had added to their lives—the new car, Teddy's wardrobe, the possibility of a new apartment—would disappear.

But Teddy seemed like a stranger. They fought rarely, and she had never seen him so angry. He was her husband, and they should be able to communicate. Yet she didn't know how to make him feel closer.

"Selling the baseball cards might work now, but how will you pay for the charge cards next time?" she asked, her own anger rising. Teddy had to see that he was wrong.

Teddy set the glass on the coffee table.

"If you had any respect for me, you wouldn't ask that question." He grabbed his coat. "Maybe the magazines and all those women who only want to meet me to get your autograph are right. I'm just Maggie Lane's husband. I'm hungry and I'm going to pick up Ruby Foo's." He walked to the door. "I'll eat at Alan's. Don't wait up. I expect to make it a long night."

The door slammed and the apartment was completely silent.

Maggie thought about heating up a bowl of soup for dinner. But she wasn't hungry. Teddy had walked out, and she didn't know when he would return. They had to be able to talk to each other about difficult subjects without either of them running away. It was the most important thing in a marriage. She felt at such a loss, as if she were standing on top of a precipice and didn't know how to get down. At that moment, there was nothing she could do. A feeling of exhaustion overwhelmed her. She went into the bedroom and crawled into bed.

Chapter Fourteen

Teddy came in late and slept on the sofa. She woke up in the middle of the night and wanted to go out to him. But what would she say? He shouldn't have run up the charge cards without telling her, and he shouldn't have stormed out. If there was a problem in their marriage, they had to fix it.

He was gone again before she got up. She made a cup of coffee and toast and went to the studio. The morning on the set was terrible. She forgot her contacts and couldn't read the cue cards. Luckily, she had already baked pecan spice brownies and didn't need the recipe. But she accidentally set the oven to 450 degrees instead of 350 and almost burned the entire batch. She took them out of the oven and said into the camera that baking was easy, as long as one followed the directions on the side of the Deluxe Baking Company box.

During her lunch break, she bought a sandwich and sat on a bench in Central Park. A woman approached and asked her to sign her *Good Housekeeping* magazine. When Maggie saw the article, with the accompanying photo of her and Teddy smiling at each other in a restaurant booth, tears sprang to her eyes. She scribbled her signature and jumped up before the woman could gush how Maggie was an inspiration to wives everywhere.

The rest of the lunch hour she spent walking around the lake. She thought of all the lunchtimes she spent with Teddy, feeding breadcrumbs to the ducks and talking about everything. Without him beside her, she felt somehow empty. She wondered how she would respond to a viewer with the same problems. Women needed to be independent, but at the same time, she and Teddy were a team.

Now, the workday was over, but she wasn't ready to go home. She'd go to Woolworth's and buy something small for Teddy. A bottle of shaving cream or a bag of Mounds, his favorite candy bar. Something that signaled that she loved him and wanted to talk.

"Our men's colognes are popular," the saleswoman in the men's department said. She held up a bottle of gold liquid for Maggie to smell. "Old Spice is our bestseller."

Before Maggie could stop her, the saleswoman sprayed the cologne into the air. Maggie inhaled and felt a little dizzy. It was the same scent that she had bought for Jake when they met.

The saleswoman recognized her. "You're Maggie Lane. I'll ask my floor manager. I'm sure she'd be happy to give you a special price."

Maggie shook her head. "Thank you, but my husband is very particular about his cologne."

The saleswoman looked disappointed. "Could I get your autograph? I watch *The Maggie Lane Baking Show* every morning. I took this job part-time because of you. I was tired of doing housework all day. Now I'm around people, and I have my own money to buy things for myself."

Maggie signed a piece of paper for the saleswoman and paid for her purchases.

Later, she sat in a diner and ordered a cup of tea. Her hands were shaky, and it all came back to her. The turkey sandwich that she and Jake shared at the Woolworth's lunch counter the day they met. His last leave before her accident, and moving into Charles's apartment. She had been so confident in their love, certain that nothing could come between them.

~

Maggie had been working for Charles for two months. Her typing skills had improved, and she enjoyed the work. Charles was a fair boss. He never started work until Maggie had a nutritious breakfast, and he insisted they take frequent breaks. Charles's new play was very good. The work was more interesting than typing up reports or adding ledgers, like the secretarial jobs that had been available through the temp agency.

Besides the dinner at the 21 Club, she and Charles rarely ate together in the evenings. A few times, when he had an idea for a new scene and it was past five o'clock, he asked Maggie if she wouldn't mind working through dinner. Then they moved to the dining table, and Ellen served cream of broccoli soup and pork chops and apple pie for dessert. Maggie enjoyed those evenings more than she acknowledged to herself. Ellen's cooking was delicious, and Charles grew so animated. He bounced scenes off her and was so pleased with her feedback, she felt like she was contributing something important.

She suggested a few times that she should get her own apartment, but Charles wouldn't hear of it. It would cause all sorts of inconveniences. They'd have to start later in the mornings, and on the nights that they worked through dinner, it wouldn't be safe for her to take the subway. He'd have to drive her home. It was better for both of them if she stayed in the room in Charles's apartment.

And she was happy there. She loved the grand proportions of the rooms—the high ceilings, ten-foot doors, and floor-to-ceiling windows. Whenever she felt guilty that her bedroom had a view of the Empire State Building, while Jake was somewhere in the South Pacific, she reminded herself that the money she was saving was for both of them.

She missed Jake. Often, she walked by the jewelry store where he'd bought the engagement ring and wondered if she made the right decision. Her reaction at the time might have been fueled by her anxiety rather than logic, but she hadn't been able to do anything else. She would have done anything to keep him safe.

The only cloud in her happiness was that it had been weeks since she received a letter from him. She figured it was because he was busy at the naval hospital, or the mail was even slower than usual. Then she remembered the curt tone of his last letter and wondered whether it was something else. She had done everything she could to assure him that there was nothing going on between her and Charles. The only reason she was living in his apartment was to save money for their future. She described the dates that Charles went on, and the fact that Ellen was always there. Jake had to understand. He knew how much she wanted to stay in New York.

It was midafternoon, and Maggie was sitting at the desk in the living room. Charles entered. He wore a navy blazer and yellow tie.

"This afternoon we're going for a drive to Long Island," he announced. "Please wear one of your prettiest dresses. Maybe wear a bow in your hair, and wear that pink lipstick."

Maggie asked what they were doing in Long Island.

Charles couldn't keep the excitement out of his voice. "Nothing special. Just meeting Lou Magnolia to talk about him directing my new play."

On the drive, Charles told Maggie all about Lou. He had directed four Broadway smash hits and then disappeared. Rumors circulated he had retired to the South of France or joined an ashram in India. Charles knew someone with a house in East Hampton who had seen Lou on his bicycle.

"How will we meet him if he doesn't see anyone?" Maggie asked.

Charles glanced over at her. "I'm going to park by the road and wait in the car. You'll walk up to the house and pretend you have a flat tire."

"I can't lie!" Maggie exclaimed. "What happens when he sees you at the car?"

"He'll either throw us out or admire our determination." Charles drummed his fingers on the steering wheel. "Lou is what this play needs. I'll never forgive myself if we didn't try."

Charles drove past estates with views of the Atlantic Ocean. Driveways were flanked by hedges, and Maggie caught glimpses of tennis courts and swimming pools.

"Here we are." Charles parked at the foot of a sloping driveway. "If a housekeeper answers the door, don't let her turn you away."

Maggie hiked up to the house. It was built in the Tudor style, with vines clinging to the walls. In the front, there was a stone fountain and a pergola.

She knocked twice, but there was no answer. She was about to turn away when a man opened the door. She guessed it was Lou. He was in his midfifties, with dark hair and a hefty build. He wore a knit sweater and gray slacks.

"Who are you?" he asked.

Maggie flushed. She felt guilty. "My name is Maggie Lane. I have a flat tire, and I wonder if you can help me."

Lou frowned. "A pretty young girl shouldn't be driving out here alone."

Maggie tried to think of something to say. "It's a beautiful day. I wanted to go for a drive. It's not my car, and I don't know how to change the tire."

Lou wavered, and Maggie was afraid he wasn't going to help her. But he closed the door and walked ahead of her.

"You're lucky. I'm good with cars. I'll see what I can do."

When they reached the road, Lou saw Charles sitting in the driver's seat. He glanced from Maggie to Charles. His eyes narrowed, and he stepped back.

"What's going on?" he demanded.

Charles jumped out of the car. "Charles Grey." He held out his hand. "I'm a playwright and one of your biggest fans. I wanted to talk to you about directing my new play."

Lou turned to Maggie angrily. "You lied to help your friend?"

"Maggie isn't my friend. She's my secretary," Charles corrected. "I asked her to lie. This play is trickier than my previous plays. It needs a director with vision. Someone like the great Lou Magnolia."

Lou's features softened slightly. He shrugged.

"You drove all the way out here to see me. Come on up to the house. We'll discuss it over a late lunch."

They sat on the terrace overlooking the swimming pool. A maid brought out sandwiches and a pitcher of margaritas.

After his last Broadway hit, Lou had gone to the South of France, but he didn't like the language, and the butter made him fat. So he returned and bought the estate in East Hampton.

"I thought I'd be happy out here. But I miss the bustle of New York, and I miss the theater." He sipped his margarita. "Tell me about the play. If it's about the war, I won't do it. I can't stand another insipid comedy about an enlisted man who falls in love with a nurse, or one of those tearjerkers about a young woman pining for her fiancé whose plane was lost somewhere over Germany."

Charles explained it was nothing like that. It was a retelling of *Romeo and Juliet* set in 1890s Philadelphia. The lovers' families were on opposite sides of the picket line to unionize the railway companies.

"It sounds dreary," Lou said dubiously.

"It's the opposite," Maggie piped in. "The heroine, Julia, comes from a wealthy railway family, but she gives it all up to be with Adam. He's ready to abandon everything he's worked for to marry her. In the end, they bring both sides together."

"A *Romeo and Juliet* with a happy ending?" Lou raised his eyebrows.

Charles nodded enthusiastically. "I wanted to show that even in the face of the greatest obstacles, love is the best weapon we have."

Lou gave them a tour of the grounds, and they talked about Broadway during the war. Audiences packed the theaters, needing relief from the newsreels. Most of the shows were matinees or early-evening performances to avoid the timing of the precautionary blackouts.

"I can't spend my whole life staring at this swimming pool, and I'm never going to learn to play tennis," Lou said when they were seated again on the terrace.

"Send me the script when it's finished. If I like it, I'll do it on one condition." Lou pointed at Maggie. "That Maggie is at opening night. Anyone with the spunk to do what she did will bring the show luck."

The whole drive back, Charles hummed Frank Sinatra songs, "Bye Bye Baby" and "Some Enchanted Evening." She had never seen him so happy. The critics were waiting to declare that his new play would be a flop. If a playwright was successful for too long, he developed a large ego.

With Lou as the director, it would be Charles's biggest hit so far.

"You heard Lou, it's because of you," Charles said when they entered the apartment.

Maggie shook her head. "I didn't do anything."

"Of course, you did," Charles replied. "You're special, Maggie. You have the freshness of youth, combined with an innate sophistication."

Maggie hung up her coat. Charles was a little drunk from the margaritas. He was only talking as her boss. He'd never done anything inappropriate. He was almost ten years older than she was, and she was quite sure that the women he dated were glamorous and worldly.

"Let's write a few more scenes." Charles took off his blazer. "First, I'm going to make a pot of coffee."

Charles disappeared into the kitchen, and Maggie walked over to the typewriter. It was out of ribbon so she went to the study, where Charles kept the office supplies. She opened the drawer and noticed a small pile of mail. An envelope with familiar handwriting poked out. It was from Jake.

Charles must have been going through the mail and got called away. He didn't like a messy desk. He probably put the letters in the drawer and forgot them.

She opened it and scanned it quickly. There wasn't time to read the whole letter. Jake ended it by saying he loved her. Relief and happiness washed over her. She'd been worrying for nothing.

She heard Charles reenter the living room. She collected the typewriter ribbon and went to join him.

~

Maggie pulled her mind back to the present. Nothing that had happened in her past could change what was going on between her and Teddy. She finished her cup of tea and signaled the waitress for the check. She had been so sure of everything back then. That Jake would return from the South Pacific and they'd get married. That living in Charles's apartment and working as his secretary was the best way to provide for their future.

She was older now, and she had been through so much. The one thing she was sure of was that she and Teddy loved each other. But that wouldn't stop their marriage from falling apart unless they communicated. She still thought they should learn to cook, and they needed to reduce their spending. Most young couples in New York made less than they did, and they could afford the things that were important to them.

She'd stop at the butcher and pick up two steaks. It couldn't be too hard to cook a steak. They'd eat dinner at home, and then they'd talk about their argument and make sure it didn't happen again.

When Maggie got home, Teddy was sitting on the sofa. A delicious smell was coming from the kitchen.

"You're already home," she said. She suddenly felt nervous. She hadn't seen Teddy since he'd stormed out the previous night, and she had no idea what kind of mood he was in.

"If you're about to say that I took the afternoon off, you're wrong," he replied. "I worked through my lunch hour because I wanted to stop and pick up dinner on the way home." He waved toward the kitchen. "I bought two lamb chops at the butcher, and I'm making green beans."

Maggie gave a small smile. She held up her package. "I stopped at the butcher too. I got steaks and asparagus."

The lines around Teddy's mouth softened. "My mother's going to come on Sunday and teach us how to make casseroles. I'm very sorry. I shouldn't have stormed out, and there's nothing wrong with eating at home a few days a week. It will be fun to cook together."

Maggie took off her coat. She put her package on the side table and sat on the sofa. "I shouldn't have gotten so upset about the charge cards. We should have talked about it instead."

Teddy shook his head. She noticed circles under his eyes.

"You were right about that. It was wrong to use them without discussing it first," he said. "The thing is, they made me feel like a proper husband."

Maggie said she didn't understand.

"When my parents got married, my father went to work at the insurance agency. Over the years, he rose from being a clerk to an account manager, and eventually a vice president. My mother never had to work. First, they had a small apartment, then they moved to a two bedroom, and eventually bought the house in Rye. In the beginning they weren't wealthy, but he could always provide for us. My mother bought clothes whenever she liked, and my father always had beautiful suits and ties. I wanted to be able to do that for us, but I can't on my salary. Using the charge cards gave me a little boost."

Maggie flinched. Teddy sounded like Dolly talking about her pills. He was trying to believe something that wasn't true. And yet, she should be happy. Teddy was opening up and talking about his feelings. She thought she finally understood why he refused to accept financial help from his parents. He wanted to be like his father and be able to take care of himself and a family. It took courage to tell her these things, and she was proud of him. If only he could see how much she loved him and that her success didn't change how she felt. Part of it was her fault. She had to show him how much she cared.

"We don't need anything, and I work too."

"That's the thing. You earn more money than I do, and I'm okay with that. I'm proud of you, and the show. But what if you didn't want to work, or something happened to the show? I need to be able to provide for us by myself."

Maggie replied that the charge cards wouldn't help with that. They were a way of getting into debt.

"I realized that last night," Teddy agreed. "I put them in the drawer in the study. I won't use them again." His eyes crinkled at the corners. "Except the Bendel card. I like to be able to buy a present for my wife. If I do, I'll pay it off myself."

Maggie was touched. She could ask Teddy why he had given up the higher-paying job, but this wasn't the time. It was brave of Teddy to admit his insecurities about being a good husband. She loved him for it.

"I'll put the steaks in the fridge and finish making the green beans. We'll eat them another time." She stood up.

Teddy stopped her. He reached out and took her hand.

"The lamb chops take another hour to cook, and the green beans just need to be heated," he said. "I have a suggestion."

"What are we doing?" she asked. His palm was warm against hers, and a charge of sexual desire shot through her.

"If you don't mind, we're going to the bedroom." He kissed her. "I thought we'd work up an appetite first."

Maggie kissed him back. Her whole body relaxed. "That's an excellent idea. I'm not that hungry yet. And I'd love to get out of these clothes."

Chapter Fifteen

For the next few weeks, Maggie spent most of her free time preparing for the Botanical Garden gala. Teddy was very helpful. Every night she practiced her speech for him. They'd stand together in the kitchen, chopping a salad and coating crumbs on pork chops, while Maggie recited the words the speechwriter had written. Teddy made suggestions, and then they'd sit down to dinner and talk about how she should answer the audience's questions.

Ever since the night they talked through their argument, things had been better between them. They both apologized and said how much they loved each other. Together, they created a budget for clothes shopping and dining out. Teddy explained that he had inquired about the house for sale in Rye because Alan was going to propose to Dolly. Teddy hadn't told Maggie because Alan had sworn him to secrecy.

Maggie was touched that Teddy and Alan were so close. And that her best friend, Dolly, would soon be engaged.

Their argument improved their marriage in many ways. Cooking together at home was more intimate than dining at restaurants. There wasn't the fear of being interrupted by fans asking for Maggie's autograph. As their cooking skills improved, Teddy grew happier and more confident. On the nights they went out with Alan and Dolly, Teddy boasted that the restaurant's Cobb salad or meatloaf wasn't half as good as what he and Maggie whipped up in the kitchen.

When they stayed home in the evenings, their clothes didn't smell of other diners' cigarettes. They didn't have to wait for a taxi after dinner, so there was more time for lovemaking. Maggie had grown to enjoy their lovemaking very much. Sometimes, the morning after a particularly affectionate night in bed, Teddy sent flowers to the studio with a note saying how much he loved her. They were never over-the-top roses or orchids, just a sweet bouquet of gardenias from the corner florist. Maggie would inhale their fragrance while she prepared her show notes and think how lucky she was. She was married to Teddy and was the star of *The Maggie Lane Baking Show* and about to be honored alongside one of her idols, Eleanor Roosevelt.

The dressing room door opened and Dolly peered in. She was elegantly outfitted in a day dress decorated with silk floral petals. Maggie recognized it from Dior's latest collection.

"What a gorgeous dress," Maggie commented. "Is it for a special episode of the show?"

"It's not for the show. I'm finally meeting Alan's mother."

Alan's mother, Barbara, was staying at the Waldorf-Astoria and had invited Dolly to lunch. Alan was supposed to accompany Dolly, but there was a problem with the episode, and the writers had to work through the lunch hour.

"I can't face her alone," Dolly said. "You have to come with me."

"I'm not dressed for the Waldorf-Astoria, and I have to prepare for tomorrow's show."

"Please," Dolly urged. "What if Barbara doesn't like me?"

Recently, Alan's father sold his medical practice, and his parents had moved to the wealthiest suburb of Cleveland. They were beginning to travel and considering buying an apartment in New York. Alan was their only son, and Barbara had gushed over the phone that she couldn't wait to meet the young woman he was spending so much time with.

"She made it sound like she was interested in me as a person, but I'm sure she's sizing me up as a potential daughter-in-law," Dolly fretted.

She glanced at her reflection in the mirror. "I should have gotten the nose job. No one has a nose like this in Cleveland."

Maggie hated to see Dolly upset. She could go over her show notes in the evening.

"All right, I'll go to lunch," Maggie agreed. "But remember, you're beautiful. Your children will be lucky to inherit your features."

Barbara was in her early fifties with shoulder-length brown hair and hazel eyes. Maggie had expected her to be tall and thin like Alan, but she was Dolly's height. Her two-piece suit fit snugly around her waist and hips.

She wore a smart hat, and a pair of silk gloves was folded over her handbag.

"This is my first trip to New York," Barbara said when Dolly and Maggie were seated in the booth opposite her. "I never saw a reason to come. Cleveland has everything we need. A symphony hall and art galleries and museums. My husband, Carl, insisted I visit. Alan has been so sweet, showing me around. Last night, after my train arrived, he took me to Katz's Delicatessen. It's in all the guidebooks. I have to admit, their Reuben sandwich was better than anything one can find back home."

Dolly looked surprised. Maggie guessed that Alan and Dolly had never eaten there. All the dishes had Jewish origins, and most of them were made with lots of butter and cream.

"How long are you staying?" Dolly asked.

"Until Friday. Carl was supposed to be here, but something came up. He'd already booked the Waldorf-Astoria, and it's not the kind of place you cancel."

"It's one of the best hotels in New York." Dolly nodded. "All the movie stars and celebrities stay here. Last week, I was on Park Avenue and saw Kirk Douglas walking down the steps. A few days ago, that pretty new actress, Janet Leigh, was getting out of a limousine."

Barbara picked a breadstick from the bread basket.

"Did you know Kirk's name was Issur Danielovitch?" Barbara buttered the breadstick. "He changed it to Kirk Douglas when he entered the navy. As if anyone wouldn't know that he was Jewish with that face. Janet Leigh is sweet, and at least she doesn't starve herself like some of those other young actresses. I read that she's dating Tony Curtis. He's a popular new actor too, but they'll never get married. Tony Curtis's real name is Bernard Schwartz. His parents are Jewish Hungarian immigrants."

There was an uncomfortable silence, and Maggie waited for Dolly to say something. Dolly sat and played with her water glass.

Maggie tried to think of a way to change the subject. "You must be proud of Alan. He's a brilliant writer."

"Writing was fine when he was ten and won the local writing contest, but it isn't a respectable profession." Barbara took a bite of her breadstick. "If he had become a doctor like his father, Carl wouldn't have sold the practice. Alan can be stubborn; that's why I'm here. On the phone, he says he has everything he needs, but a mother can tell when her child's not saying something. I went to his apartment and discovered his suits aren't ironed and his maid only comes once a month. A young man can't live like that. I took his shirts and suits to the dry cleaner and scheduled the maid to come weekly."

Dolly stood up abruptly. Her mouth was slightly open, and she resembled a deer staring into a car's headlights at night.

"Excuse me, I need to use the powder room."

Fifteen minutes later, Dolly hadn't returned to the table. Maggie apologized to Barbara and went to find her.

Dolly was standing in front of the sink. The little bottle of pills peeked out of her purse.

"What are you doing?" Maggie demanded.

"You heard the things Barbara said," Dolly replied. Her mouth was dry, and her eyes were very bright. "Obviously, she discovered that I'm Jewish. She came to New York to stop Alan from seeing me."

"You don't know that," Maggie answered.

"Why would she make those references to Tony Curtis and Janet Leigh and Kirk Douglas?" Dolly asked.

"She read about them in a movie magazine." Maggie shrugged.

"There are other things. She doesn't approve of New York, or Alan's career. She's going to drag him home and marry him off to some debutante."

Maggie glanced at her own reflection in the mirror. "What if you have her all wrong? She doesn't approve of actresses who starve themselves, and she doesn't appear to be worried about her own figure."

"She and her husband were high school sweethearts," Dolly reminded Maggie. "She's probably one of those women who was slim until she had children and then couldn't take the weight off. She still wants Alan to marry a blond, blue-eyed beauty queen who'll pass on her all-American genes to their children."

"Well, I don't care what she wants. You have to stop taking those pills." Maggie pointed to the bottle.

"The pills are just a little pick-me-up." Dolly dabbed cold water on her cheeks.

"You can't believe that," Maggie objected. "I never see you without them. And you're always taking more."

Dolly's expression wavered. She smoothed her hair in the mirror. "I tried to stop a couple of weeks ago, but it didn't work."

Maggie was surprised. Dolly never said she was worried about taking them. "What do you mean, you tried to stop?"

"Please don't tell my mother. She'll worry that I didn't trust her doctor," Dolly began. "I saw another doctor, and he said the pills aren't bad for me, but it's possible to get dependent on them," she admitted. "So I left them at home for two days."

"What happened?" Maggie asked.

"Nothing really. The second doctor was wrong." Dolly gazed at her reflection. She turned to Maggie. "All right, if you must know, the first day was fine. I was busy at work, and afterwards Alan and I went to dinner and I forgot about the pills. But the next morning, I woke up with a sluggish feeling and I had a terrible headache. I drank two cups of coffee, but it didn't help. Then I thought I was hungry, so I ate a bowl of oatmeal and two bananas. The feeling wouldn't go away, so I took a pill, and immediately I felt better."

"That must tell you something," Maggie said. "You were having withdrawal symptoms from the pills."

"I disagree. I proved that I could go without them," Dolly said. "And the only thing I learned is that oatmeal for breakfast makes me feel full all day." She sighed. "The pills give me energy and make everything feel easier. Why should I stop doing something that makes my life happy?"

Maggie wanted to argue, but Barbara was waiting for them in the restaurant.

When they returned to the table, the waiter had set down their plates. Dolly had ordered a turkey salad with diet dressing. Maggie was having the roasted chicken, and Barbara ordered the slow-cooked roast beef with mashed potatoes.

"So, what does your father do?" Barbara asked Dolly.

Dolly replied that he owned shoe stores. Maggie wanted to add that they were the most exclusive shoe stores in New York, but she was afraid of upsetting her friend.

"Everybody needs shoes," Barbara acknowledged. She heaped mashed potatoes on her fork. "A neighbor, the Feinsteins, own Feinstein's Shoes in downtown Cleveland. Miriam always tells me about the sales before they start."

"I didn't know Cleveland had a Jewish population," Dolly blurted out.

"Not all Jews live in New York or Los Angeles." Barbara shrugged. "Miriam and her family left Poland in 1938, just before the war." Her expression turned grim. "Many weren't so lucky. I despise the Germans. Carl wanted to buy a Mercedes when he sold the practice, but I refused."

The conversation lagged again, and Maggie tried to fill the silence.

"Have you seen Dolly on her show?" she asked Barbara.

"A few times," Barbara acknowledged. "To be honest, I don't find it funny. Dolly's character is too sharp. Why can't they just admit they love each other?"

The table went silent. Maggie concentrated on cutting her chicken. When she looked up, Dolly was gulping from her water glass.

"I have something stuck in my throat." Dolly stood up. For a moment she teetered from side to side. Then the glass dropped and she slid to the floor.

Maggie gasped. She jumped up, and the color drained from her face.

The maître d' rushed over to the table. He crouched down and picked up Dolly's hand.

"Her pulse is normal, but I'll call the hotel doctor."

Dolly's eyes fluttered open. She attempted to sit up but slipped back to the floor. Maggie and Barbara and the surrounding diners waited anxiously until the doctor arrived.

"She's fine for now. But she needs to stop the coffee or the cigarettes, or whatever she's doing to stay thin," he said to Maggie after he examined Dolly.

Dolly had gone to the powder room to freshen her makeup.

"It's probably just nerves," Maggie said and turned to Barbara. "She was anxious about meeting you today."

Barbara made a clucking sound. "The doctor's right. Dolly is too thin. I don't understand it. Young women these days think it's attractive to appear as if they're starving."

The doctor left, and Dolly returned to the table. Barbara ordered three slices of cheesecake, but the lunch was ruined. Dolly attempted a few bites, but Maggie could see the pain in her expression. They made small talk about which museums Barbara should visit, and then Barbara asked for the check.

"It was nice meeting both of you," she said stiffly. She turned to Dolly. "You have to take care of yourself. Alan has enough on his plate with his job and his new life."

Later in the afternoon, Maggie sat with Dolly's mother, Ruth, in the Meyerowitz's living room. Maggie had called the television studio and told them she was taking the afternoon off. Then she took Dolly home, and Dolly's mother called the family physician. The doctor had given Dolly a sedative, and she was asleep in her bedroom.

"I don't know what would have happened if you hadn't been there," Ruth fretted to Maggie. "Poor Dolly, that woman sounds horrible."

"Barbara just has strong opinions." Maggie sat on the sofa opposite Ruth. "Dolly was nervous, since she's in love with Alan."

Ruth let out a sigh. Maggie hadn't seen her in a while and had forgotten how stylishly she dressed. Ruth wore a belted tunic dress that accentuated her slim waist. Her hair was teased into thick waves, and she wore high-heeled leather pumps.

"She pretends she isn't, but I know she's in love," Ruth agreed. "When Alan doesn't call for a day, she hovers around the phone waiting for it to ring. When he does, she's so light and happy. She reminds me of Ginger Rogers in a Fred Astaire movie."

Maggie wished she could tell Ruth and Dolly that Alan was planning to propose. But Alan had sworn Teddy to secrecy. And it wouldn't help. Dolly would worry that even if Alan did propose, Barbara would find a way to stop the engagement.

"They'll find a way to make it work," Maggie said with more confidence than she felt. "They're a wonderful couple."

Ruth poured a cup of coffee from the coffeepot on the side table.

"This is my fault. I should never have introduced Dolly to those pills." Ruth added sugar to the coffee. "My doctor said they were harmless, but Dolly's been taking too many."

"She has been taking quite a few," Maggie acknowledged. She couldn't tell Ruth what Dolly had told her in the powder room. She had promised Dolly that she wouldn't.

"Bernie and I shouldn't have let her become an actress instead of going to college, or hide the fact that she's Jewish," Ruth continued. "I thought I was making Dolly's life easier, but I was wrong. Young women have to follow a certain path or society won't approve of them. I should have helped Dolly find a nice Jewish young man. By now she'd be happily married with children, like her friends."

"She did find a nice young man," Maggie reminded Ruth. "And she would hate to stay home. She loves working in television."

Ruth wasn't listening. She sipped her coffee.

"When Dolly was a child, I thought she'd be part of the generation of women who could do whatever they wanted. The war changed everything. Now young women are supposed to be grateful to have found someone to marry, and they're expected to be happy vacuuming the house and folding the laundry. For girls like Dolly, that's a prison sentence."

"Dolly is smarter than anyone I know. She just has to believe in herself," Maggie said firmly.

Ruth looked up from her coffee cup. There were fine lines on her forehead.

"If anything bad happens to Dolly, I'll never forgive myself."

Ruth and Maggie finished their coffee, and Maggie said goodbye. After she left, she stopped at the supermarket and picked up lamb chops for dinner with Teddy. Then she went home and worked on her show notes.

She was worried about her friend. Dolly thought she wasn't dependent on the pills, but she was wrong. And Dolly's mother and the doctor had agreed that she should cut back on them, but Dolly needed to do more than that. She had to stop taking them all together. And she needed to reintroduce foods she had cut out of her diet—steak and butter and bread. Maggie recalled the first time she and Dolly had lunch. Dolly ordered a cheeseburger with fries and a milkshake. She had seemed so happy and vibrant—her hair was shiny and her eyes sparkled. Now, Maggie could see the bones in Dolly's shoulders, and there was a lethargy about her—as if she had only enough energy to take the pills.

Maggie had to stop thinking about her. She had to answer readers' letters for the next day's show. She picked the top letter in the stack and began to read:

Dear Maggie Lane,

This letter won't make it on the air, but I had to write it anyway. Three months ago, I had a baby boy, David, and I haven't been able to lose the pregnancy weight. I tried eating only broccoli and cauliflower for dinner but I'm nursing, and David started getting gas. Then I started running five miles a day, but my milk stopped coming in, so I had to stop.

Every afternoon I bake a Deluxe Baking Company recipe from the morning's show. It's my favorite part of the day—the baby is asleep and the kitchen fills with delicious smells. My husband, Evan, loves having a slice of Deluxe Baking Company chocolate cake or a few Deluxe cinnamon brownies every night for dessert. The thing is, he makes me eat a whole dessert too. Don't get me wrong, there's nothing I enjoy more than a few bites of Deluxe Baking Company key lime pie or half a slice of Deluxe Baking Company apple pie, but if I eat a whole portion, I'll never lose the weight. It's not that I'm fat, but my pre-pregnancy clothes don't fit and I'm afraid they never will.

What should I do?

Sincerely,

Ellen Harper

Maggie replaced the letter in its envelope. Ellen was right, but if Maggie responded on the show, viewers might worry that Deluxe Baking Company products would make them fat. Tommy would be furious. But if she stayed silent, women like Ellen and Dolly would never be happy with the way they looked.

She had an idea. She picked up her pen.

Dear Ellen,

On the contrary, your letter is important for all women to hear. Many women struggle with their looks. They want their hair to be thicker, or their nose to be smaller, or their hips to be narrow. There's no perfect woman just as there is no ideal marriage. Everything in life comes with compromise.

The important thing is to be happy with yourself. Your baby, David, doesn't care if there's an extra bit of fat on your stomach. He just wants to be close to you. And if your husband really loves you, and it sounds like he does, he's more interested in you as a person than a beauty queen.

Life is to be enjoyed, and baking Deluxe Baking Company desserts in your kitchen while the people you love are safe and happy can be one of the best parts. If you and Evan can't eat as many desserts as you bake, think about donating a pie or some brownies to your local food bank.

And when you look in the mirror, see all parts of yourself. A wife who is responsible for running an entire household, a mother who has done the most miraculous thing of giving birth. If those accomplishments come with a few extra pounds, embrace them.

Sincerely,
Maggie Lane

Chapter Sixteen

It was the day of the New York Botanical Garden gala. In a few hours, a town car would pick up Maggie and Teddy and take them to the Plaza Hotel on Fifth Avenue. Reporters would be hovering on the Plaza's steps, waiting for a glimpse of the former First Lady, Eleanor Roosevelt, and last year's Miss America, Jacquelyn Mercer, and Maggie. Tommy had instructed Maggie to greet each journalist with a few kind words and a warm smile so they would write her up favorably in the next day's newspapers. Then she would slip her arm through Teddy's and they would enter the Palm Court restaurant. Maggie had been there for a rehearsal, and it was perfect for the occasion. The domed ceiling let in so much light, it was as if one was standing in a garden. Trellises covered the walls, and the marble floor was dotted with urns filled with magnolias and gardenias. The furniture had a cane accent, and giant palm trees separated the conversation areas.

Maggie was going to wear a gown designed for her by Claire McCardell. It had a tight-fitting bodice with a sweetheart neckline and a wide taffeta skirt. The skirt was decorated with floral appliques. A floral scarf would be knotted around her neck, and she was going to carry a floral satin evening bag and wear satin pumps.

Even her perfume had a floral theme. L'Air du Temps by Nina Ricci. Maggie recalled when she had seen it in the window at Macy's two years previously and had been enchanted by the Lalique bottle with its entwined-doves stopper. It smelled like an English garden—jasmine and irises, wrapped in a blend of sandalwood. The salesgirl had pressed her to buy a bottle, but back then she couldn't afford the smallest bottle of eau de cologne. Now there was a large bottle of the perfume sitting on her dressing table, sent by the perfume's creator, Francis Fabron, with a note thanking her for wearing it.

She still couldn't believe she was being honored at the gala. She spent the last week researching the accomplishments of Eleanor Roosevelt. President Truman had appointed her as the United States delegate to the United Nations, and recently she had coauthored a book about children and human rights. She had her own syndicated newspaper column, which ran in the *New York Post* and other newspapers, and a radio show on CBS, and she traveled the country giving lectures.

Every time Maggie pictured standing on the stage beside her, her knees wobbled and her legs turned to jelly.

Teddy's mother, Patty, was attending, as were Alan and Dolly. Dolly's fainting episode seemed to have scared her. She had stopped skipping breakfast and eating only a salad for lunch. But Maggie worried; there was a skittishness about her. When they all had dinner together, Dolly disappeared for ages to the powder room. Maggie wondered whether she was still taking the pills, but she was afraid to say anything. If she lost Dolly as a friend, she wouldn't be able to help her. She had to tread carefully. Often, she felt confused. How could she reach Dolly and make her see that the pills were bad for her without pushing her away?

Alan still hadn't proposed. Teddy assured Maggie that he was saving for a diamond ring, but Maggie wasn't so sure. What if Alan's mother had intervened? Dolly was in love with Alan. All Maggie wanted was for Dolly to be happy.

The apartment door opened. Teddy had been to the barber. His hair was slicked back, and he smelled of aftershave.

"You should go dressed like that. You'd steal the whole night." He joined her in the living room.

Maggie was wearing a robe and a pair of slippers.

"I don't think Tommy would approve," Maggie said, laughing.

"It would make it easier for me at the end of the evening." Teddy slipped his hand beneath the robe. "That dress you're wearing is stunning, but there are too many buttons."

Maggie felt light and happy. "I promise I'll help with the buttons," she said with a smile. Then she remembered the night's itinerary. "First, we have to get through cocktails and dinner and the speeches. What if I stumble when I read the speech?"

"You won't, but if you do, you'll make something up. You're Maggie Lane. The audience will love you no matter what you say."

A lump formed in Maggie's throat. For the last week, Teddy had been extra gentle and encouraging. He rubbed her feet at night and brought her cups of hot cocoa to help her sleep. When she got up, the coffee was already made, and there was a slice of bread waiting in the toaster.

"I love you, and I'm lucky to have you," she said.

Teddy gave a playful shrug. "If we spend any more time with you wearing nothing but that robe, we won't get to the gala on time and we'll be in trouble." He reached into his pocket. "I picked up something for you."

Maggie frowned. They had promised they wouldn't buy each other presents except for Christmas and birthdays and their anniversary.

She unwrapped the paper. Inside was a heart-shaped watch with a diamond face. It was beautiful, but it must have cost a fortune.

"Before you get out of sorts, I didn't buy it," he rushed in. "I've had it for years. I never knew what to do with it; now it seemed simple. You see, I always thought that when a woman got married, she cared about the wedding more than anything," he mused. "But our ceremony was conducted in my parents' living room. Father Darcy got a little tipsy, and afterwards my father gave a rambling toast and we ate a store-bought wedding cake. So you didn't marry me for the big church wedding with the elaborate gown and caviar at the reception. Maybe wanting to be married for the show had something to do with it, but I know you better than that. You wouldn't have gone through with it unless you loved me, and you wouldn't have agreed to have a simple wedding if you didn't care more about the marriage."

Teddy was right—once she had dreamed of a church wedding. The kind where guests lined up to throw rice at the bride and groom as they left, and a photographer followed the couple around at the reception, snapping photos of them cutting the wedding cake.

After she decided to marry Teddy, none of that had seemed important.

"Where did you get the watch?" she asked.

"In a pawnshop in London during the war. A woman was trying to sell it to the owner, but he wouldn't take it. He had a cabinet full of watches and promise rings that servicemen had given to their girls. I felt sorry for her, so I bought it." Teddy turned it over. "I had it engraved. It's yours now."

On the back were their initials, joined by a heart.

That was so like Teddy. He couldn't bear to see anyone suffer.

Maggie fastened it around her wrist.

"It fits perfectly." She kissed him. "It will look beautiful with my gown."

At the last minute, Dolly lent Maggie one of her mother's diamond necklaces. On the way to the gala, Maggie glanced in the rearview mirror at the bright stones glittering around her neck and felt like she was gazing at someone else.

"I can't go through with this. I'm not rich and famous," she whispered to Teddy when they arrived. "Everyone will know I'm an impostor."

He placed her gloved hand in his. "You're nothing of the sort. You're Maggie Lane, and everyone can't wait to meet you."

The car pulled up in front of the Plaza Hotel, and they were met by photographers. Then everything happened as Tommy had predicted. Journalists followed Maggie and Teddy up the steps, asking for a few words about the evening. Tommy greeted them at the top and led them into the lobby. More photographers took their photographs, and the president of the board of the New York Botanical Garden shook Maggie's hand and thanked her for being there.

Champagne and cocktails in the Palm Court were followed by a three-course dinner. Maggie and Teddy were seated at the same table as Eleanor Roosevelt and Jacquelyn Mercer and her husband. Maggie was so nervous, she could barely touch the food.

"You have to eat a few pieces of the steak," Teddy leaned over and whispered during the main course, "or you won't have the energy to give your speech."

Maggie set down her champagne glass and picked up her fork. Teddy had a point—she wasn't some schoolgirl there to gush over the decor and the menu. Tommy and everyone at Deluxe Baking Company were counting on her.

Maggie ate a few mouthfuls of steak and felt better. By the time dessert was served and the board president introduced the guests of honor, she was beginning to enjoy herself.

Eleanor Roosevelt was in her midsixties, with short brown hair and wrinkles around her mouth.

"Until my husband's presidency, the role of First Lady was about decorating the White House and chatting with wives at political dinners. From the beginning of Franklin's term, I championed my own causes, focusing on women's and children's rights. At first, Franklin's press secretary would have been quite happy if I got a case of laryngitis that lasted four years." She laughed. "Gradually I found an audience that was as passionate about my causes as I was. What I learned most from that time and from the last five years since Franklin died is that women are capable of doing anything.

"So, tonight I stand here not to be honored for my accomplishments, but to honor all of you. For what you have given to your families, to your communities, and to this country."

Eleanor folded her notes, and the room erupted into applause. Maggie blinked and realized there were tears in her eyes. Eleanor had been the wife of the president of the United States. From afar, her life seemed so gifted. Yet she and Franklin had struggles like any other married couple. Now that Eleanor was alone, she had to be stronger than ever. She was so passionate about the things she believed in, it gave Maggie hope to achieve her own goals.

Jacquelyn Mercer spoke next about growing up in Arizona and assuming she'd get married and become a teacher or librarian. While those were fine professions, she wanted something else. It was only when she entered the Miss America contest and rode a bus to Atlantic City that she realized the world was bigger than she imagined. Dozens of opportunities were available, and it was up to her to find them.

The best part about her year as Miss America was meeting other young women and talking to them about their goals. She was thrilled to be standing up there tonight, and she hoped that her time as Miss America encouraged all young women to follow their dreams.

It was Maggie's turn to speak.

Teddy squeezed her hand. She stood up and walked to the podium.

The ballroom seemed too bright. The women in their cocktail dresses and the men in tuxedos were elegant and distinguished.

Maggie shouldn't be up there. There was nothing she could say that would come close to Eleanor Roosevelt's speech. Even Jacquelyn Mercer had accomplished more than she had. She couldn't simply read the words that Deluxe Baking Company's speechwriter had prepared. This was her chance to stand up in front of a room full of people and open her heart. Even if it was in a small way, she wanted to show her gratitude to the people who supported her.

Then she glanced at Teddy, who was looking at her with so much love. And at Patty, and Alan and Dolly, who were beaming proudly as if they were partially responsible for her success. She suddenly knew what to do.

She set aside the speech.

"This is a big night for *The Maggie Lane Baking Show* and a big night for our sponsor, Deluxe Baking Company," she began. "In fact, they hired a speechwriter. They were worried that a young woman who grew up on a farm and never went to college wouldn't know what to say to a room full of important people.

"I was going to read the speech and return to my seat. But these aren't my words, so I'm not going to read them after all." She crumpled up the paper. "Instead, I'm going to tell you why you asked me to be here tonight and why *The Maggie Lane Baking Show* is important to women everywhere.

"Deluxe Baking Company recipes may not seem special on the cake box at the supermarket, but they turn into something different in your kitchen. Whisking eggs and flour, or dusting an orange pound cake with powdered sugar, are expressions of love."

Here Maggie took a breath. She looked directly at Teddy's mother.

"All of us want to be loved. Whether I'm baking my mother-in-law's favorite pineapple upside-down cake to celebrate her talent." She paused and addressed Dolly. "Or I'm making a lemon tart for my best friend to show her how much I care. Or I'm baking something I've never tried before, a rhubarb pie, for my husband, because I'm grateful that he believes in me. A Deluxe Baking Company recipe isn't just about baking a dessert; it's about filling a home with love.

"That's why I'm standing here tonight. Yes, on the show, I teach women how to spread icing on a pound cake, but mainly I want to share in their struggles and joys. I want to be their friend.

"I can't thank you enough for watching the show. America is a great country when a girl from rural Pennsylvania comes to New York with nothing, and all her dreams come true."

There was a silence, and a pit formed in her stomach. She should have read the speech.

Someone in the audience started clapping. The clapping grew louder. A few people stood up. Soon, the whole audience was clapping. Maggie glanced around and saw Tommy clapping and beaming at her.

She returned to her seat. Her legs trembled and her chest tightened with emotion. She took deep breaths to calm herself. Eleanor Roosevelt leaned across the table.

"That was a wonderful speech." She took out a card from her purse. "Come see me at my townhouse on Fifth Avenue. We'll have afternoon tea and a chat."

Maggie took the card and tried to hide her amazement. Eleanor Roosevelt had approved of what she said! It was a moment out of a storybook.

The band started, and couples moved to the dance floor. Teddy and Maggie danced to Frank Sinatra's "Some Enchanted Evening."

Finally, guests started to leave. Maggie went to the cloakroom to get her coat. It was a silver fox that Aladdin Furs had lent her for the evening.

"What a beautiful jacket," a woman complimented her. She was about thirty, with shoulder-length dark hair. She pointed to Maggie's diamond necklace. "I envy you. You get to attend these fancy dinners, wearing beautiful gowns, and furs, and diamonds. But doesn't all that go against the advice you give on your television show?"

"I beg your pardon," Maggie said.

"*The Maggie Lane Baking Show* is about baking for your family. It seems to me that if cooking and cleaning made a woman happy, you wouldn't spend your days in a television studio and your evenings attending fancy galas."

"Sometimes it's fun to dress up and go out," Maggie responded.

"You and your husband do it so frequently. When you're not going to dinner, you're taking drives in that fancy car," the woman continued. "My husband and I have been married for four years, and we're still saving for a new car. Maybe if your viewers had careers, they'd be able to afford nice things too." She gave a small smile. "That wouldn't be good for the show's ratings, or for its star."

"I'm sorry, my husband is waiting for me." Maggie finished buttoning her coat. The woman was wrong—Maggie didn't enjoy her career because of the trappings of fame. Being the star of her own television show allowed her to give advice to women who needed it. All her happiness about the evening drained away. She felt as if she had been punched in the stomach. She needed to get away from the woman as quickly as possible.

"That's another thing. You don't care enough about your marriage to take your husband's last name," the woman persisted. "And why did he stop being a radio host to take a producing job? I'm guessing it's because you didn't want two celebrities in the marriage."

Maggie's face grew hot. The woman's words had struck a nerve. She cared so much that Teddy was comfortable with her career. She was about to turn away when Teddy strode toward her.

"Hello, Helen, what are you doing here?" Teddy said to the woman. He turned to Maggie. "This is Helen Jacobson. She's a reporter with the *New York Times*."

Helen took a camel-colored coat from the rack. "I'm working. These are my favorite gigs. I get to eat steak and potatoes while my husband stays home with the baby." She turned back to Maggie. "You can keep baking those Deluxe Baking Company desserts and giving advice, but you don't fool me. All you want is fame and fortune and a handsome man on your arm."

Teddy and Maggie went home and sat together in the living room. Maggie was still shaken up by the encounter with Helen.

"Helen and I competed for the same job several years ago," Teddy explained "I got the job, even though she was more qualified."

"What if she writes terrible things about me in the *New York Times*?" Maggie asked worriedly.

Teddy shook his head. "She won't. It would look like a spite piece. It was a wonderful evening. Don't let her spoil it."

Teddy was right. Maggie couldn't let Helen Jacobson ruin their night.

"It was a wonderful evening," she agreed. It had been the best night, but meeting Helen had cast a black cloud over it. Helen was the wicked godmother appearing at Sleeping Beauty's christening. She wouldn't let Helen take away their joy. Tomorrow was a new day; everything would seem brighter in the morning. "I'm tired. Let's go to bed."

Chapter Seventeen

In the weeks following the gala, Maggie's picture was everywhere. Photographs of her and Eleanor Roosevelt and Jacquelyn Mercer appeared in *Life* and *Newsweek*. There were articles in *Woman's Day* and other women's magazines. Ratings for the show shot even higher, and Maggie received a bonus and a raise. She used the bonus to pay off the charge cards.

She worried that Teddy would be upset about the added attention she was receiving and by Helen Jacobson's harsh comments. But he didn't mention Helen again. Everything else about the night of the gala had been so perfect, it would have been foolish to dwell on it. On the contrary, he seemed thrilled with Maggie's growing wealth and fame generated from the articles about the gala. Now that the charge cards were paid off, there was no excuse for her not to carry the Henri Bendel handbag. She agreed and took it to work every day and placed it on the dressing table to remind herself how much she and Teddy loved each other.

He hadn't started smoking again. She told herself that alone should make her realize she was doing the right thing. For a week after the banquet, she found herself checking Teddy's pockets for a packet of Camels. She even rehearsed a little speech in her head for if she found them. Helen Jacobson had said hurtful things, even if they weren't true. It would be natural if Teddy felt like a cigarette now and then. Then she'd suggest they take an evening stroll around the neighborhood or go out for a late-night burger, and by the next morning the desire for a cigarette would be gone. But she didn't need the speech, because Teddy's pockets were always empty.

But she still had her own doubts. Sometimes, in the evenings when she was standing in line at the butcher after a long day at the studio, or waiting behind a mother and her smiling baby at the pharmacy, she wondered if Helen had been right. Would she and Teddy be happier if she stayed home? They could buy a little house in the suburbs and start a family. Teddy's parents would help with the down payment if they asked, and when the children were older, she could get a part-time job.

But she loved everything about working in television. The camaraderie on the set, meeting celebrity guests, the feeling of accomplishment when a show went particularly well. The warm glow she experienced when they finished filming, and sitting in her dressing room with a cup of tea and a stack of viewers' letters.

It was lovely to get dressed up occasionally at night and attend a movie premiere or a Broadway show. After the gala, she had treated herself to a pair of diamond earrings. They were the first diamonds she ever owned, and she had paid for them herself.

She was sitting in the dressing room. There was a knock.

"I thought you'd still be on the set with Perry Como." Dolly entered. "Every secretary in the building is there, waiting for his autograph. One woman started swooning, and she needed smelling salts."

Perry Como had been Maggie's celebrity guest. They baked a lemon supreme cake. While it was in the oven he sang his latest hit, "'A' You're Adorable."

Perry had the deepest-brown eyes. When he looked at you, if felt as if he were singing just for you and not for the thousands of fans that bought his albums.

"You're lucky that Teddy isn't the jealous type." Dolly sank onto a chair. "I wish Alan was. Maybe I should ask Perry out to dinner; then Alan would propose. He keeps hinting he's going to, but he never does."

Maggie had stopped asking Teddy when Alan was going to propose.

"He's saving for the ring," Maggie suggested.

Dolly shook her head. "Alan makes enough money. It's something else. I've asked him, but he avoids the question. So I pretend to enjoy going out every evening, but it's exhausting. Some nights, I'd rather stay home and watch television together."

"You can stay home without being married," Maggie pointed out.

"What if we get tired of each other's company?" Dolly demanded. "That's all right once we're married. While we're dating, we have to keep everything fresh and interesting."

Maggie laughed that Dolly had too high expectations.

Dolly gazed at her reflection in the dressing room mirror.

"Alan's mother has something to do with this. She's the queen bee of Cleveland society now. Alan sent me the newspaper clippings. I wish I could send Sally Knickerbocker to write a gossip piece about her. Nothing terrible, just a small article that would make her less sure of herself."

Maggie asked who Sally Knickerbocker was.

"You haven't heard of her? She's the big gossip columnist, like Hedda Hopper and Louella Parsons in Hollywood. She lived in Palm Beach and Washington, DC. She just moved to New York. The *New York Post* hired her to compete with Walter Winchell."

Walter Winchell wrote a gossip column for the *New York Daily Mirror*. If Winchell cut you, you were banished from New York society forever.

"Speaking of Walter Winchell, you received a small mention in today's column. It's only a few lines, but that makes you an official New York celebrity." Dolly handed her a folded newspaper.

Maggie set it on the dressing table. She would read it later.

"I should go. I have to buy a red cocktail dress for Saturday night's CBS dinner." Dolly stood up. "An article in *Vogue* said that more women get engaged when they're wearing red than any other color."

Maggie frowned. "You should stop worrying about Alan proposing and do something for yourself."

Dolly's mouth wobbled. Maggie noticed she was looking thinner again. Her cheeks were sharp, and her wrists seemed very small.

"It's not about the diamond ring, or the fancy wedding, or even children." Dolly's eyes widened. "I'm in love with Alan. I don't want to live without him."

Dolly left, and Maggie picked up the newspaper. A paragraph caught her eye.

> After several years, Broadway might see another Charles Grey play. There are rumors that a script is circling the Theater District, though there is no word of a financial backer or director yet. This columnist can't help but wonder if the script is as brilliant as his early successes, or, in reverse, a play reminiscent of why he left New York. Only time and the box office will tell.

Maggie read it again. Her stomach dropped, and the newspaper shook in her hands. She hadn't had any contact with Charles in ages. The panicky feeling rose to her throat. What if he tried to see her?

She gazed at the photo of him and recalled the early days of living in his apartment and being his secretary. Charles had been so handsome and debonair. Everything about him—from the cashmere sport coats hanging in his closet to the invitations that piled up on his desk—were part of a life Maggie had never imagined.

～

It was the start of theater season on Broadway, and Charles's play had just finished a trial run in Boston. In the days leading to his departure, Maggie had never seen Charles so anxious. Instead of writing in the mornings, he took long walks around the neighborhood and insisted Maggie accompany him. They crisscrossed the Upper East Side, and he went over the things that could go wrong. The lead actress could come down with the flu, and her understudy wasn't ready to take over her role. The set design might be all wrong, or the audience might not appreciate Lou Magnolia's directing.

Maggie tried to calm him down. Lou was enthusiastic about the play, and the few backers who had been allowed into rehearsals were full of praise. Charles couldn't be appeased. He became superstitious. He stopped wearing the blue blazers in his closet because wearing the color blue in the theater was bad luck. He put away the mirrors in the apartment because breaking a mirror meant the play was going to flop.

When he finally left for Boston, Maggie was relieved. She spent the week writing to Jake. The war in the Pacific continued, and sometimes Maggie wondered when Jake would ever come home. Then she reread one of his letters, or pulled out the photos they'd taken together, and felt in her heart that he would return soon.

The one request Charles made while he was away was that Maggie read the Boston and New York newspapers. He was too agitated to read reviews of the play himself, but he didn't want to miss anything.

The first few days, there was no mention of it. Then Maggie found a positive review in the *Boston Globe*. The next day there was a piece in the *New York Times* about the play coming to Broadway. It was accompanied by a photo of Charles with an attractive woman on his arm. Charles wore a dinner jacket, and the woman was dressed in a black velvet cocktail dress.

The article read:

> New York playwright and man-about-town Charles Grey is in Boston this week for a trial run of his new play with famed director Lou Magnolia. It's not all work and no fun for Charles. He's been seen every night with recently divorced socialite Rebecca Marshall. Rebecca was the subject of one of last year's messiest breakups. She now seems happily recovered and has sunk some

of her ex-husband's money and much of her energy into the production. Her investment might pay off in other ways. She and Charles have been seen looking intimate at Boston's best restaurants.

Maggie studied the photo more closely. Rebecca appeared to be in her late twenties. Her blond hair was styled in a pageboy, and she wore a diamond pendant.

Charles hadn't mentioned her, but he never talked about any of the women he dated in New York. It wasn't any of Maggie's business. He could date whomever he pleased.

Now Charles was back from Boston, and the play opened this evening.

She was sitting at the kitchen table when the front door opened.

Charles entered, carrying a shopping bag.

He unloaded his purchases. There was a bouquet of white lilies and a tin of sardines with a box of crackers. "I ate these on opening night of my first Broadway production." He held up the sardines. "I swore to myself, if the play was a success, next time I'd have caviar instead. But I found I prefer the sardines.

"The flowers are for Margot, the lead actress. I can't give them to her until the final curtain call. If she receives flowers before the play ends, it's bad luck. During my previous play, I had to send someone to the lead actress's dressing room to get rid of the bouquets she had received. She only got them back after the night's performance ended.

"This is for you." He handed her a long, flat box.

Maggie opened it. Inside was a silver bracelet.

"You can wear it tonight. Decades ago, wearing expensive jewelry near the stage was bad luck, because thieves could try to steal it when the theater went dark. Silver jewelry was the only kind that was acceptable."

"It's beautiful." Maggie turned it over. "But I'm not going to the play."

They hadn't talked about it. Maggie had barely seen Charles since he returned. He'd spent the last few days at the theater. But all of Charles's wealthy friends would be there. She didn't feel like it was her place.

"Of course you are," Charles said. "Lou insisted before he agreed to direct the play."

Maggie argued that was ages ago. Everything had been going so well, she didn't need to be there.

"One can't change anything about opening night." Charles shook his head. "Afterwards we're all going to Sardi's to wait for the reviews. You'll come with us."

Maggie wanted to ask whether Rebecca would be there, and what she would say if Maggie tagged along. But Maggie realized she wanted to go. She'd been working on the play for so long.

She nodded. "All right, I'll come."

Charles beamed. "I have to get to the theater early, so I've arranged for a car to pick you up at seven."

Maggie went to her bedroom to choose a dress. Her latest letter to Jake sat on her bedside table.

She wondered what Jake would say when she told him that she was going to the opening of a Broadway production. She missed him so much. She wanted to show him everything—her pretty bedroom with its floral wallpaper and views of the Empire State Building. The fresh towels Ellen always put in her bathroom, and the flowers in the vase on her bedside table. She imagined introducing him to Charles and Ellen and leading him around the townhouse.

They'd sit in the living room and plan their future. There wasn't time to think about it now. She had to get ready for the evening.

Maggie had never been to a Broadway show before. When the town car pulled up in front of the theater on Forty-Second Street, she could feel the excitement in the air. Men were dressed in tuxedos; women wore evening gowns with fur stoles. They stood in groups in the lobby, clutching their programs and sipping champagne. Maggie was about to go inside when a blond woman wearing a full-length silk gown approached her.

It was the woman from the photo with Charles in the newspaper article.

"You must be Maggie. I'm Rebecca Marshall," she introduced herself. "Charles has talked about you so much, I feel like I know you." She eyed Maggie's cocktail dress. "Though you're more mature and even prettier in person."

Maggie wondered what Charles had said about her.

"I have to thank you. I have a lot of money invested in the play," Rebecca continued. "Charles insists that if it wasn't for you, it would still be a pile of unfinished pages." She gave a small smile. "I should find him. We have a box in the front. It's lovely to meet you."

Maggie finished her champagne, but it tasted flat. She had assumed that she would be sitting with Charles. She entered the theater, took her seat in the far left, and waited for the lights to go down. Halfway into the first act, she knew the audience was hooked. They set down their programs and stopped searching for friends in the dark. Instead, their eyes were glued to the stage. They laughed in the right places. During a particularly moving scene, she could almost feel them holding their breath.

At intermission, Charles was surrounded by so many people, clapping him on the shoulder, Maggie couldn't get close to him. But when the final curtain came down, and he and Lou stood on the stage, she glowed with happiness. Charles's fears had been for nothing. The play was a success. In her own small way, she had been part of it.

Dinner at Sardi's was a parade of people approaching the table and congratulating Charles and Lou. The waiters set down plates of oysters Rockefeller and Peruvian chicken, but Maggie hardly ate a bite. It was too exciting to be surrounded by the glamorous men and women she had seen only in the society pages, to listen to conversations about extended runs and overseas performances in London.

When the newspapers arrived, the reviews were predictably favorable. Charles read excerpts out loud. "In Charles Grey and Lou Magnolia, Broadway has found a writing/directing duo who are more charismatic than fictional Gotham City's Batman and Robin." "Grey's play has all the attributes of great theater. This reviewer sees a bright future for Grey and Magnolia." "Hands down, tonight's production will be the hit of the season."

It was only at the end of the night, when Maggie was waiting for her wrap, that the evening turned sour.

Rebecca Marshall joined her at the coat check.

"Charles is waiting for you in the hire car out front," Rebecca said. "Thank God he didn't drive. He's quite drunk." She chuckled. "I suppose we all are. Success and champagne is a heady concoction."

Maggie answered that she wouldn't drive with Charles and Rebecca. She'd get a taxi.

Rebecca raised her eyebrows. "Don't be silly. You and Charles are going to the same place. Or did you think he was coming to my apartment?"

"I assumed . . ." Maggie paused lamely. She wasn't comfortable talking about Charles's love life.

"That Charles and I are sleeping together?" Rebecca finished for her. "Charles is good looking, and we did have a little fling in Boston," she conceded. "But he's not my type. In fact, I'm going home with Lou." She studied Maggie closely. "Anyway, it wouldn't matter how I feel about Charles. After this evening, it's obvious that he has feelings for you."

Maggie felt her cheeks get hot. She fiddled with her earrings. She wondered whether Rebecca was right and Charles did have feelings for her. That was impossible. Charles only saw her as his secretary. He always had a beautiful, sophisticated woman on his arm. And it didn't matter anyway—she was in love with Jake.

"You're wrong. Charles hardly talked to me at dinner. And he knows that I'm in love with someone. Jake is stationed in the South Pacific. As soon as the war is over, we're going to get engaged."

"It was the way Charles talked about you at dinner. Everyone at the table could see how he felt."

Charles had been very complimentary. He told the story about how Maggie got them in to see Lou at his house on Long Island, and how easily the writing came to him when he was dictating to her.

"That was strictly professional," Maggie said firmly.

"You could do a lot worse," Rebecca said. "What if Jake never comes home, or he meets someone else?"

The coat check girl handed Rebecca her cape. She draped it around her shoulders and turned to Maggie.

"You're young and pretty. Enjoy life now. You never know what the future will bring." She paused. "But be careful. One of the most important things to Charles is how he looks to other people."

"What do you mean?" Maggie asked.

"It's common with people in the arts. They create an image of themselves, which is the only one they let others see. The expensive apartment, the fancy cars, dinners out every night at the best restaurants. And most importantly, the adoring woman on his arm. As long as you make Charles look good in public, he'll worship you. But if you ever embarrass him, he'll stop at nothing to get back at you." She gave a vibrant smile. "Goodness, I'm getting ahead of myself." She squeezed Maggie's arm. "That must be the champagne talking. I can tell you're not that kind of woman. You'll do fine."

Maggie accepted the ride home from Charles, but they hardly talked in the car. When they arrived at the apartment, she claimed a headache from the champagne at dinner and went straight to her room.

She set her wrap on the bedside table and laid out the photos of her and Jake. Then she took out his letters and read them from the beginning.

By the time she finished, her eyes were scratchy, and her heart pounded.

Maggie couldn't stay in Charles's apartment. It had never occurred to her that Charles might have feelings for her. From the beginning, he knew that she was only waiting for Jake to come home from the war. Charles saw her as his secretary. He counted on her for everything to do with his plays, just as he counted on Ellen to take care of the cooking and cleaning in the apartment. Even if Rebecca was right and he did have feelings for her, it would never work. They came from different worlds. She could never fall in love with a man like Charles. His life was glamorous, but she wanted to build her own life in New York, with a career and a family. And she was in love with Jake. That would never change.

But what would she do for an income without Charles? And what if Rebecca was right, and Jake never returned?

She took off her dress and went to take a bath.

~

Maggie folded the newspaper and placed it on the table in her dressing room. She had stayed in New York all these years, and Charles never tried to contact her. There was no reason to think he would now because there was a mention of her in Walter Winchell's column.

She had to buy a dress for the CBS dinner on Saturday night. And she'd stop by the Realtor's office. The charge cards were paid off, so she and Teddy could look for an apartment.

Charles had nothing to do with her life. She was the star of *The Maggie Lane Baking Show*. She and Teddy had friends and family. Nothing was going to ruin their happiness.

Chapter Eighteen

Maggie glanced at her reflection in the bedroom mirror. She wore a green cocktail dress with a wasp waist and full skirt. She bought it at Saks, and it was perfect for tonight's CBS dinner.

The dinner was being held at the Rotunda restaurant in the Pierre Hotel. CBS was honoring employees who had been nominated for Peabody Awards in New York. There was a separate category for CBS Radio. Teddy was nominated for his work as a content producer.

Teddy entered behind her. He looked handsome in a tuxedo and silk bow tie.

"You look stunning in that dress," he said admiringly.

"A new gossip columnist will be there tonight. Her name is Sally Knickerbocker. Dolly thinks it's important that my photograph ends up in her column."

"Sally Knickerbocker?" Teddy repeated.

"Do you know her? Dolly said she aims to be as influential as Walter Winchell."

"You know, I don't read gossip columns. It's like eating sugared cereal for breakfast. It leaves a bad taste in your mouth all day." He shrugged.

There was something odd in Teddy's expression. His eyes were hooded, and lines formed on his forehead.

"I have something for you." Maggie opened the drawer and took out a small package.

Teddy opened it. Inside was a rabbit's foot.

His eyes darted up. "Where did you get this?"

It was from the gift department at Saks. It had been in the display case and caught her eye.

"You're up for an award. You can keep it in your pocket for good luck."

Teddy's expression softened. He set the rabbit's foot on the bedside table. "Of course. That was very thoughtful."

The Pierre was Maggie's favorite hotel in New York. It was on Sixty-First Street on the Upper East Side. Coco Chanel lived there during the 1930s, and all the famous actors and actresses—stars like William Holden and Betty Grable—stayed in the suites overlooking Central Park.

Cocktails were being served in the upstairs lobby, followed by a sit-down dinner in the Rotunda. The Rotunda's floors were four different colors of imported marble. The domed ceiling was decorated with murals by famous American artists.

"They shouldn't hold parties in a place like this," Dolly said. "What if someone gets tipsy and knocks over one of those marble busts? It would cost more to replace than most employees' annual salary."

Maggie glanced at the busts of Greek gods and goddesses scattered around the space.

"I like it. I think it's inspiring," she said.

"That's because you make a decent salary." Dolly sipped her champagne. "There's a rumor going around that you're one of the highest-paid female stars on television."

"Where did you hear that?" Maggie asked sharply.

She didn't discuss her salary with anyone except Teddy. Even Dolly didn't know how much Maggie earned. Dolly wasn't terribly interested in money—her parents were happy to subsidize her income. But neither of them wanted their salaries to get in the way of their friendship.

"Sally Knickerbocker was in the powder room," Dolly said.

"She was talking about me?" Maggie asked.

"She seemed to know all about you and Teddy. She didn't stay long, so I didn't hear much more," Dolly said.

Maggie wondered why Sally was interested in them. There were more famous couples in New York.

"Maybe she read Helen Jacobson's piece about you in the *New York Times*," Dolly suggested.

Maggie winced. The article that Helen wrote pretended to be complimentary—Maggie was setting an example for other young women who wanted to be on television—but it included references to Teddy being a "house husband" and what it must feel like for him to know that his wife could travel anywhere in the world, while he could only afford a vacation on the Jersey Shore.

"Just be careful," Dolly cautioned. "If you get on Sally Knickerbocker's bad side, she'll make Helen's article seem as light and airy as a soufflé at La Bourgogne."

The Maggie Lane Baking Show won awards in three categories. Maggie was chosen as CBS's female star of the year. She gave a warm speech, thanking Tommy for taking a chance on her, and Dolly for always being in the adjoining dressing room, and Teddy for making her life complete.

The awards for CBS Radio came next. When the award for best content producer was announced, Teddy lost to a young man fresh out of college. The producer bounded up to the podium and gave a speech, and Teddy joked that he was relieved because he specifically became a producer so he wouldn't ever have to talk into a microphone again. But Maggie could sense his disappointment.

Tommy whisked her off to meet some executives from Deluxe Baking Company. When she returned to the table, Teddy was gone. She was about to take the elevator when she noticed him sitting with a striking woman wearing a red ball gown. A mink cape was draped over her shoulders, and she was smoking a cigarette.

The woman glanced up and their eyes met. She had a long, elegant neck like a swan.

"You must be Maggie. I'm Sally Knickerbocker," she introduced herself. "I'm sorry I borrowed your husband without asking. I found him standing near the exit. I needed a cigarette, and I asked him to join me."

Maggie noticed the cigarette in Teddy's hand. She wondered how many he had already smoked. An alarm went off in her head. Teddy hadn't smoked in ages. Why was he smoking now? And how had Sally known that Teddy would accept a cigarette? They must already have been friends.

"You know each other?" she asked.

Sally nodded. "Since the war, though we haven't seen each other in years. I was an American journalist in London, and we met during an air raid at the Savoy. I was terrified and desperate for a cigarette. Teddy shared his pack of Camels."

"Teddy didn't tell me," she said to Sally.

Sally leaned forward. "We moved in the same circles in London for a while. Then the war ended and we lost touch. I got married and moved to Palm Beach. My husband had an affair, so I divorced him. He wanted to pay me off, but I refused and kept his last name instead. The name gets me in everywhere. Now I make my own money, and I'm not dependent on any man."

Maggie wondered why Sally was telling her all this. They had just met.

"After that, I moved to Washington, DC. But politics are boring. All the men were afraid that their wives would divorce them and ruin their chances for higher office if they talked with any single women." She inhaled her cigarette. "New York is much more interesting. There's museums and art galleries and theater. I was just saying to Teddy that he must be proud of you."

"I'm just on a baking show," Maggie said.

Sally fascinated Maggie and made her uncomfortable at the same time. She was so glamorous, in her ball gown and mink cape, she could be any of the society wives that one reads about in the social pages. But there was something about the way she talked and even the way she held her cigarette that made Maggie feel as if Sally wanted to be noticed by everyone she met.

"You're the best-loved television hostess in the country," Sally countered.

They talked about Sally's gossip column and her apartment on Riverside Drive.

"I came this evening with the Whitneys, and they'll wonder where I am." Sally stood up. "I'm having a cocktail party at my apartment next month. I'll send you an invitation."

Maggie and Teddy said goodbye and left. They barely talked on the way home. Maggie sensed an uneasy tension between them that she couldn't put her finger on. They were climbing the steps to their apartment when Teddy felt inside his pocket.

"I borrowed Alan's cigarette case," he said. "I'm going to take it to him."

It was late. Teddy could return it in the morning.

"I could use a walk," he continued before she could say anything. "Don't wait up. You must be tired."

When Maggie entered the apartment, the latest *Vogue* sat on the coffee table. She felt too restless to read. She debated making a pot of coffee, but the coffee would make her even more anxious. Instead, she sat down and kicked off her shoes.

She and Teddy should be curled up on the sofa, talking about the gala. At some point, he would play with the zipper of her dress, or she would undo his bow tie, and they'd kiss. One of Maggie's favorite things about attending black-tie events was their lovemaking afterward. They'd both be slightly intoxicated from the champagne and conversation. Teddy would pick her up and carry her into the bedroom. She'd laugh that she was too heavy and he'd regret it in the morning. He'd kiss her again and say he'd never regret anything they did together.

Maggie was quite sure they wouldn't make love tonight.

Ever since she saw him with Sally Knickerbocker, Teddy had been acting strangely. In the back of the town car, he sat as far from Maggie as possible. And it was obvious he didn't want to be in the apartment together. Returning Alan's cigarette case could have waited until the morning.

She wondered again why he hadn't told her that he knew Sally. Even if they had an affair in London, it wouldn't have mattered. That was years ago. It was his silence about Sally that disturbed her.

All she wanted now was for Teddy to hold her. But he told her not to wait up. She walked to the bedroom. She thought about Arabella and Ian, and Oradour-sur-Glane. Sally said she had been a journalist in London during the war. What if seeing Sally brought up old memories? Teddy's night sweats had eased lately. Maggie attributed it to how busy and happy they were. But now she feared the night sweats would return, and he'd start smoking again.

If only she could ask him about the war. Every time she started to, she stopped herself. Teddy was at his happiest when he was living in the present. Exploring New York with Maggie, going to dinner with Alan and Dolly, playing squash at the club. Bringing up tragic events that happened years ago could only upset him.

But now she thought differently. Sally had come into their lives, and Maggie felt instinctively that she was bringing the past with her. If Maggie didn't do something, Sally could find a way to come between them. From everything Dolly had told her, Maggie guessed that was the kind of woman that Sally was.

Before Maggie could stop herself, she went into Teddy's dressing room and took out the notebook. The envelope of photos was stuck to the back cover. She shook them onto the bed and arranged them on the bedspread.

There were more photos of Teddy at Pathé News. He was sitting at a desk and smiling. But his eyes looked tired, and Maggie could tell the smile was forced. Several photos were of a country house. There were a few photographs of the house's interior. Large rooms with heavy wooden furniture and crystal chandeliers. A library with two walls of bookshelves, and a living room with a brick fireplace and Oriental rugs. She studied a photo of a group of young men and women seated at a dining table. Teddy wore a blazer and tie. Arabella and Ian were seated on either side of him. Another photo was of the same group playing cricket on the lawn. A third was of them eating a picnic beside a river. All the photos had the same caption: "House party at Cousins Manor. July 1944."

Maggie set them down thoughtfully. The house party had been after the events in Oradour-sur-Glane. Teddy and Arabella and Ian had still been together. She glanced at the photo of the picnic. One of the women resembled Sally. She had Sally's wavy hairstyle and slim figure. But she was too far from the camera for Maggie to see her face.

Sally said that they moved in the same circles in London. Where was the house party, and had Sally been a guest too?

She slid the photos back in the envelope and went into the living room. In the morning, she'd ask Dolly what else she knew about Sally Knickerbocker. If Sally posed a threat to her marriage, she wanted to be as prepared as possible.

Chapter Nineteen

Maggie sat at a diner on the Upper East Side waiting for Dolly. She had an appointment with the Realtor, and Dolly was going to accompany her.

In the two weeks since the CBS dinner, she and Teddy had grown close again. She had been anxious and wary at first. The morning after the dinner, she had been determined to ask Teddy why he hadn't told her about Sally and why he had been so distant on the way home.

But when she woke up, Teddy presented her with coffee and donuts. They sat in bed and did the *New York Times* crossword puzzle together. Then they spent the afternoon at an exhibit at the Metropolitan Museum of Art, followed by dinner at Ruby Foo's. She was so glad to sit in the upstairs booth and have the waitstaff bring out their favorite dishes—chicken chow mein, Peking duck—instead of at one of the trendy restaurants they had been frequenting, she couldn't bring herself to mention the previous evening.

The following week, Teddy was so thoughtful. He took her blouses and skirts to the laundry. When she arrived home, they were neatly folded on the bed. On the day that she had a late taping and wouldn't be home for dinner, he ordered a steak and baked potato from Delmonico's and they were waiting, piping hot, in the dressing room.

He even canceled their plans to spend the weekend in Rye. Maggie protested that she enjoyed visiting his parents. Teddy replied they weren't going to spend two days baking casseroles and raking leaves when Maggie had been working so hard, and instead Teddy managed to get tickets to see the hit musical *Along Fifth Avenue* on Broadway.

Maggie glanced at the door of the diner. Dolly still hadn't arrived. She pulled out a viewer's letter from her purse and spread it on the tablecloth.

Dear Maggie Lane,

I live in Scarsdale and watch *The Maggie Lane Baking Show* every morning. Sometimes I feel that I know you so well, I'm tempted to take the train into New York and ask you to lunch. I'd bring you a box of my homemade pecan cookies, and after lunch we'd go shopping together at Macy's.

I know that's a fantasy. You probably dine at fancy restaurants with movie stars and celebrities. You shop at Saks and Bloomingdale's, and a town car takes your packages home so you can go straight to cocktails with your husband, Teddy.

You may wonder why I'm writing to you, when we lead such different lives. The thing is, Scarsdale is a small place and there's no one I can confide in. You might be able to answer my question without anyone in town knowing. It's about my husband, Arnold.

Arnold and I were high school sweethearts. We have an eight-year-old daughter, Susan. I'm the leader of Susan's Girl Scout troop.

Recently, a divorcée, Denise, and her daughter, Joanie, moved to Scarsdale. Joanie comes over often after school and for sleepovers on the weekends. Sometimes, I'm running errands when Denise picks Joanie up. When I arrive home, Denise and Arnold are sitting and talking in the living room.

I never thought anything about it. But something happened recently. When I bake cookies for the Girl Scouts, I always bake an extra batch to have at home. Last week, a few women came over for coffee and cake. One of the women, Laura, brought a plate of chocolate crinkle cookies. They were my cookies. I know, because they were from a Deluxe Baking Company recipe, with little waves of chocolate and cinnamon.

Laura said she bought them at the Girl Scouts bake sale. After the women left, I went into my pantry. The box of chocolate crinkle cookies that I had baked was gone.

I assumed Susan had given them to Joanie, but she knew nothing about it. Arnold admitted he had given the cookies to Denise. Denise works part-time in the undergarment department at Woolworth's and didn't have time to bake her own cookies.

If Denise had asked, I would have been happy to bake extra cookies. What disturbs me is that Arnold didn't tell me. Should I say something to him or keep my worries to myself? As I mentioned, Scarsdale is a small place and I don't want to cause a fuss.

Sincerely,
Roberta Perkins

Maggie set the letter down and sipped her coffee. If Roberta didn't say anything to Arnold, the same thing might happen again. Maggie could see it clearly. A pretty young divorcée moves to town and drives a wedge between a couple who had been married forever. But if Roberta did say something and Arnold was just being kind to a new face in the community, he might become angry that she didn't trust him.

She was about to reply when Dolly entered. She looked very pale. Her eyes were large in her small face. A pillbox hat was perched on her head.

"I'm sorry I'm late." Dolly sat opposite her.

Dolly eyed the slice of key lime pie that Maggie had ordered with her coffee. Her mouth trembled, and tears welled in her eyes.

"It's Alan. We're finished, and it's my fault."

Dolly told Maggie the whole story.

They had driven up to New Rochelle in Westchester County and parked in front of a new split-level house. Inside, there was a step-down living room with a built-in bar. The kitchen had an eating nook with a bay window. Upstairs, the master bedroom had an adjoining dressing room and a small room that could be used as an office or nursery.

Dolly sat in the living room while Alan went to the kitchen to make a pitcher of lemonade. She was certain that he was going to propose. She loved him and wanted more than anything to get married. But she'd have to tell him that she was Jewish.

Dolly toyed with her gloves. "It was Alan's house. His parents had helped with the down payment. He could take the train into the city, and on weekends he'd play golf and tennis at the country club."

Dolly glanced up at Maggie. Her expression was full of anguish.

"Then he asked if I would furnish it. I was so good at interior design. He wanted it to be sleek and modern, but comfortable at the same time."

"What did you say?" Maggie asked, horrified.

"I told him the truth. I thought he brought me there to ask me to marry him," Dolly continued. "He'd been planning to propose for months. He even bought the ring. A square-cut diamond from a diamond merchant on Seventh Avenue. Then his mother visited and said if he married me, he'd be cut off from the family." Dolly took a long breath. "He had to marry someone who would raise their children in the same religion. Alan is Jewish."

Maggie stared at Dolly. "I don't understand."

Alan's great-grandparents had emigrated from Russia. They fled to America to escape the pogroms.

When Alan told her, Dolly felt so foolish. Everything she had done to make her seem like the girls Alan knew in Cleveland—considering a nose job, using the pills to lose weight—had been wrong.

"He loves me, but he can't defy his parents," Dolly said miserably.

"How could you not know that he was Jewish?"

"I never dreamed he was Jewish. Like I said, I didn't know there were any Jewish families in Cleveland. That's why his mother ate at Katz's Delicatessen when she was in New York and why she made those odd comments about Tony Curtis and Janet Leigh. But Alan never lied to me. I made up whole stories about how my family celebrated Christmas and that I'd been going to church for as long as I could remember." Dolly wailed. "I can't tell him that I'm Jewish now. I've lied to him all this time. He'll never forgive me."

"He didn't tell you he was Jewish right away either," Maggie reminded her. "There must be something you can do. You love each other."

"That's the worst part," Dolly said. "If only I'd told the truth from the beginning, both our families would be happy. I ruined everything."

Maggie glanced at the letter from Roberta Perkins.

"I was just answering a viewer's letter," she said to Dolly. "I was going to tell her that no matter how hard it seems, the most important thing in a relationship is to communicate. Invite Alan to Friday night Shabbat dinner, and tell him then."

Dolly had never invited Alan to her parents' house. She had been afraid that he would discover that she was Jewish. Alan had met Dolly's mother, but Dolly had sworn Ruth to secrecy.

"Do you think that will work?" Dolly asked.

Maggie nodded. "Alan will see the table set with those beautiful silver candlesticks and listen to your mother give the prayers in Hebrew, and he'll feel like he's come home. We all make mistakes. He loves you. He'll understand."

They met the Realtor, Nancy, in a third-floor apartment on Lexington Avenue. The living room had a sectional sofa, and in the kitchen there were all new appliances.

"I'm glad you started looking again." Nancy walked around the apartment. "Prices are going up, especially at this time of year. Buyers want to be settled before the holidays." She eyed Maggie. "Though I'm sure you can afford whatever you like. You must be so successful. You and your husband are featured in all the gossip columns."

Maggie started to answer, but Dolly cut in.

"Maggie isn't one of those women who can be won over by pretty paint in the bedroom. Her bank manager has her on a strict budget," Dolly announced. "The apartment has to be a wise investment or she's not interested."

Nancy coughed nervously, and Maggie shot Dolly a grateful look.

They visited four more buildings before Maggie found the perfect apartment. It was in a doorman building on Park Avenue, a fifteen-minute walk to the Metropolitan Museum, and a few minutes to the entrance of Central Park.

The entry had a white marble floor. A potted palm stood on a pedestal, and there was an art deco mirror. In the living room, one wall was floor-to-ceiling windows overlooking the street. The sofas were red velvet, and there was a television cabinet and cocktail cart. A maid's room sat off the kitchen, and the master bedroom had his-and-her walk-in closets.

Nancy told her the price. It was more than she wanted to spend, but it was within the budget.

"I want to make an offer," Maggie blurted out.

Nancy and Dolly glanced at her in surprise.

"Don't you want to show it to your husband first?" Nancy asked.

Maggie knew she should show it to Teddy, but she couldn't bear the thought of losing it to another couple. And she was certain he'd love it. It was the kind of apartment one saw in movies from the 1930s, where everyone dressed in black tie for dinner, and there was a butler and a maid.

"Teddy will approve," Maggie said confidently. "Let's go to the office and sign the papers."

After Maggie left the office, she stopped and bought a bottle of champagne. She'd surprise him when he arrived home. She couldn't remember the last time they celebrated anything that didn't involve her career.

The new apartment would give them something to share. Teddy could add his records to the television cabinet. Maggie would buy vases and keep every room filled with fresh flowers.

She went into the bedroom and hung up Teddy's shirts and folded his ties. The rabbit's foot that she had given him sat on the bedside table. She opened the drawer and noticed a silver cigarette case. It was Alan's. Why hadn't Teddy returned it on the night of the CBS dinner?

What if Teddy hadn't gone to Alan's that night? What if he had gone to Sally Knickerbocker's apartment instead? Maybe he came home and put the cigarette case in the drawer so that Maggie wouldn't find it. Then he forgot about it.

She remembered lying awake for ages, waiting for the sound of the front door opening. The next morning she'd said something about Alan appreciating getting his cigarette case back, and Teddy hadn't corrected her.

She closed the bedside drawer. A memory came back to her. It was of Charles, and the jewelry box she found in his chest of drawers. She still wondered if she had never seen it, would everything in her life that happened afterward have been different?

～

Charles's and Lou's play was the hit of the Broadway season. Maggie had sent Jake a long letter telling him about opening night, but he hadn't replied. Every day when she went through the mail, she looked for the familiar blue-and-white airmail envelope. She told herself the holidays slowed the mail down. It could take weeks for letters to cross the ocean. She longed to see Jake's handwriting and find out whether he was going to be home for Christmas.

Since the play opened, she was so busy there wasn't time to think about getting a new job and moving out of Charles's apartment. Every day, the stack of mail grew higher. Fan letters and requests for tickets from film stars and movie producers. When Cary Grant sent a handwritten letter requesting two tickets, Maggie almost fainted with excitement. Cary Grant was her favorite actor. Charles dictated a response inviting him to dinner after the performance. He instructed Maggie to make sure Cary's box at the theater had a humidor filled with the finest cigars.

Charles was working on a new play. He would go out early in the morning and return with a bag of pastries. They would sit at the kitchen table while Charles talked about plot and character. Maggie couldn't write down his ideas fast enough. When she'd read them back to him, his eyes became the color of bright sapphires.

Rebecca was right—something had changed between them on opening night. Maggie couldn't put her finger on it. Charles's dating life was busier than ever. A few nights a week, he put on a tuxedo and went to dinner at the Stork Club or Tavern on the Green. He was invited to parties given by New York socialites and was photographed with actresses and models.

Part of Maggie's job became ordering flowers for his dates. He rarely took out the same woman twice, but there was a pretty cousin of Gloria Vanderbilt that he dated for three weeks. They were photographed at intimate restaurants, and the gossip columns predicted a Thanksgiving engagement.

Maggie told herself she was glad for Charles. He was successful and generous and deserved to be happy. But after he left in the evenings, she'd gaze at the gowns in her closet and wonder what she would wear if he invited her to dinner. She started reading *Vogue* to follow new designers like Claire McCardell and Norman Norell and spent a few afternoons browsing in the dress department of Bloomingdale's.

The biggest change was the atmosphere in the apartment when he arrived home after a date. Maggie would often be reading in the living room, and Charles would insist on pouring them each a nightcap. Then he would describe the evening, including the wine at dinner and the music the band played at the nightclub. Maggie expected to feel uncomfortable, but somehow they grew closer. As if the dinners and parties were events Charles had to participate in, and the real pleasure was sharing it with Maggie afterward.

Tonight, Charles was late for a cocktail party. He had called and asked Maggie to lay out his tuxedo. She took his shirt and jacket from the closet and opened the set of drawers. A jewelry box sat next to his bow tie. She clicked it open, thinking it was his cuff links. Instead, there was an engagement ring. The center stone was an emerald-cut solitaire, flanked by two rubies.

Maggie's eyes opened wider and she gasped.

Whom was Charles going to propose to? He had broken up with Helen Vanderbilt a few weeks earlier, and since then he had gone on only a few dates. He often said that one of the perks of success was that he could employ Ellen to do the cooking and cleaning. He didn't need a wife.

Without thinking, she slipped it on her finger. It felt heavy and elegant at the same time. She quickly took it off and put it back in the box.

The front door opened.

"Thank God you're home." Charles entered the bedroom. "Fifth Avenue is stop-and-go traffic, and I was afraid I was going to be late."

Maggie felt guilty. She shouldn't have been snooping in Charles's chest of drawers.

"Everything you need is laid out on the bed," she said awkwardly.

Charles walked to the mirror and untied his tie. He took off his blazer and slung it over the chair.

"Do you mind calling the car service while I get ready?" he asked. "Babe has booked a table at the dining room in the Plaza Hotel. She wants to introduce me to Anita Colby."

Anita Colby was a top model, with more magazine covers than any other model in America.

Babe Cushing Mortimer was the fashion editor at *Vogue*. She practically ruled New York society. When she was young, she was one of the wealthy "Cushing sisters." Recently, *Time* magazine named her the second-best-dressed woman in the world, behind Wallis Simpson.

Maggie walked to the telephone in the study. It had been foolish to try on the engagement ring. Tomorrow, she would donate the cocktail dresses and evening gown that Charles had given her to a local charity. He had plenty of women to date. He didn't need her to accompany him to theater openings and galas.

She was about to dial when there was a knock. She went to answer it. A man wearing a gray uniform stood in the hallway.

"Special delivery letter for Maggie Lane." The postman handed her an envelope.

Charles appeared in the entry. "Who was at the door?"

Maggie scanned the letter. Hospital Corpsman Third Class Jake Pullman had been fighting in the Battle of Leyte Gulf and was missing in action, presumed dead. Maggie's name was listed as his next of kin. Any further updates would be sent to her by the US Post Office Department.

A throbbing sounded in her ears, like a waterfall she had visited with her parents as a child. It couldn't be true. Jake had to be all right. It was the most important thing in the world. She read it again, the words swimming in front of her eyes.

The letter slipped to the floor and for the second time since she had known Charles, she fainted.

~

Maggie remembered that day so clearly. Waking up on the sofa, with Charles hovering over her. The weeks that followed, when she spent every second that she wasn't taking dictation or answering mail wondering if there had been some mistake and Jake was alive. And the guilty feeling that perhaps if she hadn't been infatuated with Charles's lifestyle, if she hadn't tried on that engagement ring, Jake would have been kept safe. She recalled the diamond ring Jake had hidden in the banana split at the Woolworth's lunch counter. Then, she had taken it back to the jeweler because if she'd kept it, Jake wouldn't return from the South Pacific. It had been one of the few times in her life that she was superstitious, but she told herself it was wartime, and she was allowed to believe in those kinds of things. She had worried that somehow Jake being missing was her fault. Gradually, she had relaxed and enjoyed herself with Charles and his circle, when she should have spent every moment being vigilant.

Even if Teddy loved her, he could be distracted by another woman. Just like she had been distracted by Charles. She slipped Alan's cigarette case back in Teddy's bedside drawer. She'd ask him about it tomorrow.

Chapter Twenty

Maggie sat in her dressing room at the television studio, drinking coffee.

Teddy had been gone before she woke up. He often went for an early-morning jog around Central Park. She wanted to wait to ask him about Alan's cigarette case, but Tommy's secretary called and said he needed her immediately at the studio.

Tommy poked his head in the door.

"I'm sorry I asked you to come in early," he apologized. "I've got some news, and it couldn't wait."

Maggie set down her coffee cup.

"Sally Knickerbocker wants to interview you for her gossip column in the *New York Post*. It's a special feature about the women who are changing television."

A feeling of dread passed through her.

"Sally Knickerbocker?" she repeated.

"My secretary scheduled it for this afternoon. A car will take you to her apartment."

"I can't," Maggie protested. "Doris Day is tomorrow's celebrity guest. I was going to spend the afternoon watching her movies."

"You can do that this evening," Tommy replied. "Sally's column is syndicated around the country. We can't pass it up."

Maggie knew that Tommy wouldn't back down. This was the kind of press that made *The Maggie Lane Baking Show*'s ratings climb even higher.

"No, of course not," Maggie agreed.

Tommy turned to the door.

"Deluxe Baking Company is very pleased with you, Maggie," he said. "If the show continues to be a success, there'll be more opportunities."

Maggie asked what he meant.

"They want to sponsor a prime-time variety hour, with you as the star." Tommy beamed. "You'd be on the air right after the evening news."

Being on a show during the family dinner hour was every television actor's dream. The pay was better than daytime, and she'd have triple the number of viewers.

"I'm already more successful than I ever imagined," Maggie said.

"You can never be too successful. Think about that apartment you and Teddy want to buy. With a prime-time spot, you could afford a penthouse on Park Avenue."

When Maggie arrived at Sally's apartment, she was greeted by a maid wearing a black-and-white uniform. The maid ushered her inside and asked her to wait in the living room. The living room was furnished in bold colors. A Lucite writing desk stood near the window, and there was a glass bar. A large portrait of Sally hung over the fireplace.

"Maggie, I'm glad you came." Sally swept into the room. She wore a yellow blouse over a pencil skirt. A scarf was tied around her neck.

"Your home is lovely," Maggie commented, taking off her gloves.

"Do you like it? The *New York Post* wanted to rent me something furnished, but I insisted on bringing my own things."

Sally sat on the sofa and motioned Maggie to sit opposite her.

"Teddy said you moved into his apartment when you got married," Sally continued. "That must be difficult. Couples often have different tastes."

For some reason, Maggie felt like she had to defend herself.

"His apartment was bigger than mine. I like his furniture. It's very comfortable."

"Still, I'm sure you'd rather decorate your own place," Sally persisted. "I heard you and Teddy want to buy something."

Maggie wondered whether Teddy had told her.

"Where did you hear that?" Maggie asked.

"New York is a small town. It's my business to know everything." Sally waved at the tray of cheese and crackers on the coffee table. "I had my maid prepare a snack while we get to know each other."

Sally picked up a notepad. "I want to know everything about you. When did you learn to bake, and what was it like growing up on a farm?"

Maggie tried to keep to her usual responses. She had been an only child. She was close to her parents, but it was still lonely. Some of her favorite times were when she and her parents listened to radio shows—*The Jell-O Program, The Pepsodent Show*—together in the evenings. That's when she developed her desire to go to New York. But her mind kept drifting off. She wondered whether Teddy had been in Sally's apartment.

"You and Teddy are lucky you found each other," Sally was saying. "It's hard for career women like us to find a husband. Most men are intimidated by successful women."

"I wasn't successful when Teddy and I met," Maggie said without thinking. She pulled her eyes away from the framed photographs of Sally displayed on the sideboard.

"That must be even more difficult." Sally picked up a cigarette. "Do you mind if I smoke?"

Maggie shook her head. She wanted to change the subject, but she didn't know how.

"On the contrary, Teddy is thrilled that I have my own television show. He's never been ambitious in his own career."

Sally lit her cigarette. She inhaled the smoke thoughtfully.

"My husband said the same sort of thing. He inherited his money and insisted he was happy playing polo and serving on charity boards. All men are competitive in one way or another. It wasn't that he was in love with the women he had affairs with, he just wanted to know he could have them if he wanted."

They talked about Maggie's old radio show and the commercials she did for Westinghouse.

"Why do you do *The Maggie Lane Baking Show*?" Sally stubbed her third cigarette into the ashtray.

Maggie could see how Sally stayed so slim. She hadn't touched the cheese and crackers.

"Before you answer, I'm not talking about Helen Jacobson's silly article in the *New York Times*," Sally said. "Of course, being on television is more interesting than being a housewife. Why a baking show? You're intelligent. You could host a program about art or theater."

Maggie shifted on the sofa. She wondered whether Sally was trying to make her feel uncomfortable.

"There's nothing wrong with being a housewife," Maggie disagreed. "And I don't know anything about the arts."

Sally looked at Maggie steadily. "Didn't you work for Charles Grey years ago? You must have learned something about the theater."

Maggie let out a gasp. No one had ever mentioned Charles before. She was tempted to lie and say she didn't know what Sally was talking about. But it was clear that Sally knew something about her past.

"I was his secretary for a short while. I answered letters and took dictation."

Sally opened her mouth to say something, and then seemed to change her mind.

"I saw one of his plays on Broadway," Sally replied. "He was very talented. Then he disappeared."

"That was after I stopped working for him," Maggie said.

Sally lit another cigarette. She leaned against the cushions.

"He left New York and just vanished," Sally continued. "I love a mystery. I suppose that's why I became a gossip columnist. You get to dig up so much dirt."

Maggie and Sally talked about the current plays on Broadway and the celebrities Sally had interviewed for her column. Finally, Maggie said goodbye and took the elevator down to the lobby. On the way home, she picked up a roasted chicken and salad for dinner. Teddy wasn't there when she arrived. Her mind reeled with questions. How did Sally know about Charles? Why was she interested in Maggie and Teddy's search for an apartment?

The front door opened as Maggie was tossing the salad. Teddy looked handsome in a pair of tan slacks and V-neck sweater. She was reminded of how much she loved him.

She was tempted to tell him everything about Jake and Charles. She'd ask whether he had an affair with Sally and what had happened with Arabella and Ian. But the morality clause she had signed meant she would probably lose her job. Teddy wasn't happy at work; he would probably quit and find something else. If they couldn't afford to live in New York anymore, they could move up to Rye. Teddy could do local radio, and Maggie would stay home and have children.

It sounded so easy, and they would be happy. Life would become a round of squash games and barbeques at the country club. But she loved being the host of *The Maggie Lane Baking Show*. And she would miss her friendship with Dolly, the ease of having Dolly just next door in the adjoining dressing room.

Teddy set a shopping bag on the kitchen counter.

"My mother called. She wants us to come to Rye this weekend." He unloaded the groceries. "She's having a dinner party. Everyone wants to meet her famous daughter-in-law."

"Of course. I'd love to go," Maggie said. "We could stop by that new development near Willow Road. The one with its own playground and tennis courts."

Teddy put a ketchup bottle in the pantry.

"Why would we do that?" His voice was tight. "It sounds like you already picked out our next apartment. The Realtor called. She had some news about your offer."

"I'll call her back after dinner." Maggie tried to keep her voice light, but Teddy's tone made her uneasy. The Realtor had suggested that she consult her husband first. But Maggie had been so excited about the apartment, she didn't want another buyer to make an offer. Now she wondered if she had made a mistake.

"You didn't tell me you were making an offer on an apartment." Teddy turned to her. His brow was furrowed, and she had never seen him look so angry. A feeling of foreboding overcame her. But she hadn't done anything wrong, and Teddy would love the apartment as much as she did.

"It's on Park Avenue. I saw it with Dolly and the Realtor yesterday," Maggie answered.

She described the television cabinet in the living room where Teddy could keep his record albums, and the his-and-her walk-in closets in the bedroom.

"I'm very sorry. It's all my fault. I wanted it to be a surprise. I was going to tell you tonight."

"Buying an apartment is one of the biggest decisions of our lives, and you didn't think to include me?" Teddy's voice bristled.

Maggie's stomach turned over.

"You helped Alan look at houses in Rye without telling Dolly," she reminded him. She knew it wasn't the same thing, but she had to do something to make Teddy less angry.

"That was between Alan and Dolly. They weren't even engaged," Teddy said. "You're my wife. I expect we'd make those kinds of decisions together."

Maggie wondered whether Sally had something to do with Teddy finding out about the offer on the apartment. She didn't know how to ask him. Instead, she decided to change the subject. She told Teddy about the interview and going to Sally's apartment.

"I haven't spoken to Sally since the CBS dinner," Teddy said.

Maggie's pulse throbbed. This was her chance to learn more about Sally. If she didn't ask about her now, she never would.

"After the dinner, you were going to return Alan's cigarette case. I found it in your bedside drawer. But you still came home late. When I asked if Alan thanked you for returning it, you didn't correct me."

Teddy's brow knotted together, as if he was working out what she was talking about.

"You think I went to Sally's," he said. "Sally was staying with the Whitneys. She went with them from the party to their house in East Hampton. She only got back a few days ago. If you don't believe me, ask Stephen Whitney. I saw him at the squash courts and he told me."

Maggie took the salad bowl into the dining alcove. She felt so miserable, she didn't know what to say.

"You don't trust me." Teddy followed her. "Ever since you became the star of *The Maggie Lane Baking Show*, you've been waiting for me to make a mistake. You want to fall out of love with me so you can find someone more suitable, like that brash young producer at the CBS awards dinner. The thing is, I'm squeaky clean. I might have run up the charge cards, but we talked about it and I stopped. Now all I do is clap at the right time during your speeches and pose for photographs so the gossip columns can write that Maggie Lane has a handsome husband.

"Well, I'm tired of it. And I'm tired of pretending that I'm happy being a content producer when my responsibilities are being taken over by younger men. I'm going to do some thinking." He walked to the door. "I'll stay at Alan's tonight. You don't need to stay up."

The front door banged.

Maggie was too shocked to move. Her skin felt icy, and a prickle ran down her neck. She stared at the dining table set with salad plates and water glasses. Her eyes went to the coffee table, where the latest *Vogue* sat next to Teddy's magazines. The living room looked so warm and inviting, she wondered why she wanted to live somewhere new.

The problem in their marriage wasn't about finding the right apartment. It was about becoming close to each other. Teddy said his behavior was squeaky clean, but Maggie wasn't sure if that was true. There was something between him and Sally. She could feel it.

Teddy could get a new job and they could move to Rye, but it might not solve anything. There would be more fights, and Maggie would be alone, without Dolly to talk to. She would have given up her career and her life in New York.

She had to find another way to solve whatever was bothering Teddy. It went back further than when she got the role on television. The nights before they were married when he tossed and turned in bed were caused by something that happened during the war.

She placed the salad bowl in the fridge and went into the bedroom. If she confronted Teddy about the photos, she'd have to admit that she had looked at them without telling him. He'd be furious, and she wouldn't blame him. It was unlike her. She respected people's privacy. But once she had discovered the notebook, she kept going back to it.

This time, she detached the envelope from the back cover. In the bottom was a folded piece of paper.

Maggie smoothed it on the bed. It was a magazine article from August 1944.

~

Many people believe the British aristocracy had an easier war than the rest of the population. They suffered some hardships, of course. Their country estates were borrowed by the British government and became field hospitals and command centers. They were asked to take in young children, who often misbehaved because they longed for their own parents. And even though many young men used their family connections to avoid the fighting and get safe office jobs, a significant number went overseas and fought valiantly for their country.

For the young women of the British aristocracy, the war was just as difficult. They could join the Auxiliary Territorial Service or become a Wren, which was the naval equivalent, but that meant performing tasks they had never done before in strange, new surroundings. During my years as a war correspondent in London, I met many young duchesses living in some unheated dormitory, without any of the comforts of home. They seemed as lost and frightened as Alice in Wonderland in the famous children's book.

To make matters worse, many of the young women got engaged at the beginning of the war, so they weren't able to ease the tension of blackouts and air raids by having a wartime romance. And in the back of their minds was the constant dread that one of the men brought on a stretcher could be their own fiancé.

But I met a few aristocratic young women who were so brave, and so unaware of their own bravery, they left an impression that will stay with me.

Lady Arabella Cousins was one of these women. She was nineteen, the age that most American young women are in college, or living at home and attending secretarial school. She had already seen more tragedy and heartache than many women see in their lifetimes.

I met Arabella through a mutual friend, Teddy Buckley. Teddy was the voice of Pathé News. We at home all heard Teddy's reports about the war in Europe. For many, his evening programs, delivered in his honeyed voice, were one of the few bright spots during that dark time.

Arabella was the typical lovely English rose. Fair hair, peach-colored complexion, and the widest hazel eyes, like Scarlett O'Hara in *Gone with the Wind*. She knew she was beautiful, so she flirted outrageously with men.

She was flirting with Teddy when we met, and I almost thought they were a couple. But then another man entered the bar at Claridge's. He was handsome, reddish-blond hair, blue eyes, an aquiline nose. His name was Ian Macmanus. He was Irish, and a lieutenant in the army.

Arabella was in love with Ian. Her parents would never approve because of his background, so she was using Teddy as a go-between. The three of them spent all their free time together. Ian was in love with Arabella too, but she didn't encourage him. She was afraid that he would propose and she would have to turn him down.

Then Ian was sent on a secret mission, which turned out to be D-Day. Arabella was a Wren, so he asked her to come and she agreed. But only if Teddy went too. Arabella was afraid she would reveal her feelings to Ian if they were abroad together, and their wonderful flirtation would be over.

Teddy had no interest in going to France. He had been there earlier in the war, and it frightened him. But he was the kind of man who would do anything for a friend. He agreed, and the three of them crossed the channel together.

D-Day was a success, of course. Teddy got some good material for Pathé News, and Arabella and Ian spent time together. Then Arabella had the idea to take a jeep and visit a vineyard in the Haute-Vienne region that she'd read about. They'd have a few more days together and then return to England.

But they stumbled across one of the most terrible tragedies of the war. The massacre of the village of Oradour-sur-Glane.

The Germans believed that resistance fighters had killed a German officer. To retaliate, they entered the little village and killed all its inhabitants. It was the tenth of June, and by the end of the day, 643 men, women, and children were dead.

Arabella and Teddy and Ian were staying in the barn of a local couple overnight. Arabella walked into the village and saw everything that had happened. She rushed back to the barn and told Teddy what she had seen. They ran back to the village to see if they could help any survivors, but it was too late. All the women and children had been taken into the church and burned. The men were led to barns and sheds and shot in the legs so they couldn't move. Then they were doused in fuel and set on fire.

Arabella would never forget it. One never knew how long one had to live. The important thing was to lead a life of love and kindness.

The next time I saw Arabella was at a house party in Sussex. The party was to announce her engagement to Ian. She had convinced her parents to let her marry him, even though he was the furthest thing from the British aristocracy. She was not only brave enough to return to the village when the Germans could have been nearby, she was also brave enough to stand up to her aristocratic parents in the name of love.

It's stories like Lady Arabella's that give me hope for a better world after the war.

Maggie skipped to the end of the article. The byline was Sally Matheson. Matheson must have been Sally's maiden name, before she married her husband.

The paper was wet, and she realized that she'd been crying. How could Teddy live with such a memory? No wonder he had nightmares and woke up bathed in sweat. The entire event was unimaginable. If only he had told her, she would have tried to help him through it. Were there other reasons he hadn't told her? Was Sally there to comfort him, and had something occurred between them?

Somehow, she always thought Teddy would tell her what happened during the war when he was ready. But he never had.

Chapter Twenty-One

Maggie hardly slept all night. She couldn't stop thinking about what Teddy and Arabella and Ian had witnessed in Oradour-sur-Glane. If only Teddy had told her, they could have faced it together. But how could she be angry with him when she never said anything about Jake and Charles?

The next morning, he wasn't home before she left for the television studio.

Her dressing room felt cold. She buttoned her cardigan and turned on the radio. They were playing an episode of *Father Knows Best*. It was one of her and Teddy's favorite radio programs.

Dolly poked her head in. She wore a pleated skirt and cotton blouse. Her hair was styled in a wave that curled at her shoulders.

"I called the apartment, but no one answered." She took a piece of dry toast from the sideboard.

Maggie watched her. "You could add butter to that toast."

"No, thank you." Dolly shook her head. "I shouldn't be eating bread at all. The wardrobe department complained that my skirts are too tight. But I can't just drink coffee in the mornings, because my hands start shaking."

"Your hands wouldn't shake if you stopped taking those pills," Maggie said firmly.

"Remember, I tried that before. Stopping the pills didn't do anything except make me feel sluggish."

"You only stopped taking them for two days," Maggie reminded her. "You need to give it longer than that."

"And risk not being my best in front of the camera?" Dolly raised her eyebrows. "I'd be fired and replaced by some perky young actress. The doctor said the pills are harmless as long as I don't take too many. I cut down on how many I take. I'm fine."

Maggie didn't believe that Dolly had cut back. She was still too thin. Her hips were narrow beneath her skirt.

She told Dolly about her fight with Teddy. He had stormed out of the house, and she didn't know where he had spent the night.

"What are you going to do?" Dolly asked.

"Teddy can be stubborn. He won't talk until he's ready," Maggie reflected. "What if he went to see Sally?"

Dolly ate a bite of toast. "Teddy is smart enough not to jeopardize his marriage over a woman like Sally. She only cares about herself and that column. He just needs time. Give him a few days to think it through. I promise, he'll come home and apologize. Why don't you come to dinner tonight to get your mind off it? My mother is making matzo ball soup and roasted chicken."

It was Friday night. Dolly's mother was preparing the Shabbat dinner.

"I thought you were going to invite Alan."

"I asked him. He said he had to work late, but I found out that he's going on a date. Her name is Rachel Silverman. Her mother is friends with Alan's mother in Cleveland." Dolly's eyes were wide. "She's Jewish, of course. But I can't blame him. I met her. She's a customer at the shoe store. She's pretty and intelligent. She's studying to be a doctor."

Maggie reminded Dolly that Alan was in love with her.

"Alan is too nice to break up with me formally," Dolly fretted. "But he won't marry outside the religion. When he finds out I lied, our relationship will be over." She played with her pearl necklace. "We're going to lunch today. I'll tell him then. I can't put it off any longer."

Maggie felt terrible for Dolly. "I'll come over for dinner tonight," she promised.

"You can help me break the news to my mother." Dolly sighed. "She spends half her time standing near the telephone. She keeps expecting Alan to call to ask for my hand in marriage."

After Dolly left, Maggie went over the show notes. Her celebrity guest was Barbara Hutton. Any other time, she would have been thrilled. Barbara Hutton was one of the most sought-after socialites in New York. The gossip columns said that at her dinner parties, the courses were served on 24-karat-gold plates. She kept bottles of Chanel No. 5 in every room of her Fifth Avenue townhouse. And she never went anywhere without her Hermès handbag and her poodle.

But today, Maggie couldn't stop thinking about Teddy. She called the apartment, but there was no answer. She was about to go on the set when the phone rang.

"Maggie, this is Nancy," the Realtor said. "There's been another offer on the apartment."

"That's impossible. You said it wasn't officially on the market."

"It wasn't," Nancy replied. "The owners didn't want just anyone tromping over their parquet floors. But when there's an apartment in such a coveted building, word gets out. The offer was waiting on my desk this morning."

Maggie recalled the gracious proportions of the rooms. The shiny new appliances in the kitchen. The bedroom with mirrored walls and matching glass pineapples on the bedside tables. She'd never find another apartment like it.

"I haven't shown the other offer to my client yet," Nancy confided. "There was something odd about it. The buyer wants to meet with you. He left his phone number."

Maggie wound the phone cord around her wrist.

"If he's trying to start a bidding war, I'm not interested," she said. "I already offered more than I want to pay."

"His name is Charles Grey. He's at LE7-5000. I don't usually condone this kind of thing, but I know how much you love the apartment. It wouldn't hurt to meet with him."

Maggie said goodbye and hung up. A chill passed through her, and she sank onto the chair.

She hadn't heard Charles's name in years; now she heard it twice in a few days. Sally must have had something to do with this. It didn't make sense. If Maggie refused to meet with Charles and took back her own offer, Charles would be left with an expensive apartment that he might not want.

If he was so anxious to see her, he could have phoned the television studio. But he would know that she would have refused to take his call.

Her mind went to the months after the letter came that Jake was missing in action. Charles had practically smothered her with care and attention. She had been so young, and she had been in love only once before. How could she have known what to do?

~

For weeks after Maggie received the letter about Jake, she barely left her bedroom in Charles's apartment. Ellen brought bowls of soup and sandwiches on a tray. Maggie sat up in bed, eating chicken soup, and wondered when the choking feeling would go away.

She went over her actions in the month before she received the letter. Attending the opening of Charles's play, lunches with Lou and Charles while they discussed their next project, afternoon strolls with Charles around Central Park. She recalled trying on pretty dresses at Macy's and sampling perfumes at Lord & Taylor.

She couldn't help wondering if she had thought more about Jake, if she had written to him daily, would he be alive. There was no one she could talk to. Charles wouldn't understand that if she had stopped buying *Vogue* or reading the society pages of the *New York Times*, Jake would appear at the door. Maggie knew she was being silly. But she had refused

Jake's marriage proposal because she wanted to keep him safe, and she had failed. Every morning she woke up and pictured finding the diamond ring in the banana split at the Woolworth's lunch counter. Going with Jake to the jewelry store and demanding the jeweler take back the ring. Now her behavior seemed so young and starry eyed. But she had told herself she had to return the ring to keep Jake from becoming distracted and putting himself in danger. If only she had been right and it had worked.

After a few weeks, Charles insisted she get dressed and go outside. They visited the New York Public Library and went to exhibits at the Metropolitan Museum of Art. He took her for long drives to Long Island. Lou gave them lunch, and on the way home they picked up crab from a crab stand in East Hampton.

Every weekend, Charles went away. He never said where he was going. She kept expecting him to return with an attractive woman on his arm and announce that he was engaged. She didn't check if the diamond ring was still in the drawer. It wasn't any of her business.

It was late on a Monday afternoon. Maggie sat at the desk in the living room, responding to letters. After the weekend, Mondays were almost a relief. It was easier to take dictation and pick up office supplies than to wander around the neighborhood and pass the apartment buildings where she had dreamed of living with Jake.

Charles entered. He was holding a cup of coffee. The pages of his new play weren't working. He had rewritten them three times, and he still wasn't pleased.

"Pack an overnight bag," he said. "We're going away."

"Going where?" Maggie asked.

"You'll see when we get there." He filled a briefcase with a notebook and pens. "I don't know why I didn't think of this sooner."

They drove out of Manhattan and onto the Taconic Parkway. The car wound through the Hudson Valley. Barns dotted the countryside. Fields were white with a thick layer of snow.

Charles turned at the sign that read WELCOME TO RHINEBECK. He stopped in front of a hotel with white columns and a slanted black roof.

"The Beekman Arms is one of the oldest inns in America," he said, stepping out and opening Maggie's door.

Maggie stayed in the passenger seat. She wasn't going to stay at a hotel with Charles.

"I promise, it's perfectly innocent. I called ahead and asked for two rooms," Charles said.

Maggie swung her overnight bag out of the back seat. A stone path led to the front door. Oak trees were covered with snow. Through the hotel windows, Maggie could see a fireplace and a table with books.

The lobby was furnished with upholstered armchairs. A map of the Hudson Valley during the eighteenth century hung on the wall. In a corner was an old-fashioned writing desk. A plate of cookies sat next to a backgammon board.

Charles had stayed there years before, when he was writing his first play.

"Our rooms are on other sides of the hotel." He handed Maggie a key. "Go change and meet me in the dining room." He smiled for the first time since they left New York. "Dinner is casual. I didn't bring a suit and tie."

Maggie's room was in the original carriage house. There was a four-poster bed and an ottoman draped with a blanket. The window overlooked the garden. Maggie changed out of her dress into a wool sweater and skirt. She brushed her hair and put on lipstick.

Charles was waiting when she reentered the lobby. He looked debonair in a blue turtleneck and plaid sport coat.

"You look lovely," he greeted her. "Let's go eat. The fresh country air always makes me hungry."

The maître d' seated them at a table near the fireplace. Charles ordered oysters to start and a rib eye steak to share.

The Beekman Arms was built before the Revolutionary War. George Washington and Alexander Hamilton had stayed there. It had been a hotel ever since.

"You still haven't told me why we're here," Maggie said after the waiter took away their oysters.

"If I don't turn in finished pages soon, the producers will withdraw their funding." Charles sipped a glass of red wine. "At first, I thought I couldn't write because I was taking care of you. But Ellen did the cooking and brought your meals; I hardly did anything. Then I thought it was being in New York during the winter. So I accepted Lou's invitation and spent the weekends in his guest cottage."

"That's where you've been," Maggie said before she could stop herself.

"I should have told you, but I was embarrassed. I hoped all I needed was a change of scenery. Lou's guest cottage is outfitted like a suite at the Beverly Hills Hotel. Smoked salmon and caviar in the fridge. A small study with whiskey and cigars. But every weekend he held a party. Limousines would drive up and the most beautiful men and women would spill out." He paused. "Rebecca was often there. You met her at the play's opening."

Maggie glanced down at her plate so Charles didn't see her expression. Charles and Rebecca had a fling in Boston. Maybe they rekindled it. He bought the engagement ring for her. Maggie wondered why the idea bothered her. She wondered if she was jealous.

Maggie had become deeply fond of Charles. She thought about the last few months. Opening night of the play, with the after-party at Sardi's and waiting anxiously for the reviews. Charles telling everyone at their table that without Maggie the play would still be pages in his notebook. The following weeks when the days hummed with fan mail to answer and requests for tickets to the play. The interesting gifts that arrived at the apartment and the parade of fascinating people stopping by for cocktails.

Then the letter came that Jake was missing in action and presumed dead. Maggie lay in bed and believed that his fate was her fault. She tried to push aside her guilt. Deep down she knew that it didn't accomplish anything and only made things worse. She had to focus on what was real. Charles had been a great help. He was so kind. He let her grieve, and then he slowly brought her back to life. The walks around the neighborhood, the delicious crab and clam chowder they brought back from Long Island. Afternoons at museums where for a while she could put Jake out of her mind.

Charles had been there when she needed him. He never asked questions about Jake, and he didn't comment when she spent hours sitting on her bed and going through photographs of them together. And Maggie had fun with Charles. He was bigger than life, and he belonged to a world that was intoxicating. When he threw a cocktail party at the apartment or took her with him to shop for a new blazer, she was reminded that life could be enjoyable. She didn't know what she would have done without him.

She recalled Rebecca saying that Jake might not return, so Maggie should grab happiness when she found it. She opened her mouth to say something, but Charles was still talking.

"Rebecca wants to invest in an overseas production of the play. Once the war ends, we're going to Paris and London to check out theaters."

Her thoughts were cut short.

"You and Rebecca are going to Paris?" she repeated.

"It was Rebecca's idea. People will be clamoring for entertainment." He nodded. "I've never been to Paris, but Rebecca has an apartment there."

She wanted to ask if Lou would go too.

"It's too soon to think about. I've got to get the damn thing written," he continued. "This afternoon I remembered the Beekman Arms." He looked at Maggie. "I didn't want to go alone. I need you, Maggie. You've come to mean so much to me."

Charles was looking at her. His expression had changed. He was about to say something else, but the waiter set down their plates.

Charles took a bite of the steak. He put down his fork.

"I want to ask you something. No matter how you answer, I promise I won't ask again."

The dining room felt so quiet, she could hear her heart pounding.

"You can ask me anything."

His face broke into a smile. "I've never asked you to work after dinner before, but I wondered if tonight we could make an exception.

We're only going to be here a few days, and I don't want to waste a minute."

Maggie cut into her steak. It was rarer than she liked.

"Of course we can work after dinner. Isn't that why we're here?"

They ate steak with creamed spinach and talked about the war and the plays on Broadway. Maggie wasn't listening. She felt silly for thinking that Charles was interested in her. The address book he kept on his desk was filled with the most beautiful women in New York.

She tried to conjure Jake up in her mind. The first time they met at the Strand Bookstore. Jake was boyish and handsome, with his blue eyes and that wonderful smile. He gave her a book to read, and afterward they ate lunch at the counter at Woolworth's.

She remembered the last day of his leave, when she planned a special steak dinner at Keens but he insisted they go to Woolworth's instead. She had been disappointed because she thought she didn't mean anything to him. Then the clerk brought out the banana split with the diamond ring on top, and she realized that Jake brought her there to propose.

It felt so long ago. She wasn't even twenty. She couldn't mourn Jake for the rest of her life.

Charles was only interested in her as his secretary. As soon as the play was finished, he'd start dating again. Charles was almost thirty. He was rich and successful. He could have any woman he wanted.

Charles suggested they have a nightcap after dessert, but Maggie refused. She wanted to get straight to work. It would be less painful to sit opposite Charles holding a pen and notebook than across a candlelit dining table.

She waited for him in the hotel's library while he went upstairs to get his notes.

He handed her a small package when he returned. "This is for you."

Maggie opened it. Inside was a silver locket. There was a charm of the Empire State Building.

"It's your birthday next month. I wanted to get something special," Charles said. "I told Rebecca how much you love New York, and she picked it out."

Maggie tried to be happy, but the gift felt childish. It wasn't the type of necklace that someone who was elegant and worldly like Rebecca would wear.

"Thank you." She fastened it around her neck. "It's lovely."

Charles paced around the room.

"Rebecca and I had a long talk." He slid his hands in his pockets. "She's a big admirer of yours. In fact, she said I couldn't choose anyone better. You're beautiful and smart."

"I enjoy being your secretary," Maggie acknowledged.

"She wasn't talking about being my secretary. We were discussing something else. I told her I wanted to ask you to marry me." He gave a sheepish smile. "She said it was about time. That I'd been in love with you for ages."

Maggie gasped. Charles just admitted that he was in love with her. She was so unprepared for his revelation that his words barely registered. She looked at him and her eyes were wide. "She said that?"

Charles nodded. "I started falling in love with you the first months you were at the apartment. Everything was new to you, and I saw New York through fresh eyes," he continued. "And you were loyal to Jake. Even if I was jealous, I admired that. You worked so hard on the play without complaining. On opening night, all I wanted was to be alone with you."

He drew a jewelry box out of his pocket.

"That's when I bought this. I practiced a hundred times how I would propose." He opened it. "Then the letter came about Jake. And I couldn't do it. I didn't want you to think I was taking advantage of the situation."

It was the emerald-cut diamond and ruby ring she found in his drawer. It looked beautiful in the yellow light of the library.

"Maggie, I don't know if you have feelings for me. But if you say yes, I promise I'll give you a life of happiness." Charles got down on his knee. "Will you marry me?"

Charles gazed up at her. His expression was so hopeful. He seemed nervous, not his usual confident self. She asked herself if she had feelings for him. It was so hard to tell. She would never have survived the months since she received the letter about Jake without Charles's warmth and support. But being in love with Charles was a different thing entirely. She had only been in love once with Jake, so she had almost nothing to compare it to. She did find Charles attractive, and they got along so well. Surely that was a type of love. Perhaps what she had felt for Jake was rare. Perhaps her feelings toward Charles were more similar to what most married couples felt for each other.

Until recently, Charles's way of life had been so foreign to her. She thought about the women he had been photographed with in the gossip columns. If the next play was a success, there would be more rounds of cocktail parties and dinners. Would she ever fit in, or would Charles and his friends always see her as his secretary? A girl who grew up on a farm, whom he rescued like Eliza Doolittle in the George Bernard Shaw play *Pygmalion*.

If they got married, they'd live in Charles's world. She'd never have the opportunity to achieve anything of her own. But she didn't know what she wanted to do. They could start a family. Wouldn't that make her happy?

She remembered Rebecca's warning about Charles. The most important thing to him was how he was perceived by others in his circle. What if she did something that embarrassed him? He could turn on her, and then she'd have nothing. That was being silly. She and Charles would be a team, the way they were now.

She couldn't think of a reason to say no.

"Yes, I'll marry you," she answered.

Charles wrapped his arms around her and kissed her. It was different from Jake's kisses. His had been uncertain and urgent. Charles placed his mouth firmly on hers. His lips were warm, and she could smell his cologne. Her body seemed to be lit by an inner flame, and she was reminded again of how attractive he was. She must be in love with him. It was almost impossible to believe that he was holding her, that he wanted her to be his forever.

"I'm too excited to work. Let's take a stroll around the grounds," he suggested.

They put on their coats and walked around the gardens. The sky was bright with stars. The moon was completely round. They talked about the wedding. Charles insisted on a church wedding. They could get married at Trinity Church and have a dinner dance at the Pierre.

"I hardly know anyone in New York," Maggie said pensively. "We could get married at city hall and host a small lunch afterwards. I'll ask Rebecca to be a witness. Lou could be one too."

"I don't care if the whole church is empty." Charles squeezed her hand. "I want to see my beautiful bride walk down the aisle in a white dress."

Charles was right. She had always dreamed of a church wedding. And once the gossip columns found out that Charles was getting married, everyone would want an invitation.

"All right, I won't argue," she said with a laugh. "I'll ask Rebecca to help plan the reception. We can't have any mistakes at a Charles Grey production."

They did another lap around the gardens, but Maggie was cold even with her coat. Charles suggested they go up to his room for a nightcap. This time she said yes. She and Charles had been alone in the apartment's living room dozens of times. There was nothing to worry about.

Charles had a suite in the Old Firehouse, which had once been the firehouse in Rhinebeck. The walls were exposed brick. There was a small sitting room with a fireplace.

He poured two glasses of brandy and handed her one. She had been in his bedroom before, but this felt more intimate. Ellen wasn't somewhere in the apartment, and there was no television or phonograph.

"We should get to work." She set her glass on the coffee table.

"Let's think about the play later. We have so many details to work out." Charles sat on an armchair. "We can move to a new apartment if you like, or you can furnish the apartment in your taste."

"I like it the way it is," she said truthfully. "And I don't want to move."

"I'm glad. Neither do I." He stood up. "Maggie, you're so lovely. Is it all right if I kiss you again?"

She nodded, and he put his mouth on hers. As his hands caressed her blouse, a shot of desire ran through her. She wondered whether Charles knew she was a virgin, or did he think she and Jake had made love?

The kiss ended and Maggie stepped back. It had started to snow. She would have to walk outside to reach her room in the carriage house.

"You can stay here tonight," Charles offered, as if he were reading her thoughts. "I'll sleep on the sofa in the sitting room."

Charles looked so sophisticated. The turtleneck and blazer suited him. The flame that had licked her body earlier grew stronger. Perhaps it was the wine combined with the brandy, but all her inhibitions fell away. She tried not to think about whether they should wait until they were married to make love. At this moment, she wanted to go to bed with Charles more than she had wanted anything.

"I'd rather not walk back to my room." She tried to sound confident and mature. "You don't have to sleep on the sofa."

Charles hung up his blazer. He moved over to her and unbuttoned her blouse. Maggie stood on tiptoe and brought her mouth to his. His arms wrapped around her and he groaned.

Maggie stepped out of her skirt and unrolled her stockings. Charles unfastened her bra. His hands moved from her breasts to her stomach, and down to her thighs. She felt a yearning and pressed her body against his.

Charles kissed her again, deeper this time. He took off his turtleneck and slacks and they walked to the bed. They lay together and explored each other's bodies. Maggie ran her hands over his chest. She wanted to touch the hard thing between his thighs, but she was too embarrassed.

Then, his kisses became more insistent, and he rolled on top of her. His body was strong and warm. Her legs opened and he was inside her, and her thoughts slipped away.

She grabbed his shoulders and tried to catch his rhythm. But he moved faster, and she couldn't catch up. The hot, white flare of desire became a pain that overwhelmed her. She let out a yelp and her body tightened. Charles pushed harder and fell against her.

They lay together for a long time before Charles spoke. "You didn't tell me you were a virgin."

"I never thought this would happen," Maggie answered. A wave of remorse overcame her. Jake had never asked her to go to bed with him in the short time they were together. This was different. She and Charles were engaged; soon they'd be married. There was nothing to be ashamed about.

Charles propped himself on his side and kissed her.

"Then we'll take it slowly. We have all the time in the world."

~

Maggie glanced at the piece of paper with Charles's phone number. If she ignored it, he would find another way to contact her. She turned to the dressing room mirror and gave her hair a quick brush.

First, she'd record today's episode of *The Maggie Lane Baking Show*. Then she'd call Charles.

Chapter Twenty-Two

After the show finished taping, Maggie left a message with Charles's answering service. Then she walked home to the apartment.

Teddy was in the bedroom when she arrived. His eyes were bloodshot, and he hadn't shaved. He wore a striped sweater and tan slacks.

"Maggie, you're home," he said.

"I live here," she tried to joke.

Teddy glanced at his watch. "It's not even six o'clock. You usually stay later at the television studio."

Maggie noticed Teddy's overnight bag in front of the closet. She took a breath.

"Are you going somewhere?" she asked evenly.

Teddy folded a shirt into the bag. He sat on the bed, and rubbed his forehead.

"I spent last night at Alan's. I think it's better if I spend more nights away. Just while we sort things out."

Her heart beat a little faster. She turned her head so Teddy wouldn't see her surprised expression. How had things gotten so bad between them? She wondered if Teddy was leaving her. Her knees buckled, and she put a hand on the wall to steady herself. She couldn't let herself fall apart in front of Teddy; it would only make things worse. She tried to keep her voice from shaking.

She turned back to him. "If you don't want to stay married, you can tell me."

"Of course I want to stay married." His voice was impatient. "But this isn't working. It's not your fault. I pushed you to get married in the first place. And it was my idea that you do *The Maggie Lane Baking Show*." He stood up and took a sweater from his drawer. "But if you don't dislike me now, you will soon. I'm holding you back, Maggie."

Teddy looked so determined. As if they were discussing how she should ask for a raise. But they were talking about their marriage. Maggie wanted to tell him that nothing that happened in her career could change her feelings for him. Anyway, he was wrong. He had always been supportive. He arranged the surprise dinner at the Carlyle Restaurant with Alan and Dolly, and he defended her when they ran into Helen Jacobson at the gala. She could tell by his expression that he wouldn't listen. He might even argue that any husband would do what he had done, that she needed more and should be married to someone who was as successful as she was. It was better not to say anything.

"We've been married for a while, and we never talk about having children," he continued. "I want a family soon."

Teddy was right. When Maggie got the role on television, they stopped planning their future. She did want children, but she didn't know when.

"We're still young," she said.

"Our friends are having babies," Teddy countered. "It's not going to happen if we keep buying bigger apartments in New York. Children need fresh air and a place to play."

Maggie was shocked. They both wanted to stay in New York. Teddy was changing how he felt.

"I know that couples raise children in New York. But if we have a choice, I'd rather move to the suburbs," he continued. "That won't be possible if we're both working in the city."

For the first time since she arrived home, Maggie was angry. Teddy was negating everything that they had been working toward. Until now, he wanted to live in New York as much as she did. And how could he be upset about not having children yet when they hadn't even discussed it? He wasn't being fair. He was blaming her for things that he found wrong in their marriage that weren't her fault.

"You sound like Helen Jacobson. I'm supposed to chain myself to the kitchen and only leave the house to drive to the supermarket." She paced around the room. "Well, you're right. I do love my job, and I love New York. There are plenty of apartments on Park Avenue or Fifth Avenue that are big enough to raise a family. And Central Park is outside the door. Not to mention the museums nearby. You're using all that as an excuse. You don't love me."

Teddy was quiet for a long time. He finished packing.

"I'll call you before I go to sleep. For the record, I do love you, Maggie. That's not what this is about."

After Teddy left, Maggie sank onto the sofa in the living room. Her whole body felt numb, and there was a dullness in her head. She tried to remember their previous argument. Then she had said she would move to Rye if he wanted to, and this time she insisted they stay in New York. They were talking in circles.

She wished she could call Teddy's mother. Patty knew Teddy so well, she might be able to help. But that wouldn't be fair to anyone.

The apartment felt so empty. She grabbed her jacket and handbag and locked the door. Couples had fights all the time. Whatever they were going through, they would work it out. Yet she couldn't escape the feeling of dread. Even if it was only for a few nights, Teddy had actually left. What if he didn't come back?

She ordered a bowl of soup in a diner, but she couldn't finish it. After dinner, she strolled down Lexington Avenue. There was a painting in an art gallery that would look wonderful in the new apartment. It was modern with splashes of color, the kind of thing that she and Teddy loved. But she couldn't get excited.

What advice would she give a viewer? Most of her audience loved being wives and mothers. The best part of their day was turning on the television and watching her show after they had seen their husband off at the train station and put the baby down for a nap.

Helen Jacobson was right—Maggie was an impostor. But she had worked hard to get where she was, and she loved her career. She didn't want to give it up. Marriage was about compromise. Shouldn't Teddy support her, like she supported him?

On the way home, she stopped at the pharmacy. Sally Knickerbocker was standing in the aisle. She wore a stylish wool coat and long gloves. Maggie was about to walk out, but Sally stopped her.

"Maggie, this is a coincidence." Sally approached her. A scarf covered her dark curls. Her cheeks were powdered, and she wore lipstick.

Maggie couldn't ignore her. She had to be polite.

"It's nice to see you," Maggie replied.

"I usually shop at a pharmacy closer to my apartment. This is your neighborhood, isn't it?" Sally inquired.

"Teddy and I live a few blocks away," Maggie acknowledged.

"It's very convenient, and there are lovely buildings. But I can see why you want to move. There's nothing like being on Central Park."

Maggie wanted to ask if Sally had told Charles about the new apartment. But she didn't even know if Sally and Charles knew each other, though she suspected it.

"By the way, your interview comes out next week," Sally continued. "I hope you'll be pleased. My editor loved it. You and Teddy are the 'it couple' of New York."

Sally drifted off. Maggie picked out a lipstick and face cream and stood in line for the cash register. Sally was talking to the clerk.

"Do you carry Bayer aspirin? A friend has a terrible headache."

The clerk handed her a bottle with a pink label. Sally set it on the counter along with her other purchases.

Maggie froze. Teddy took Bayer aspirin when he had a headache. Sometimes he used it at night if he couldn't sleep.

What if Teddy had lied? He wasn't staying at Alan's. He was at Sally's. She tried to imagine how she would feel if they were having an affair. Would it be possible to continue in their marriage even if Teddy wanted to? Teddy had always been so loyal and loving. She had never worried about him being with another woman. But now her fears about Sally and Teddy's shared past returned, and a chill ran through her. She put the lipstick and face cream on the counter and hurried outside.

She entered the apartment and walked to the bedroom. The bed looked too large without Teddy. She missed seeing his slippers at the foot of the bed and his slacks draped over an armchair.

She made a cup of tea and brought it back to the bedroom. Seeing Sally had shaken her more than she realized. She kept thinking about Teddy and Arabella and Ian. And about the house party in the summer of 1944 where Arabella and Ian had announced their engagement. Sally had written about it in her article. It had taken place a couple of months after the tragedy of Oradour-sur-Glane. Teddy must have still been devastated from what he had witnessed. His two best friends were getting married, and he was alone. Sally was a fellow American and beautiful in her way. Perhaps they started a love affair.

Then the war ended, and they went on with their lives. But what if they still had feelings for each other? Sally was the kind of woman who would ignore the fact that Teddy was married to get what she wanted.

She thought of all the instances when Teddy had asked her to marry him before she finally said yes. In a small way, Maggie blamed herself that their marriage was in trouble. She hadn't shown Teddy enough how much she cared about him. At the same time, she hadn't allowed herself to feel confident in their love. Instead, she spent too much time dwelling on what happened with Jake and Charles. If only she could talk to Teddy and make him see the good things in their marriage, she knew they could make it work.

But what if it was too late to tell him how much she needed him?

Chapter Twenty-Three

The next morning, Charles's answering service called and said Charles would meet her for lunch at Tavern on the Green. Maggie wondered why he hadn't called himself. Perhaps he was afraid that if Maggie heard his voice, she would hang up.

She wished she could have asked Dolly what to wear, but her friend knew nothing about Charles and Jake. She decided on a calf-length pencil skirt and cashmere sweater. She accessorized it with her Bendel handbag and a silk scarf.

Charles was sitting at the bar when she arrived. He looked the same. His blond hair was worn a little shorter, and there were lines on his forehead. But he still had those emerald-green eyes and firm jaw.

Maggie wished she hadn't come. She put her hand on the wall to steady herself. When she had walked out of the apartment for the last time, she thought she'd never see him again.

Charles jumped up and walked over to her.

"Maggie, you're here." He leaned forward to kiss her cheek, but she moved away. He picked up his cocktail and pointed to a table in the back.

"I asked the maître d' if we could sit far from the window. You're so famous we won't be able to talk." He took her arm. "I would have chosen a different restaurant, but I thought it was better this way. So that your husband, Teddy, doesn't think you're hiding something."

Maggie flinched. "How do you know Teddy's name?"

She let him lead her to the table. They sat opposite each other, and she placed her handbag on the floor. The waiter appeared and took her order for an orange juice.

"You and Teddy are in every society section and gossip column," Charles said. "Whoever would have thought that Maggie Lane would become one of the most well-known faces on television?"

Maggie protested that she wasn't really an actress. She was the host of a daytime cooking show.

"I'm in show business, remember." Charles sipped his cocktail. "You're America's sweetheart. The other day I was at the supermarket, and there was a life-size cardboard figure of you in the baking aisle. You were on the cover of *Life* magazine, and you started doing nighttime talk shows. Every actor in America would kill to be on *The Ed Sullivan Show*."

Tommy had been over the moon when Maggie was asked to be on *The Ed Sullivan Show*. The week following her appearance, *The Maggie Lane Baking Show*'s ratings climbed higher than ever.

Maggie couldn't let Charles's praise sidetrack her. She had to know why she was there.

"How did you know about the apartment, and why did you want to meet me?"

Charles looked at her for so long, she lowered her eyes to the table.

"The apartment was a coincidence," Charles began. "I had dinner with a friend and his wife. The wife works at the real estate firm and saw your name on the sales offer. She's a huge fan, and she mentioned it at dinner." He paused. "I told her she had to keep that kind of thing confidential. But when I got home, I couldn't stop thinking about it. If I made an offer, I'd be killing two birds with one stone."

Maggie said she didn't understand.

Charles leaned back in his chair. "I left New York after my last play failed. Lou knew a movie director in Italy who was looking for a scriptwriter. I'd never written a movie script, but the whole thing sounded so cosmopolitan. Being on a movie set in Rome, working with

Italian actors and actresses. But Rome was dreary after the war, and the director and I clashed. I ended up living in Venice, but that didn't work out either."

"Why Venice?" Maggie asked.

Charles played with his drink. "I met a countess whose husband died just after the war. She owned a palazzo and invited me to stay. In his will, the count left the palazzo to his children from his first marriage. They kicked her out, and I had nowhere to go. So I came back to America. I spent the last few years in a cabin in the Hudson Valley."

Maggie remembered when Charles's life had been endless rounds of dinners and weekend house parties on Long Island.

"Why didn't you stay with Lou?" she asked.

"Lou got sick and left the business. He's living in a small house in Florida," Charles replied. "My newest play is the best that I've written. I showed it all over town, and no one will touch it. Once you have a flop, it's as if you have a contagious disease."

"What do I have to do with this?" Maggie wondered.

For the first time, Charles smiled. "I decided to fund it myself. Once I have a hit, I'll be Broadway's golden boy again. I don't have any money. You do. You're Maggie Lane, America's girl next door."

Maggie sucked in her breath. Charles couldn't be serious. He wouldn't dream of asking her for money. He was behaving as if they had parted on good terms, when he had practically ruined her life. How could he reappear after all these years and expect her to be civil to him?

"You owe me, Maggie," Charles said as if he could read her mind. "I picked you up off the sidewalk after your accident and gave you everything. And I loved you, don't forget that."

Maggie wanted to say so many things. That she had been naive and trusting, and he had taken advantage of her. That she could never forgive him for what he did. It had taken her ages to put her life back together. But there was no point. Charles had always done exactly what he wanted.

"I could provide a little bit of funding . . ." she suggested. She didn't want anything to do with him, but Charles was so stubborn. It might be easier to make him go away if she promised him something.

"I need a lot of money. I have to hire the best director and actors and set designers." He frowned. "If I move back to New York, I need to project a certain image. The right apartment, expensive clothes, being seen at the best restaurants. All that takes the kind of money you have."

Maggie's stomach turned over. She took a deep breath.

"I don't have that kind of money. I make a salary, and television isn't secure. The ratings could drop, and I could get fired."

"You're riding high, Maggie. No one can touch you," Charles scoffed.

"Teddy and I want to buy a bigger apartment," she tried again. "We have other expenses."

Charles set his glass on the table. His voice took on a different tone.

"I thought we could be nice to each other. So much time has passed, and I'm not unreasonable." His eyes became darker. "Do you know the real reason why my last play failed? The newspapers might have given it bad reviews, but plenty of plays have withstood a few scathing comments from the *New York Times* and the *Boston Globe*. I was run out of town because of you."

Maggie asked what he meant.

"I was the laughingstock of New York. It wasn't just the theater circle. It was anyone who read the *New York Post*. 'Playwright Charles Grey left at the altar by Pygmalion bride.' 'Playwright Charles Grey jilted by his own secretary.' 'Charles Grey double failure, in life and on the stage.' The headlines all came with photos. Do you want to know the worst part?" he demanded. "I provided many of those photos to the newspapers. You were so lovely, and we had so many wonderful times together. We were going to be the golden couple of New York theater."

He leaned closer. "You ruined it, Maggie. And you ruined me. No one ever looked at me in the same way. I'm guessing it didn't stop you from getting a job afterwards. You were just the pretty brunette who typed my manuscripts. But everyone who read the *Post* and the *New York Times* had seen the reviews of my plays for years. After that, I became an outcast."

An old memory came back to Maggie: Rebecca saying the most important thing to Charles was the image he created for others in his circle. Why hadn't she been more careful at the time? She had been so young. She hadn't thought about the consequences.

"I trusted you with everything, and you lied to me about Jake," she said. "You knew how I felt about him. It was the worst thing I ever went through." Maggie's throat constricted. "I had to turn away. I didn't have a choice."

He gave a bitter laugh. "Everyone has choices. You could have waited and left me privately. We could have invented a story. You got sick on our honeymoon. We had to send you to a health farm to recover. Months later you could have returned, and we could have got divorced."

"I couldn't walk into that church," Maggie said. "I was in shock. My world turned upside down, and I didn't know what to do."

Charles ignored her. "You ruined my life in New York, and now I want it back."

He spread his hands on the table, as if he was making a decision.

"I'm guessing you never told Teddy about us," he ventured. "What would happen if the story came out now? I know all about those morality clauses. You're supposed to be a housewife, with an innocent past. It wouldn't be good for *The Maggie Lane Baking Show*, and it wouldn't be good for your marriage."

Charles's face was close; she could smell his aftershave. A bolt of dread shot through her, and she pulled away. Her stomach turned and she felt sick.

"I have to go." She stood up.

"Think about it. It could be good for everyone." Charles's eyes were bright. "You'll be backing a hit Broadway production. I'll even withdraw the offer on the apartment. You and Teddy will have the life you always dreamed of."

Maggie left the restaurant and walked through Central Park. She sank onto a bench and took deep breaths. Her hands were shaking and it was hard to swallow.

She wished there was someone she could talk to. There had been Rebecca, but she got married years ago and moved to California.

Maggie recalled the day of her wedding to Charles. Getting ready in the bridal suite of the Pierre Hotel with Rebecca and feeling for a few hours like she was stepping into a fairy tale.

~

It was Maggie's wedding day. She stood in front of the mirror in her Chanel wedding gown and couldn't believe that any of it—the large bottle of Chanel No. 5 perfume that had been a gift from Coco Chanel herself, the bouquets of flowers accompanied by notes from New York's top socialites, Consuelo Vanderbilt and Barbara Hutton—was real.

In the months since their engagement, Charles and Maggie had been invited everywhere. They attended weekend parties at ocean-front estates in the Hamptons and ate dinner at the best restaurants in New York. They sat in a box at Rodgers and Hammerstein's musical *Oklahoma!*, and Charles was a guest of honor at a dinner at the governor's mansion.

Charles had been good about keeping her last name out of the newspapers. He said that once the reporters focused on her, they might try to contact her parents on the farm in Pennsylvania. They could be so pushy when they wanted a story, it was better if Maggie remained in the background. Maggie wondered if that was true or if Charles was afraid that the spotlight would shift away from him. It didn't matter either way. She was perfectly content being photographed on his arm without her full name in the caption.

Maggie had been afraid she would be uncomfortable around Charles's friends. But he always led her around the room and introduced her to everyone. Whenever someone praised the play, he gushed that Maggie had made it possible.

He gave her money to buy a new wardrobe. She was so overwhelmed by the selection of designer gowns at the high-end department stores that she came home with only a few cocktail dresses and a fur stole. After that, Charles accompanied her. He sat patiently while she tried on dresses by Jacques Fath and Chanel. They left Saks with so many boxes, their purchases had to be sent to the apartment in a separate taxi.

One of the happiest surprises was her friendship with Rebecca. Soon after Charles proposed, Rebecca invited Maggie to her apartment for lunch. She lived in a three-story townhouse in Sutton Place designed by the well-known architect Rosario Candela.

"You're probably wondering why I invited you," Rebecca said.

They were seated in Rebecca's living room. Tapestries hung on the walls, and the white marble floor was covered by Oriental rugs. Tall windows overlooked a private garden. The drapes had wide sashes, and the ceiling was painted with a mural.

Maggie pulled her eyes away from the chandelier and the bookshelf filled with leather-bound books.

"It's a beautiful apartment," she said.

"I love being surrounded by pretty things. So I decided to invest some of my money in this apartment instead of the theater or the stock market." Rebecca smiled. "I asked you here because I thought you might need a friend. I was like you once. I was raised in a small town in Vermont. When I came to New York, I was as green as the mountains during the summer. You're smart. You'll learn like I did."

Maggie admitted that she had been overwhelmed by all the invitations.

"I thought I knew how Charles lived, but I was only his secretary."

"No matter how rich or famous someone is, they all want the same thing. To be loved." Rebecca sipped her tea. "The only difference is they're used to being spoiled."

An uncomfortable feeling shot through Maggie. She asked what Rebecca meant.

"Don't get me wrong, I adore Charles. He's witty and handsome and kind," Rebecca said. "But I've seen a different side of him. Men like Charles don't stop until they get what they want. Just remember what I told you once. Charles's image means everything to him. As long as you act adoringly in public, he'll give you everything you ever dreamed of."

They talked about the upcoming theater season and new restaurants opening near Broadway.

"I don't have many female friends. Women can be competitive, when the most important thing is to support each other," Rebecca said when the maid had brought out watercress sandwiches. "I have a silly question." She ate a bite of the sandwich. "I wondered if I could be your maid of honor."

Maggie said she couldn't think of anything she'd like more.

"Good, that's settled," Rebecca said, pleased. "Now, let's talk about the wedding day. You should get your hair done at the salon at the St. Regis, and you'll need some silk lingerie for your honeymoon."

For the next few months, they did everything together. Rebecca gave Maggie advice on entertaining and decorating and sex. They visited galleries and spent afternoons browsing at Macy's and Bloomingdale's.

Now Maggie glanced at her reflection in the suite's mirror. Her hair was styled in waves. She wore thick mascara, and her lips were painted with pink lipstick.

Rebecca stood behind her. "You look stunning."

Maggie did look lovely. She had settled on a ballerina-length lace gown with a sweetheart neckline. She wore a pearl necklace, and a wreath of rosebuds was wound through her hair.

Her only regret was that her parents weren't attending the wedding. Her father injured his back, and her mother had to take care of him. When her mother called, Maggie didn't quite believe her. Her parents were probably afraid they wouldn't feel comfortable at the Pierre Hotel.

"My parents weren't at my wedding either," Rebecca said, as if she could read her mind.

"I should have insisted on a smaller wedding." Maggie sighed.

"Charles wouldn't have agreed. This is his big moment. He might never get another like it."

Rebecca had a point. The play was selling out at the box office, and Charles was the darling of the Broadway season.

Maggie fastened a diamond bracelet around her wrist.

"Where did you get that?" Rebecca asked.

"Charles gave it to me yesterday." Maggie admired it. "It's beautiful, but it must have been expensive."

"I told you, men like Charles think they can buy love," Rebecca mused.

"Charles could have almost any woman in New York." Maggie fiddled with her pearls. "I'm lucky that he chose me. We have a wonderful time together."

Maggie enjoyed being with Charles. He was a very good dancer, and he had excellent taste in art and movies. She loved being part of the conversations at dinner parties, and she adored the charity galas where she had the chance to wear one of her new evening gowns and listen to big band music.

And she was happy during the evenings at home when they worked on the new play. Charles would make hot cocoa, and they'd sit in the living room and bounce ideas back and forth.

She wasn't in love with him the way she had been with Jake. That love had been all consuming. She and Jake could talk for hours. But it had been months since she received the letter saying that Jake was missing in action and presumed dead. She had to move on, and she did have feelings for Charles. When they were together, she felt happy.

Maggie finished getting ready. The white Rolls-Royce that Charles had hired to take her and Rebecca to the church was waiting at the curb.

When the car pulled up in front of Trinity Church, most of the guests were already there. Maggie fastened her veil and smoothed the folds of her gown. She stepped outside, and that's when she saw him.

Jake was standing on the sidewalk. She barely recognized him. His face was gaunt. His uniform jacket hung on him, and his trousers were baggy.

Their eyes met, and Maggie's heart leapt. For a moment, she thought she was imagining things. It was wedding-day jitters, and she had conjured up his image to calm herself. She blinked, and when she opened her eyes he was still there. Then she couldn't wait another minute. She picked up her skirt to run over to him, but he was already getting into a taxi. Before she could reach him, the taxi drove away.

Maggie stood in front of the church. Her white satin heels teetered on the cement. The throbbing in her head was so loud, she could barely hear the traffic. She felt dizzy, but she wouldn't let herself faint. She climbed into the Rolls-Royce and instructed the driver to take her back to Charles's apartment.

~

Now it was hours later. Rebecca had gone home, and Maggie sat in the living room. She had changed out of her wedding dress and into a sweater and skirt. Charles had left the church soon after Maggie. He spent the last few hours canceling the reception. She could hear him on the phone in the kitchen, talking to the band leader.

When she had arrived at the apartment, Ellen was waiting. The story came out. Jake had appeared at the door and asked for Maggie. Ellen thought that Jake was an old friend of hers. She told him it was Charles and Maggie's wedding day.

Now, Charles entered the living room. He still wore his tuxedo. His hair was neatly brushed, and there was a yellow rose in his buttonhole.

"Everything has been canceled," he announced. "We can get married at city hall on Monday. We'll have a small wedding lunch afterwards. I booked a table at the Colony."

Maggie had barely said anything since she arrived home. She glanced up at Charles.

"We're not getting married, Charles. I have to find Jake." Her thoughts were reeling, and she found it hard to concentrate. "The navy might know where he's staying. I'll tell him that I hadn't received a letter in months and thought he was dead."

Charles poured a scotch from the bottle on the sideboard.

"I can understand why you couldn't go into the church. You were in shock." His brow knitted together. "We're still getting married. I rescheduled our honeymoon. Everything is all set."

Maggie smoothed her skirt. She had never felt so tired.

"You know I can't. It wouldn't be fair to you. I'm in love with Jake. I always have been." She played with the sofa cushion. "I'm sorry, Charles. You can return the diamond ring and the bracelet. That will pay for the reception. I'm sorry I agreed to marry you. It's my fault. You've been so good to me. I do care for you. I can even keep working for you, until you find another secretary."

Charles sat beside her. His eyes were darker than she'd seen them.

"You don't understand. I'm madly in love with you, Maggie, and we're getting married. Over time, you'll forget Jake. I promise we'll be happy."

Maggie remembered what Rebecca said about Charles always getting what he wanted.

She tried again. "I'm going to try and find Jake in the morning. I can stay at a hotel tonight, if you like."

"It won't matter if you find him; he'll never talk to you." Charles stood up and walked to the desk. He took out a piece of paper and handed it to her.

It was a letter from the War Department. Hospital Corpsman Third Class Jake Pullman had been located at a prisoner of war camp. He was in decent health, and the government would keep her updated.

"Where did this come from?" she gasped.

"It arrived in the mail two weeks ago," Charles replied. "At first, I was going to show it to you, but there was no point. You didn't talk about Jake anymore. It had been a wartime romance. And he may never have come home. Those prisoner of war camps were full of disease and infection."

"He was alive, and you didn't tell me." She breathed. A heavy weight pressed on her shoulders. The magnitude of Charles's betrayal was becoming clear. How could he have said that he loved her while he was keeping from her the news that Jake was alive. And what about Jake? She pictured him standing on the steps of the church, and her heart turned over. She couldn't imagine what he must be thinking. She had to find him and tell him what happened.

"I just explained that there was no reason to show it to you. I couldn't let it interfere with our wedding. The invitations had been sent out. And I'm in love with you." Charles placed his hand on her wrist. "You love me too. You may not realize it right now. It's the shock of seeing Jake. In a few days, the feeling will go away, and our lives will proceed as we planned."

Maggie tried to move her hand away, but Charles gripped it tighter. She had a sudden feeling of fear. This was the side of Charles she hadn't seen before. He was being completely delusional. She wondered to what lengths he would go to keep her from leaving.

"I'll leave now," she said.

"Maggie, don't," Charles implored. "Why don't you take a sleeping pill? Everything will look brighter in the morning."

She wrenched her hand away and stood up. She had to get away from him.

"I'm fine, Charles." She walked to the bedroom. "I'll take a few things for tonight. I'll come back tomorrow, and we can talk about everything."

Maggie threw a few personal items into an overnight bag. Her heart was pounding.

She walked back through the living room, keeping her eyes averted from Charles. Then she ran through the entry, down the stairs, and onto the street.

A taxi idled at the corner. She gave the driver Rebecca's address.

"One Sutton Place."

She sank against the seat and watched Charles's redbrick apartment building recede through the window.

~

That had all happened years ago. If only Maggie had told Teddy everything when they were first together.

She had no idea what to do. But she had to think of something. If she didn't, her marriage and her career would be over.

Chapter Twenty-Four

It had been the worst week that Maggie could remember. Teddy hadn't come home. On the second night, he called and said he needed more time to think. She was about to ask where he was staying, but he hung up before she could reply.

The following morning, she called the radio station. If they could meet for lunch and talk, they could work things out. The receptionist said that Teddy called in sick and expected to be out all week.

Maggie was shocked. No matter how much Teddy complained about his job, he always went to work. Why had he lied to the receptionist, and why had he said that he would be out all week?

She hadn't heard from the Realtor or from Charles. Charles wouldn't wait forever. If she didn't give him an answer about funding the play soon, their story would end up in the newspapers and all over town.

Maggie wished she could talk to Dolly. But Dolly had gone away, and not even her mother knew where she was. Maggie guessed things had ended badly between Dolly and Alan and she went somewhere to recover.

The taping of the day's show was over. Maggie sat in her dressing room, reading letters from viewers. She was more popular than ever. The New England Women's Club in Boston wanted to host a "Maggie Lane Weekend." Participants would stay at the new Buckminster Hotel. In the mornings, Maggie would give baking lessons; in the afternoons, there would be excursions around Boston. A chapter of League of Women

Voters in Palm Beach offered to pay Maggie's expenses if she lectured about her life in television. She would have a suite at the Breakers, and her evenings would be free to do whatever she pleased.

There was a knock. Dolly entered. She looked very smart in a powder-blue jacket with shoulder pads and a pleated skirt.

Maggie had never been happier to see her. "Where have you been?"

"There was a break in filming, so I took a short vacation." Dolly pulled off her gloves and held out her hand. "Alan and I drove up to Niagara Falls."

A diamond ring accompanied by a gold band sparkled on her ring finger.

Maggie's eyes flew up to Dolly's face. "You got engaged?"

"Alan and I eloped. We're married," Dolly corrected.

The previous week, Dolly and Alan had met for lunch, and Dolly admitted everything. That she said she attended church, when the only times she'd been inside a church was to admire the architecture. That Christmas was her favorite holiday. She did love the Christmas season in New York because it was so festive, but her family had never had a Christmas tree. And that she made up different excuses about being busy on Friday nights because her parents kept Shabbat dinner. She hadn't meant to lie, but she had been afraid Alan wouldn't marry her if she was Jewish. Alan needed a wife who could accompany him to the country club, and who enjoyed boating and playing squash.

"We both laughed that even with Teddy's lessons, I was terrible at squash," Dolly said, smiling. "The country club that Alan joined was founded by a Jewish banker whose family wasn't permitted at another country club."

They talked about the Jewish community in Cleveland and how Alan's mother had raised money to bring European orphans to the city after the war. Dolly's mother had done the same thing in New York. Alan predicted they would become good friends.

"Why did you elope?" Maggie asked.

"Our parents would have argued over who gets to pay for the wedding. It was better to just get married." Dolly chuckled. "We're going to let our mothers plan the reception. Alan's mother is coming to New York next month."

Dolly and Alan had discussed raising their children in the Jewish faith but allowing them to explore other cultures and religions.

"Alan is proud of being Jewish, but it can be difficult. At school, he was teased for being skinny and having a long nose. At first, he didn't tell anyone at work that he was Jewish. They might assume he could only write a certain kind of humor. We're going to try to change things for the next generation." Her eyes were bright. "People should be judged on their skills and accomplishments, not on stereotypes based on their religion."

Everything that Dolly said made sense, but Maggie still worried about her. Dolly's happiness started with her health.

"What about the diet pills?" Maggie asked.

Dolly took a deep breath. She sat up straight.

"When we got to Niagara Falls, I jumped out of the car and threw the pill bottles into the water. I promised Alan that I'd never use them again." Dolly held up her hand. "Before you say that I've tried to stop and failed, this time will be different. I'm stopping for both of us. It won't be easy, and maybe I'll slip, but I realize I can't go on like this. It wouldn't be fair to our marriage or to our children, when we have them. Alan is going to help me. We're going to prepare meals together. Healthy dinners, like chicken and salad, but delicious things too. Alan's mother has a recipe for carrot cake, and my mother is going to give us her crepes recipe."

Maggie hugged Dolly. Dolly was right about the pills. It wouldn't be easy to break the habit. But she was strong, and Alan would support her. She always knew that Dolly and Alan were perfect for each other.

"It was nice of Alan to let Teddy stay at his apartment while he was away," Maggie said.

Dolly frowned. She asked what Maggie meant.

"Teddy and I had an argument. The last time we fought, he stayed at Alan's," Maggie said.

Dolly shook her head. "Alan's old roommate is in New York. He's staying at the apartment for a few weeks."

"Maybe they're both staying there," Maggie suggested.

"Alan's landlord wouldn't allow it. He can only have one guest."

Maggie recalled the night she ran into Sally at the pharmacy. What if Teddy was staying with her?

"It's because of Charles," she said out loud.

"What are you talking about?" Dolly asked.

There was no reason to keep her secret any longer. If she didn't give Charles what he wanted, he would tell everyone about their past. Dolly was her best friend, and she didn't want to keep it from her any longer.

"It's a long story." Maggie sighed.

Dolly sat down. "Alan is catching up at work. I have plenty of time."

Maggie told Dolly how she met Jake while he was on leave and they fell in love. She was struck by the car, and Charles rescued her and offered to let her live in his apartment. Becoming Charles's secretary, and the play's success. The day the letter came, saying that Jake was missing in action and presumed dead, followed a few months later by Charles's proposal. The heady weeks of dinners and parties, and then the wedding day. Getting ready in the bridal suite of the Pierre Hotel, climbing into the white Rolls-Royce, and seeing Jake on the steps of the church.

"For several months, I tried to find Jake. My friend Rebecca used some of her money and influence to track him down. He had reenlisted in the navy and was stationed in the Philippines. He married a girl there."

Maggie had wondered whether he had met his wife during the war. For a while, the knowledge of his marriage wounded her so badly, she had to drag herself through her days. She had been so sure of their love for each other. And yet Jake had easily found someone else. Once she passed a young couple on the street in New York. The man resembled Jake, and his arms were around a pretty Asian woman. Maggie had stumbled home and gone to bed. Gradually she pulled herself out of it. She reminded herself that appearances didn't tell the whole story. She didn't know anything about Jake's life or his marriage. And she was still living in New York. She had to find a way to be happy again.

"Then, I met Teddy," she continued. "I knew quite soon that I was really in love. It was different than Jake or Charles. Teddy and I are equals, and we have so much in common. With Jake, I was so young and it was all so sudden, I think now I was in love with the idea of love. Teddy and I have been together for three years, and my feelings have only grown stronger."

When she was with Teddy, she felt completely herself. She couldn't wait to see him at the end of each day, and when they weren't together, she had a physical ache. She knew that he had her best interests at heart, and he had never stopped telling her how much he loved her.

"You have to tell Teddy the truth," Dolly counseled. "He loves you. He'll understand."

Maggie was doubtful. Teddy was proud. She had kept the most important part of her past a secret for their entire marriage. Then there was Tommy and Deluxe Baking Company to think about. Maggie had signed the morality clause, saying she had nothing to hide.

"It's not just my marriage. If this gets out, my career will be over."

Dolly twisted her wedding band. "I wish there was something I could do."

Maggie fiddled with the stack of viewers' letters. If a woman wrote to her with a similar problem, Maggie would tell her she had to tell her husband the truth. That's what marriage was about.

Dolly was right. Maggie couldn't sit and wait for Teddy to come home. She knew what she had to do.

"Can I borrow your hat?" Maggie pointed to Dolly's pillbox hat.

"My hat?" Dolly repeated.

"I'm going to ask Sally Knickerbocker to lunch. She's the most fashionable woman I know. I need to be wearing a smart hat."

Dolly took off her hat and handed it to Maggie. "What are you going to say?"

"I'm going to find out if she told Teddy about Charles and Jake," Maggie replied with more courage than she felt. "Then I'll figure out what to do."

An hour later, Maggie was seated at Delmonico's waiting for Sally. She had been surprised that Sally agreed to meet her right away.

The restaurant door opened, and Sally entered. She wore a belted wool dress and fur-trimmed stole. Her hair was worn smoothly against her neck, and she carried a leather handbag.

"Maggie, I was surprised by your call." Sally joined her at the table. "If this is about your interview, it's already gone to press. I can't make any changes."

Maggie wished she had ordered a cocktail for courage. She took a deep breath.

"It's not about the interview. It's about Teddy." Maggie looked at Sally. "Is he staying at your apartment?"

Sally sat down. She set her handbag on the chair.

"What if he is?"

"Teddy is my husband. I want to know if he's at another woman's apartment."

"He swore me to secrecy. But you did ask, and I don't like to lie," Sally said slowly. "He came a week ago and asked if he could stay."

Maggie sat back in her chair. The whole time she had hoped that she had been wrong. Teddy was staying at a hotel, or had gone up to his parents' house in Rye.

"Is he . . . are you . . ." She couldn't get the words out.

"Are we sleeping together?" Sally prompted. "He sleeps in the guest room. I'm not as awful as you think." Her eyes flickered. "I haven't told him about Jake and Charles."

Maggie let out a gasp. Sally did know about Maggie's past. She had to be careful and find out how much Sally knew before she said anything.

The waiter appeared, and they ordered rib eye steaks and ice tea.

"I met Charles in Rome. I was there with my husband. Charles had fled New York after his last play was a disaster." Sally buttered a bread roll. "My husband was running around Rome with some Italian model, so Charles and I spent a lot of time talking. He told me that you jilted him at the altar."

"I couldn't marry Charles. He hid from me that Jake was alive," Maggie defended herself.

"Charles was in love with you." Sally shrugged. "I told you, all men are competitive. He couldn't lose you to another man."

"I've been in New York all this time, and I never heard from him again," Maggie said.

"Charles has a big ego. He wasn't going to come crawling back," Sally replied. "Unless there was something he could gain. Like the money to resurrect his career."

Maggie sipped her ice tea. Sally was so calm, as if they were discussing an upcoming fashion show at Macy's. But she was talking about the men who had been so important in her life.

"I would never have used the information. I'm a fan of *The Maggie Lane Baking Show*," Sally continued as if she could read Maggie's thoughts. "The problem is Teddy. If you remember, I met him years ago in London. He was different than the other Americans I knew. There was a sensitivity about him. We ran in the same social circles for a while and became quite close. You might even say there was something between us. When I saw him again at the CBS dinner, I remembered how attractive and enjoyable to be with he was."

"So you decided to steal him from me?" Maggie demanded.

"You can't steal a man who's happily married," Sally remarked. "There was trouble between you even then. He came to see me that night and told me about it."

Teddy had said that Sally had gone straight to Long Island with the Whitneys.

"I did go to Long Island, but I stopped at my apartment first. Teddy came over, and we had a drink," Sally said. "Nothing happened. He didn't even kiss me."

Maggie remembered finding Alan's cigarette case in Teddy's drawer. Teddy had lied to her. He said he hadn't seen Sally.

"I wouldn't have pursued Teddy. I was hurt enough in my own marriage," Sally kept talking. "But Teddy came to me a week ago. The first night, he sat on the sofa and talked about you for hours. He must have smoked three packs of cigarettes."

"All couples have fights," Maggie blurted out.

"It was more than a fight. He felt that you didn't trust him. When you don't trust someone you fall out of love," Sally said. "That's when I began to realize I have feelings for Teddy."

The hair on the back of Maggie's neck bristled. "What do you mean, 'feelings'?"

"I'm falling in love with him," Sally announced. "With a little push, he could be in love with me too. We almost had a fling, once. We were at a house party together, the summer before the war ended. I got quite drunk and entered his guest room. Nothing happened. He was too much of a gentleman. But I know, this time it could work."

Maggie realized Sally was talking about the house party where Arabella and Ian announced their engagement. She couldn't say that she already knew about it. Sally might go back to Teddy and tell him that Maggie had been snooping.

Sally was still talking.

"That's where Charles comes into things. I read about Charles's new play in Walter Winchell's column. I decided it was worth meeting him again, and my instincts were correct. Charles was still bitter about you, and he was out of money. It didn't take much prompting to suggest he get in touch with you."

Maggie's stomach dropped. "What about the offer on the apartment?"

"That was a lucky coincidence," Sally said. "I knew from your interview how important it was to find your dream apartment. If Charles interfered with that, you wouldn't ignore his call."

Maggie stirred her ice tea. "Women are supposed to support each other."

"I agree." Sally nodded. "You don't know how many talks I've given about career women helping young women who are just starting out. When I got divorced, I donated money to the women's shelter in Palm Beach. And I support two women's charities in New York. It's different when it comes to love. Then one has to be selfish."

"Teddy and I are still in love," Maggie snapped.

"At the moment, Teddy can't see a future with you. He wants a family, and he's tired of being Maggie Lane's husband." Sally cut her steak. "I have enough money to support both of us. If Teddy and I were together, I could still write my gossip column and have children."

An icy fear shot through Maggie. "What are you saying?"

"Tell Teddy that you want a divorce and I'll never breathe a word about Charles and Jake to anyone. I'll give Charles the money he needs, if he signs a paper that he'll never reveal your past. You'll continue to star in *The Maggie Lane Baking Show*, and Teddy and I will move away from New York. I prefer living somewhere sunny. I could start a new column in Hollywood."

"And if I don't?" Maggie asked.

Sally put down her fork. "Then I'll devote an entire column to Maggie Lane's scandalous past. You'll be fired from the show, and Teddy will know that you never trusted him enough to share everything about your past."

Maggie's heart hammered. She was trapped.

"I'll give you a few days to think about it," Sally said smoothly. "In the meantime, don't worry about Teddy. He can stay in my guest room."

Maggie left the restaurant and walked back to the apartment. Sitting across from Sally, and hearing her talk about Teddy, made her more determined to get Sally out of their lives. She had always known that she loved Teddy; now that realization became even stronger. She couldn't let Sally influence him. There had to be a way to save her marriage and her career. She passed the Strand and gazed in the window. There was a display of books about influential women.

Suddenly, she had an idea. She ran back to the apartment. Her evening bags were arranged in the closet in the bedroom. She searched each one but couldn't find what she was looking for.

She went to the desk in the living room where she kept business cards. The card was in the stack in the drawer.

She turned the card over and wondered if she could go through with it. She was Maggie Lane. All the women who watched her television program would expect nothing less.

She picked up the phone and dialed the number on the card.

"Is this Mrs. Roosevelt's secretary?" she asked. "This is Maggie Lane. Mrs. Roosevelt said I should call."

Maggie waited while the phone was silent. Eleanor was probably on a book tour. Even if she was in New York, she might not remember giving Maggie her card.

Eleanor's voice came over the line. "Maggie, what a pleasant surprise."

"I'm sure you're busy. But I wonder if I could take you up on your offer for a chat," Maggie said.

"I'd love to, but I'm leaving for San Francisco in the morning. Can it wait until I get back?"

Maggie recalled the wonderful times with Teddy. When they first met at the CBS charity function, and he brought her a glass of champagne without asking because he didn't want another man to steal her away. The early weeks of their courtship, when they visited every museum in New York and ate at Ruby Foo's and Delmonico's. The impromptu wedding at his parents' house and her first week on the set of *The Maggie Lane Baking Show*. Strolling in Central Park, and the evenings with Dolly and Alan.

She didn't want to live without Teddy. They belonged together.

"I'm afraid it can't." She clutched the phone. "I promise, it won't take long."

Eleanor paused before she answered. "I have to give a speech at the Plaza Hotel tonight. Why don't we meet in the Palm Court. Say five o'clock?"

Maggie's pulse slowed. She smiled into the phone.

"Five o'clock is perfect."

Maggie arrived at the Plaza Hotel early and sat in the Palm Court. She had been there a few times, and at each visit the grand marble columns and crystal chandeliers took her breath away. Now she barely noticed. She kept staring at the entry, wondering whether Eleanor Roosevelt would show up.

"Maggie," a woman's voice came from behind. "I came through the back entrance. Five o'clock is such a busy time at the hotel, I didn't want to cause a fuss."

Eleanor was dressed in a two-piece crepe suit. Her hair was crimped, and she carried an alligator-skin handbag.

Maggie stood up awkwardly. "I feel awful for asking you to come when your calendar is so full."

"Nonsense. I told you to contact me. Besides, I can't think of anything I'd like more before my speech than a Bloody Mary."

The waiter brought a bowl of salted nuts and two Bloody Marys garnished with celery sticks.

"I don't know where to begin," Maggie hesitated. She felt foolish. So many women faced bigger problems. They were homeless and without jobs. Their husbands abused them and they had no safe place to go. In other countries, there was famine and disease.

Eleanor smiled warmly. "We're not in a hurry." She held up her cocktail. "I need at least two of these before I greet two hundred guests at the charity dinner."

Maggie told her about Jake and Charles. Signing the morality clause for *The Maggie Lane Baking Show* and marrying Teddy. Teddy's dissatisfaction with his career and his growing distaste for being known as Maggie Lane's husband. She recounted meeting Sally Knickerbocker and seeing Charles again after so many years.

"I don't want to ask Teddy for a divorce," she finished. "But when he discovers what I've done, he won't want to stay married to me. Sally could cause so much damage. The Deluxe Baking Company put their faith in me. If she writes about me and Charles and Jake in her column, *The Maggie Lane Baking Show* will lose its viewers. I couldn't do that to Tommy."

"What do you want?" Eleanor asked.

Maggie hadn't thought about it in a while. But nothing had changed. She told Eleanor that she wanted Teddy, and a career she loved, and a lovely apartment. Someday, she wanted to start a family.

"Then you have to fight for it," Eleanor said. "Franklin and I faced obstacles throughout our marriage. His mother didn't want him to marry me. I wasn't suitable. We had to go behind her back and marry secretly. One day I discovered a pile of love letters in his suitcase from my social secretary, Lucy Mercer. He had been planning to leave me." Eleanor jiggled her glass. "We worked it out, but it still wasn't easy. He came down with a paralytical disease, and his mother wanted him to retire and become a country gentleman. Being idle would have killed Franklin, so I had to fight his mother to allow him to stay in politics.

"There were many times I wished I had a different life altogether. Moved to Europe by myself and pursued my art. But I loved Franklin. Now that he's dead, I wouldn't have changed a thing."

Maggie took another sip of her Bloody Mary. A longing for Teddy welled up inside her.

"What should I do?" she asked.

"Sally's column runs in the *New York Post* and is syndicated in newspapers all over the country."

Maggie nodded. She wondered what Eleanor was getting at.

Eleanor gave a satisfied smile. "The owner of the *Post*, Dorothy Schiff, is a good friend of mine. In fact, she'll be at the dinner tonight. Stay for my speech. The three of us will have a drink and a chat afterwards."

Maggie waited patiently until the charity dinner was over.

The three women sat in a booth in the Palm Court. The waiter brought a bottle of champagne and three glasses.

Dorothy Schiff was an attractive woman of about fifty. She had owned the *New York Post* for ten years. She was the first female newspaper publisher in New York, and under her guidance, the *Post* had become one of the most-read newspapers in the country.

Eleanor sipped her champagne and recounted Maggie's story to Dorothy.

"I'm sorry this happened to you," Dorothy said when Eleanor finished. "Our job is to sell newspapers, but I would never print a column that deliberately hurts so many innocent people."

"What can I do?" Maggie asked. "Even if you don't print it, Sally could submit the column elsewhere."

Dorothy shook her head. "Her contract with the *Post* doesn't allow it. It's quite simple. I'll summon Sally to my office and say that if she submits the column to her editor, I'll cancel her contract. I'll stop our affiliate newspapers from running it as well."

"You would do that?" Maggie gasped. She was flooded with relief. "You don't know me."

"Millions of women count on *The Maggie Lane Baking Show* to keep them company in the mornings. And they admire you. Your advice helps them sort out their lives," Dorothy said. "We can't let Sally ruin all that. I'll send a letter to Charles too. If he says anything to the press about you, I'll use my contacts to blacklist him in the New York theater world forever."

Maggie had thought about Charles. There had to be a way to stop him from going to the newspapers with his story. Dorothy's idea was better than anything she had come up with. Her feeling of relief grew stronger and was joined by a sensation of deep gratitude. Maggie could finally relax. Her past would remain a secret.

"This deserves a toast." Eleanor raised her glass. "There's nothing three strong, intelligent women can't accomplish when they put their heads together."

Chapter Twenty-Five

The following Saturday morning, Maggie sat in the apartment and flipped through a copy of *Life* magazine.

Dorothy had done what she promised, and Sally resigned from the newspaper. Maggie heard that she had gone to stay with a friend in Palm Beach before she headed out to California.

Charles had returned to his cabin in the Hudson Valley.

She heard from Dolly that Teddy was staying with Alan. Every day she picked up the phone to call him, but she always put it down. She would have to tell him everything. When she did, their marriage would be over. But maybe it was time to take that chance. If she didn't contact Teddy now, the opportunity might be lost forever. She had to be brave and risk his rejection.

She was about to pick up the phone to dial Teddy's number when it rang.

"Maggie, it's Teddy," he said. "How have you been?"

She held the phone tightly. She wondered if he was calling to break up with her.

"I'm fine," she said awkwardly. "How are you?"

"Busy. Alan is a terrible cook, so I've taken over preparing dinner."

She gave a little laugh.

"That's what I'm calling about," Teddy continued.

She frowned. "You want me to make Alan's dinner?"

"No, I wondered if you'd have dinner with me. We could go to Ruby Foo's."

"Sure, I'd like that." Maggie nodded into the phone. A pinprick of hope shot through her.

Teddy's voice became lighter. "I'll meet you there at seven p.m."

Maggie sat in a booth and waited for Teddy. She wore a green dress with a scalloped neckline. Her Henri Bendel handbag sat beside her, and the heart-faced watch Teddy had given her was on her wrist.

When Teddy entered the restaurant, her heart did a little lurch. They hadn't seen each other in two weeks. It was the longest they'd been apart since they started dating three years ago.

He looked handsome in a navy sport coat and beige slacks.

"You look lovely in that dress," Teddy commented. "Prettier than ever."

Maggie hadn't seen Teddy so nervous. She still didn't know what it meant. Teddy was so nice, perhaps he was finding it hard to tell her that he wanted a divorce.

"Do you mind if I order for both of us?" He picked up the menu. "I'm starving."

The waiter brought out chicken miso soup and beef chow mein. There was a plate of Peking duck and sides of chicken fried rice and noodles.

Maggie toyed with her food. She wasn't the least bit hungry.

"This might have been a bad idea," Teddy acknowledged, setting down his chopsticks. "The thing is, I don't want to talk about us yet. I'd like to finish dinner and show you something first."

They talked about Dolly and Alan. Maggie tried to concentrate on the dishes, but the noodles kept slipping off her chopsticks.

Teddy paid the check and they walked onto the street. A taxi took them to the corner of Park Avenue and East Sixty-Fifth Street. They climbed the steps of a redbrick apartment building, and Teddy nodded at the doorman. She recognized the building. She had seen it when she had looked at apartments.

She followed him to the third floor. He turned the key in the lock and opened the door. The white marble entry and red velvet sofas in the living room were familiar. It was the apartment that she had made an offer on.

"What are we doing here?" Maggie asked.

Teddy sat on the sofa and motioned for her to do the same. "Sally told me that she went to see you. Maggie, I'm so ashamed. I should never have lied to you, and I shouldn't have stayed at Sally's. Nothing happened. She tried, but I wouldn't have anything to do with her.

"I've been a fool for ages," he continued. "This was never about you or the television show. It was seeing myself as a failure in my career. I might not be one of those cocky young men who are taking over all the offices in Midtown, but I still have an ego. I want to love my career, and I want to be admired and respected by my work colleagues. So the last couple of weeks, I did something about it. I quit my job."

"You did what?" Maggie gasped.

"I didn't quit until I got a new one first." He grinned. "That's why I didn't come home. I interviewed at a dozen firms. I was hired as director of accounts at one of the new advertising agencies on Madison Avenue. They were impressed with my radio and television contacts. The salary is more than double what I was making, and I get a signing bonus and a company car."

Maggie was speechless.

"That's wonderful news," she gushed.

"There's more," he kept talking. "I went to see the Realtor about this apartment. I knew how much it meant to you, and I didn't want to stop us from getting it. So I borrowed money from my parents and used the signing bonus for the down payment." Teddy dangled the key. "Last night, I picked up the key."

Maggie sucked in her breath. The art deco mirror in the entry, the glass pineapples on the bedside tables, the his-and-her walk-in closets, and the all-new appliances in the kitchen were theirs.

She was about to kiss Teddy, but she froze. She still had to tell him about Charles and Jake. When she did, he might not want to be with her. But if she didn't, they could never truly be together.

"There's something I have to tell you," she began. "It's about something that happened when I was young. I did a terrible thing by keeping it a secret."

"If it's about Charles and Jake, I already know," Teddy replied.

The Realtor had told Teddy there was another offer on the apartment. Teddy and Charles met, and Charles told him everything.

"Somehow, he thought it would make a difference regarding how I felt about you," Teddy finished. "It didn't. If anything, it made me love you more."

"I don't understand," Maggie said. Teddy's words confused her. She had been so afraid that when he learned the truth about her past, he wouldn't want to be with her. A tiny seed of hope sprung inside her. Was Teddy saying that he felt the same about her, after everything she had told him?

"You were so young. You didn't know anything about love. How could you? But you were brave. You didn't marry Charles, even though that would have been easy. And you didn't grieve for Jake forever. You picked yourself up and started all over again."

Teddy was right. Maggie had scraped together enough money to rent a studio apartment and went back to the temp agency. This time, she got jobs that led to her own radio program at CBS, and then to *The Maggie Lane Baking Show*. She had done it all on her own. No one had helped her.

"I never told you what happened in France." Teddy stood up. "There are some things in our past that are so painful, if we bring them up, they'll stay with us forever."

"I know about Oradour-sur-Glane," Maggie said. "I found a notebook with some photos and a newspaper article."

Teddy paced around the room while Maggie explained that she didn't tell him because she was afraid he'd be angry that she'd been looking through his things. She hadn't meant to find the photos, but once she did she couldn't help herself. She wanted to understand what was troubling Teddy.

"I can't imagine what you witnessed," Maggie finished. "I wish you had told me. I would have tried to help you through it."

Teddy sat back down. "I wish I had too, but I couldn't. It would have clouded everything we did. The newspaper article didn't tell the whole story. The reason that Arabella went into the village that morning was to buy cigarettes. I was out of Camels, and she thought the *tabac* might sell French Gauloises. What if she had gone earlier? She would have been killed too.

"I almost couldn't live with myself. When we returned to London, I barely ate for a week. I tried to give up my Camels, but my habit grew even worse. I've had a love and hate relationship with cigarettes ever since. When I'm under too much stress, I use them as a crutch."

Teddy told her that they arrived in the village on the evening of June 9. It was a perfect summer night. Black velvet sky filled with stars, the scent of lavender blooming. Oradour-sur-Glane was one of those villages in northern France where life was conducted around the village square. There were cafés and a pharmacy, and a *tabac* that sold candy and newspapers and cigarettes. The main building in the square was the church. It was built of stone and four hundred years old.

That night, everybody in the town was out. Old men conducted a game of boules on the lawn. Children played near the fountain. Restaurant tables were set up outside, and people ate plates of local vegetables and grilled fish.

There hadn't been any fighting in a while, so the place was pretty and restful. The villagers were just going about their daily lives.

"We had a wonderful dinner," Teddy recalled. "Grilled trout with leeks and vegetable stew. We still had a long drive to reach the vineyard that Arabella wanted to visit, so we decided to spend the night. A couple offered to let us sleep in their barn, a short distance from the village.

"The next morning, Ian explored the fields, and Arabella went to the village. I had done most of the driving, so I was tired and stayed at the barn." Teddy paused. "All of a sudden, Arabella came rushing in. I'd never seen anyone look like her, not even on the battlefield. As if she'd seen a whole village full of ghosts.

"In a way she had. When she arrived in the square it was completely empty. All she saw were a few shops with '*Ouvert*' signs on the doors but no one in them. It was when she reached the church that she got frightened. A pram was parked on the steps. By then it was late morning, and the sun was high in the sky. No one would bring their baby to church when it was so hot.

"She ran back to the barn, and I went to the village with her." Teddy swallowed. "I won't tell you what we saw, because then you'd have to live with it too. The night sweats started soon afterwards. I'd wake up in the middle of the night and imagine I was there." His eyes darkened. "The church had been locked when we arrived. We had to enter through a broken window. There were bodies everywhere, and the most acrid smell. You've never smelled anything like it."

The women and children had been rounded up, taken inside the church, and killed. The men were put into barns and sheds. They were shot in the legs, and then doused in gasoline and burned to death.

Maggie had the same sick feeling that she had when she read Sally's article. Teddy explained why it had been so difficult to be on the radio after he returned home.

"One of my last segments for Pathé News was reporting on the tragedy at Oradour-sur-Glane," Teddy continued. "I broke down and cried on the air, Maggie. A radio announcer isn't supposed to cry. My job was to deliver the news. What if I continued in broadcasting back home and cried when I delivered news of some terrible world event?" he asked. "I should have done something else, but I didn't know what. All the young men were coming home from the war, so many jobs were taken."

She understood now why Teddy had been eager to give up cigarettes when he stopped being on the radio. And why he started smoking again when their marriage was in trouble and they started fighting. Why he talked in his sleep and woke up more exhausted than when he went to bed.

They talked about Arabella and Ian. Arabella told her parents that Oradour-sur-Glane taught her how precious life was. She was going to marry Ian no matter what they said, so they may as well accept him. The weekend house party at their country estate turned into their engagement party.

Sally was invited too since they were part of the same social circle in London.

The second night, all the guests got quite drunk except Teddy. After Oradour-sur-Glane, he barely touched alcohol. It would have been too easy to let a few cocktails numb the pain. He wanted to experience it, as a reminder of how terrible the world could be, and how being kind to others was the most important thing.

"Sally and I sometimes flirted when we ran into each other in London. All the young people did. It made us forget the war for a while. That night she came into my room, but I turned her away. Afterwards, she pretended there had been something between us. Sally says that she doesn't need a man and that she's all about her career, but that isn't quite true.

"It still managed to be a wonderful weekend. Arabella and Ian had been through so much, and they were so happy. I suppose I was a little jealous of them, but not because I had any feelings for Arabella. Because they were so in love. You could see it from across a room. Like fireflies on a summer night. Then I met you, and I knew exactly how they had felt. I love you, Maggie. You're the best thing that ever happened to me."

Maggie's chest expanded. They had finally opened up about their pasts. Instead of pushing them apart, the revelations had brought them closer together. There were no more secrets between them. She had a feeling of complete happiness. Teddy loved her. They would stay married, and everything would be all right.

"What about the other things? Wanting to move to the suburbs and start a family?" she asked.

"You're right—lots of couples raise children in New York," Teddy said. "My mother will be happy to come into Manhattan and help with a baby. Life isn't going to be perfect. Both of us will be working long hours. Photographers will still want to take photos of Maggie Lane's husband. I'm not getting younger, so we have to find a way to fit in children soon. But it's a start."

Outside the window, the skyline twinkled. There was the sound of cars honking. Maggie loved New York. Now she wouldn't have to leave it.

"What are you thinking?" he asked.

"If *The Maggie Lane Baking Show* taught me anything, it's that everyone has different hopes and dreams. Some couples want a big house in the suburbs, with their own tennis court and swimming pool. Others want to go on vacation wherever they like, and some are happy to sit in front of the television, watching *Fireside Theatre* at night and sharing a bowl of popcorn.

"I found the man who shares my dreams and still allows me to be myself. It's the best thing in the world." Maggie was so happy she felt like she would burst. She wondered how she got so lucky to have Teddy, and all the other important people in her life. Dolly, and Teddy's mother, Patty, and even Tommy and Deluxe Baking Company. It was almost too much to bear.

Teddy leaned forward and kissed her. He wrapped his arms around her, and she nestled against his chest.

"I love you, Maggie Lane."

"I love you, Teddy Buckley."

He kissed her again. "We should check out the master bedroom. The bed has one of those new Sealy mattresses, and the bathroom has a dual-end bathtub."

Maggie kissed him back and thought of the afternoon when they met, and Teddy offered her a glass of champagne because he wanted to keep talking to her without another man interrupting their conversation. She remembered how nervous she had been on the morning of their wedding. She had walked downstairs to his parents' living room and seen the banner congratulating them. Every step of their courtship had taken courage that she didn't know she had after everything that happened in her past. Something had kept her moving toward him, and then alongside him. She knew now that thing was love. Look at what she had gained from her bravery. A happy marriage, a wonderful career, and the apartment she had always dreamed of.

She stood up and took Teddy's hand. "If I remember, it has the best views of Park Avenue."

Acknowledgments

Thank you to the wonderful, talented people who make my books possible. My agent, Logan Harper; my editor, Alicia Clancy; and the team at Lake Union and Amazon Publishing, including Charlotte Herscher, Danielle Marshall, Rachael Clark, Jen Bentham, and Gabe Dumpit. Thank you to Johanna Castillo for years of great advice.

And the biggest thank-you to my children, Alex, Andrew, Heather, Madeleine, and Thomas; my daughter-in-law, Sarah; and my granddaughters, Lily and Emma, for bringing me happiness.

About the Author

Photo © 2019 David Perry

Anita Abriel is the internationally bestselling author of *The Philadelphia Heiress, The Life She Wanted, The Light After the War,* and *Lana's War.* She received a BA in English literature with a minor in creative writing from Bard College. Born in Sydney, Australia, Anita now lives in California with her family. Her hobbies include walking on the beach, seeing classic movies, reading, and traveling. For more information, visit www.anitaabriel.com.